THE
DRIFT BOAT
DETECTIVE

THE
DRIFT BOAT
DETECTIVE
MURDER ON THE MADISON

JEROME CHAPMAN

TATE PUBLISHING
AND ENTERPRISES, LLC

Published by Tate Publishing & Enterprises, LLC
127 E. Trade Center Terrace | Mustang, Oklahoma 73064 USA
1.888.361.9473 | www.tatepublishing.com

Tate Publishing is committed to excellence in the publishing industry. The company reflects the philosophy established by the founders, based on Psalm 68:11,
"The Lord gave the word and great was the company of those who published it."

Book design copyright © 2016 by Tate Publishing, LLC. All rights reserved.
Cover design by Lirey Blanco
Interior design by Richell Balansag

Published in the United States of America

ISBN: 978-1-68319-085-1
1. Fiction / Action & Adventure
2. Fiction / Mystery & Detective / General
16.05.16

I HAVE HAD THE PRIVILEGE OF fishing the Madison and other waters in Montana around Bozeman, Missoula, and Lincoln. Montana is a beautiful place and has a mystique all its own. The vast spaces of this big country are a national treasure. Fly-fishing is a great enjoyment to me and has been a great excuse to see Montana, Utah, Idaho, Colorado, New Mexico, Wyoming, the Yellowstone Park, Washington, British Columbia, Russia, Alaska, Florida, the Bahamas, Tennessee, North Carolina, Alabama, Missouri, and Arkansas, as well as Georgia. I hope I have enough days left to get to the great Northeastern US rivers as well.

Russell Baker made it to some of the spots I have been. Imagine that! Only those who have taken the time to wade out and cast the fly to a rising trout can fully appreciate the magic of that moment when the fly is taken and the line goes tight.

Russell Baker experienced love and life and seemingly lost it all only to emerge back from the darkness to a life of light and happiness.

I hope this book brings you a few moments that you will enjoy! Tight lines.

To Joy, for all those years...
And to Todd, Phil, and Wade

1

THE ALARM CLOCK STARTING BEEPING and a quick look at the clock showed it was 6:30 AM. Russell Baker reached out from the warm covers and hit the snooze button and pulled the cover back up over his head.

"No, you don't, Mr. Baker! You are not going back to sleep! We have to get up and get on the road before the traffic gets terrible going up 400. You promised we would go fishing today, and we are going fishing!"

Sarah Baker was trying to sound mean and tough at the same time. That's hard to do for someone as pretty and nice as Sarah, especially when she is all snuggled up next to you.

"We could just stay here and *snuggle* and forget the fishing," mumbled Russell, who was still half asleep. There was as special emphasis on the word *snuggle*.

"We *snuggled* last night and the night before that and the night before that, as I recall. And we might *snuggle* tonight if I catch some nice fish today! Might!"

Russell threw the covers back and jumped out of bed! "I'm going to hold you to that, Mrs. Baker!"

Russell stood for a minute and looked at the pretty lady lying on the bed. He could not get over, even after being married to her for eight years, how she could look so pretty even waking up with her hair all hanging around her face and sleep in her eyes. No doubt he had the prettiest fishing buddy around.

It was Monday, and normally, Russell would be on duty as a Cobb County Detective, but he had wrangled a day off. They were going to go trout fishing up around Helen on the Chattahoochee on a trophy trout section. No work today! Getting a chance to fish on a weekday meant there would be fewer people on the river.

Sarah was right, of course; they needed to get out of town before the rush-hour traffic. There wasn't much to do as they had lain out their clothes the night before and he had loaded most of the stuff in the Tahoe. Throw the cooler in the truck, fix a coffee to go, and they would hit a drive-through for a sausage and biscuit up the road.

Sarah was putting the sandwiches and waters in a small cooler, and Russell went to the garage to do a last-minute check on rods and waders and boots and fishing vests. Sarah came out of the kitchen door with a coffee mug in one hand and a cell phone in the other.

"Here is your coffee. Your phone has rung twice. I looked, and it's Alan Schreiber, I believe. He knows you are taking the day off, doesn't he?"

"Sure, he knows. He's the one who approved it."

Alan Schreiber was Russell's boss. He was Chief of Detectives Alan Schreiber of the Cobb County Police Department. And the phone started ringing again with that awful "nails on the blackboard" sound it has when it's ringing and it's your day off.

Sarah's eyes rolled back in her head. This could not be good. She knew from eight years' experience. When Russell was a uniformed patrolman, it was regular hours. But the detectives were on call around the clock based upon workload.

Although he was tempted to ignore the phone, he knew Schreiber would not be calling if it was not important.

"Hello. This is Russell Baker."

"Russ, I'm sorry to call you. I know you are scheduled to be off today, but I'm in a bind. We have a very active morning, and some people are out on leave. On top of that, the grand jury called a special session yesterday. Some of our folks have to appear there on that big gambling case. And we have what appears to be a double murder or a murder suicide that needs working right now. The uniformed guys just arrived and secured the scene over there now. If you have not left town yet, I need you to take charge of that for me. Can you do it?"

Russell hesitated and held the phone down so Schreiber could not hear him. "Sarah, Alan needs me to come in and work a double homicide. I could tell him we have already left."

"Of course, you won't tell him that! Why are you bothering to ask me? Go work your double homicide!"

Sarah spun around on her heels, went in the kitchen door, and slammed it behind her. Sarah did not get mad often, but she was mad now! Russell was left to answer on his own.

"If you can't get anyone else, Alan, I can do it. I have a mad wife on my hands to deal with, though."

"I would not have called if I had any other option at the moment," replied Schreiber.

Russell, known as Russ to Sarah and his friends, hurried back in the house to change from his fishing clothes and throw on some khakis and a blue shirt, his blazer, badge, and gun. His unmarked car was on the parking pad, and Sarah was nowhere to be seen. He grabbed the coffee mug and yelled as he went out through the garage door, "I'll call you as soon as I can."

Alan had given Russ the address, and Russ knew the area well. It was all high-end homes—full of doctors, lawyers, and businesspeople. The smell of money.

The problem with being a detective was that the rapists, murderers, suicides, and burglars did not always take into consideration how their actions might affect the fly-fisherman/detective who would have to handle the case. They were very inconsiderate that way.

Russ grabbed his phone and hit his home speed dial number. He did not like leaving Sarah upset. After several rings, the phone went to voice mail. Sarah was too angry to answer.

"Please leave a message." They had a very original message on their answering machine.

"Sarah, I am sorry about today. Please do not be angry with me, and I will make it up to you. I promise. Call me when you feel like it. I'll be on the scene in a minute and will be tied up a while."

Russ arrived at the house, which was being cordoned off by the uniformed officers who had responded to the call. The housekeeper for a local doctor and his wife had been off for the weekend, and when she arrived early this morning, she found the doctor's wife in her favorite chair with a book on the floor beside her and a bullet hole in her head. When she ran into the study to call 911, she found the doctor at his desk with a hole in his head and an old .38 revolver on the floor beside him. There was a neatly typed letter explaining that the doctor was despondent over his wife's illness and decided to put her out of her suffering, and himself too. He apologized to everyone.

It looked like a pretty clear case of murder/suicide. While not pretty, it was a lot less work for the detective. Still, that could be a day's worth of reports, forms, and waiting on the lab for info to fill in the blanks. The doctor had managed to screw up Russ's day pretty well, and he had some work to do to get back in Sarah's good graces.

Russ Baker and Sarah McKenzie had met at a fly shop in Bozeman, Montana. She was standing in the River's Run Fly Shop with her father, and Russ was there with a buddy from Marietta. Although they both were from the same town, they had gone to different schools and had never met. The folks at River's Run could not keep their eyes off Sarah, and neither could Russ. And he hadn't since. She was a great lady, a successful CPA, a beautiful wife, and she loved to fly-fish. It did not get any better than that. He was a lucky man.

Russ went by the office to do the reports on the murder/suicide. Alan Schreiber stopped by the desk where Russ was working.

"I'm sorry about having to call you in, and I am very sorry about getting you in the doghouse with the wife. As soon as possible, let me know what day you want off, and we'll arrange it. Please extend my apologies to her." He actually sounded sincere.

"When she starts speaking to me again, I'll see if we can reschedule a day, Alan. Thanks for the concern."

For probably the first time in their married life, Russ was not looking forward to going home and having to face Sarah. She had never been this angry and had never ignored his calls. But he knew she was upset that he had appeared to put the job ahead of her.

Other than her not being able to have a baby, after two miscarriages, they had a wonderful life. With her CPA business and her parents helping them buy the house, they did not have any money worries, and he did not have to moonlight.

When Russ pulled in the driveway, it was almost getting dark outside. He had been gone all day, and the house, too, was very dark. He pulled the Taurus over to the side pad and hit the garage door opener, halfway expecting her BMW to be gone. But there it was, in its usual place beside his Tahoe. He was not looking forward to going in, and he dreaded the prospects of a confrontation with Sarah.

Russ walked through the garage and opened the kitchen door, and he got quite a surprise! He could not believe his eyes! There were balloons and candles and wine and a large homemade card on the table. On the outside it said, "Russ."

Inside there was a note:

> Dear Russ,
>   I'm sorry for acting the way I did today. I know it was not your fault. I was just looking forward to our day together on the river. If you will come upstairs, you will find me waiting and ready to *snuggle*. We'll have the wine later.
>
>   Love, Sassy

Sassy was Russ's private nickname for Sarah. Russ was in no mood to argue. And he didn't!

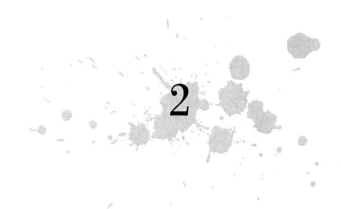

2

RUSS AND SARAH WERE RARELY ever really mad with each other very long. And the incident about the aborted fishing trip was soon forgotten.

Russ went in for a daily briefing early one morning a few days later, and following the meeting, Alan Schreiber stopped by Russ's desk.

"I have not heard back from you on rescheduling that day off that we owe your wife. I have several people wanting some time off, but I want to make sure you get the day you want, so let me know as soon as you can."

"Thanks, Alan, I'll try and get hold of Sarah and set something up and get back to you. Thanks for following up."

Russ immediately opened up his calendar program to see what might work and called Sarah. "I would like to set up another date for us to go fishing. Do you have a minute to look? And let's see what will work and I'll set it up. Alan is pushing me for an answer."

"Sure. Let's do it," was her reply. They decided on a day, and he told Alan to put him down for the extra time off. They were all set.

But the next day, Sarah called Russ at the office.

"Russ, I am sorry, but when we set up the time for our fishing date, I forgot I have my annual physical. They called today to remind me today that I was due to see them on the same day that we picked for our fishing date. You know how hard it is to get an appointment with my doctor, so I need to keep that one if you are okay with that."

"Of course you should keep it. We'll do it another time," he replied. Russ quickly knew he had best not make a big deal of the cancellation.

"Since you have that date set up, why not ask Dad or your friend to go with you and we'll do something later on or we'll just have to go on a Saturday. That will be just fine with me, and I am snowed at work."

Russ thought that would be okay, and he liked Sarah's dad. Russ's own parents had died in a house fire and her family was his only family now. No sisters and brothers.

Other than the miscarriages, they both had always been in perfect health. They both tried to eat right and stay in good shape.

As it turned out, her dad, Dan McKenzie could not go, so Russ decided to go alone to Unicoi Outfitter's Nacoochee Bend section on the Chattahoochee River and pay to catch some trophy fish. The Chattahoochee runs nearly the entire length of the state of Georgia. From just north of Helen, Georgia, it flows to a junction with the Flint River, and they form the Apalachicola River at Lake Seminole near the Florida line.

Her dad was a real man's man. A Georgia Tech graduate, Dan McKenzie went on to become an Air Force pilot and then an executive at Lockheed. He was an accomplished fly-fisherman and had passed that on to Sarah.

The morning he was going to Helen, Russ got up early to go, and he and Sarah had a coffee together before he left.

"I hope you have a great day at the river. Maybe if you are not too late getting back, we can grab dinner and you can give me a fish-by-fish report."

"Sounds great. I'll try to make sure I will be back before too late, traffic permitting. Good luck at the doctor's office."

Russ had a pretty good morning at Nacoochee Bend and caught a few nice fish. That was a spot where big fish are common, but he did not have a day with a lot of fish. He had only paid for a half day, so after grabbing a bite at lunch, he decided to run over to Unicoi Park about four miles away and try the Smith Creek section if they weren't too busy on the small stream.

Unicoi is a popular State Park with Unicoi Lake and the Anna Ruby Falls nearby. It is one of the most popular parks in the state and at times can be very crowded.

He tried to call Sarah, but the phone went to voice mail. She probably was still at the doctor's office.

"Hi. I am leaving the Hooch and I am going over to Unicoi Park for a couple hours if they are not busy. Sorry I missed you. I will call you when I am leaving and we'll go to dinner wherever you want. Why not make a reservation for about seven thirty someplace like the Canoe. Love you."

Russ got to Unicoi and paid his $3 park fee, and he was in luck as there were only two other people there. He got to the Creek and he had a spectacular day catching fish. He had caught over thirty fish in the twelve-inch to fourteen-inch size, although he really did not keep count, when a fellow walked by and Russ spoke to him:

"How is it going?"

"I caught three fish so far just down the creek. I thought I would give it a try up here just below the dam."

"Why don't you take this spot? I have caught a ton of fish, and you can take over here if you want. I have probably caught close to forty."

The fellow just kept walking. "That's okay. I'll go on up to the dam."

Well, so much for being a nice guy, thought Russ.

Russ was back to fishing and was startled by a loud clap of thunder and a flash of lightning. Standing in the water with a fly rod in a lightning storm was not a good idea, and Russ hurriedly waded out and went to the pavilion nearby to wait out the thunderstorm. The fellow who had walked by earlier came to the pavilion in almost a trot, and another fisherman came from the other direction to join them under the shelter.

After they chatted for a few minutes while the storm was passing, the first guy said he was a professor at UGA.

"When you told me to take that spot where you had caught over thirty fish, I thought you must be some kind of weirdo," he said to Russ. "No one has ever done that before."

The rain stopped, and Russ decided he'd had enough. He would get on the road home and try to be there in plenty of time for dinner with Sarah. No need to risk being late. Russ bid the other two guys a farewell and headed for his car. The UGA professor went straight to the spot where Russ had been fishing!

Russ had just reached the Tahoe in the parking lot and was removing his wet waders when his cell phone rang. The screen said, "Sassy." She just had to see how the fishing was going, he supposed.

"Hi, babe," he said.

What he heard on the other end was totally unexpected.

"Where are you and how long before you get home?" she said between sobs. Something was really wrong!

"I'm back at the truck here at Unicoi Park and taking off my waders now and will be leaving here in a couple of minutes to come home. It will take me a good two hours, depending on traffic to get there. What on earth is wrong?"

"I don't want to go into it on the phone, but get here as soon as you can. I really need you here," she said.

He asked, "Can't you just tell me what has happened?"

"Get here as soon as you can, Russ. I really don't want to say any more on the phone," she sobbed as she hung up.

Needless to say, Russ broke every traffic law getting home. He had never seen or heard Sarah like this before. He could not get her folks on the phone, so had to endure the agony of the drive home without a clue as to what had happened. His first thought was that her father or mother had died. What else could it be?

When he pulled into the drive at home, the garage door on her side was open. The car was there, as it should be, but it was not like her to leave the door open. She thought it did not look nice to leave the door open and felt it was unsafe as someone could come in and enter the house with the door open.

He was out of the Tahoe in a flash and went through the partially open door into the kitchen. Again, that was totally out of character.

Sarah was in the bedroom lying on the bed, crying. She was in a bad way emotionally. When she saw Russ, she reached for him and pulled him to her as tightly as she could; and he held her, trying to comfort her and find out what was happening.

"What's wrong, Sarah? What has you so upset? What has happened?"

"Russ, they found a mass on my lung when they did my annual chest X-ray today. I have to go tomorrow to a specialist for more tests and a biopsy, but Dr. Andrews believes it is cancer, and she really scared me!"

Russ was at a loss for words, and he felt a rush of emotion that almost took his breath away. "I need you to go with me to the hospital tomorrow for the MRI and then the biopsy. Please!"

"Of course I'll go. You know I will. It will probably be a false alarm! You've never smoked. You've never had more than a glass of wine at one time in your life. People like you don't get lung cancer."

He wasn't sure that was correct, but it was all the reassuring words he could come up with as he choked back tears.

"Did you call your mom and dad?" he asked.

"No. I wanted to wait until we got through the tests tomorrow."

It was a long night for the two of them. This had to be wrong. She had been fine. There had to be a mistake. The next morning they went to Kennestone Hospital where some test were done as an outpatient. Russ had called in and told them he had a family emergency and could not be there. Nothing would keep him from going with Sarah.

Bloodwork and an MRI were performed. Two specialists would be seen the following day. The tests confirmed Dr. Andrews's worst suspicions. She had lung cancer, and it had already spread to lymph nodes and her liver. They would schedule surgery, set her up for chemo, and hope and pray for her recovery.

Russ could not believe that this was happening to Sarah and to him. Russ's parents were both great people who were close to retirement when he and Sarah had gotten married. They took to Sarah, and she took to them, and they were all right at home together.

One night while on patrol, he heard of a fire on his radio and emergency equipment was being dispatched as well as some Cobb County Police units for traffic control, and Russ knew at once that it was his parents' house. He flew to the scene, and by the time any of the emergency and fire department personnel arrived, it was too late. Too late for the house and too late to save his parents who had been apparently overcome by smoke.

It was concluded that the smoke detectors had failed. That was Russ's only real experience dealing with the death of a loved one as all of his grandparents had died when he was small and he did not remember too much about that. The thought of Sarah dying was simply beyond his comprehension. It just wasn't possible for him to even consider it.

For the next several weeks, Sarah went through operations, tests, and treatments. She was strong and she was a fighter, but she died eight months from the day of his last fishing trip to Unicoi. Detective Russell Baker's world came to a sudden stop.

3

THE COUNTY WAS UNDERSTANDING AND gave Russ two weeks off to handle everything and to try to get prepared emotionally to return to work. The department shrink was made available to help him through the tough adjustment, and Sarah's parents, though grief stricken did what they could for Russ.

Sarah had not been able to work and her income shut down. She had a disability policy that kicked in, but the bills that insurance did not pay were enormous. Two car payments, still paying on the nice house, and all those extra bills added up to a lot. All that and the grief was taking its toll on Russ.

He had let a lot of things fall between the cracks while Sarah, who normally handled all the family finances, was sick. There was unopened mail, unpaid bills, funeral costs, and grieving that had to be handled. He had to get a grip on himself and the other stuff too.

Finally going back to work was some help, and he started back to some sort of routine. He missed Sarah terribly and found himself not sleeping, drinking more beer than he ever did, and looking like hell. Everyone could see it. He could see it but wasn't sure what to do and wasn't sure he cared.

On a Sunday, on what was to be his off day, his work phone rang. That awful "nails on the blackboard" ring he had come to hate. Someone had done something somewhere and they needed a detective.

He got in his unmarked county car and went to the gated neighborhood to a beautiful two-million-dollar house. There were ambulances, fire trucks, emergency personnel, police, neighbors, and TV crews mobbing the area. Russ arrived as officer in charge.

Inside was a gruesome scene: a dead mother, a dead father, and two dead children. Even the pet yellow lab was dead. The house was ransacked. The housekeeper had discovered the bodies when she came by to pick up her check they had forgotten to leave as they normally did on Friday.

When no one answered the door, she used her key to come in; the alarm was off and she walked in on hell. Now, Russ was doing the same thing. He had handled a number of homicide cases and had seen a number of dead and injured people, and they had never seemed to bother him before. But in his current state, he was jolted and found himself wanting to run out the front door. He wasn't sure he could handle this.

The crime scene team started putting their investigation efforts to work, and Russ started trying to see what was going on, questioning the housekeeper, getting the names of neighbors, and trying with all his might to mount a serious investigation of his own.

He called another detective that acted as a partner in larger cases and told her he needed her at the scene; and when she arrived, he told her he was ill and had to leave. He

23

handed her his notes, left her standing there overwhelmed and bewildered as he got in his car and went home.

His work phone rang several times after getting home, but he did not answer it. About an hour later, his doorbell rang, and it was Alan Schreiber, chief detective. This was his boss although the chief of Cobb County Police was the overall boss.

Schreiber had gotten a call from the detective at the scene saying that Russ had left and she was concerned about him and that he had not answered his phone. Schreiber was here to investigate the investigator, and he knew all about the trauma that Russ had been through losing Sarah. After talking for a few minutes, he told Russ to come in to his office in the morning and they would review the situation.

When Russ arrived at Schreiber's office on Monday, the department mental health doctor was there, and they sat down together. Russ gave his written permission for Alan to be present, and they all came to one conclusion: Russ was not in a mental state to carry out his duties at present. He could be reassigned to an administrative job for a while, take an unpaid leave of absence, and protect his seniority and retirement program, or he could resign. One other possibility was that the doctor could give him a medical leave of absence.

Russ had never wanted to be anything but a cop. From as far back as he could remember, he'd dreamed of wearing a uniform, riding a motorcycle, and driving a police car. Now, it looked like that dream was about to come to an end and there was little he could do about it.

Russ was ready to hand in his badge and resign, but Alan intervened and recommended that he take up to a six-month maximum medical leave of absence, and they could reevaluate it when and if Russ felt he was ready to come back and the doctors felt he was fit to carry out his duties. This was agreed to, and Russ left the office and went home to the empty house, and he sat and cried. He had lost the two most important things in his life: his beautiful wife Sarah and his job as a policeman.

By Wednesday, Russ was feeling better as he was under no immediate pressure from work. He had to sit down and go through all of the paperwork that had piled up, catch up bills, and start trying to get his life back together. Sarah's parents were wonderful to him. They came over and offered to help him financially and to help organize all the stuff that had accumulated.

Russ declined the financial help from Sarah's parents, although he was in no position to stay in the house on his detective salary alone. Sarah had made a high income, and life was easy financially when they both worked, but those days were gone.

He would no longer need this big five-bedroom house for just himself. He asked his father-in-law to help get it listed for sale. He would sell Sarah's car, although he hated to, but it wasn't being driven, and he did not need the car payment since his check was now reduced to a disability payment. What then? He did not know.

Sarah's parents were Mr. and Mrs. McKenzie. The McKenzies sat down with Russ and started going through the unopened mail, most of it junk, that was piled on the desk in the room Sarah had used as a home office. They carefully looked at all the pieces before throwing them in the big trash bag they had brought in to accommodate it all.

Sarah had belonged to several professional associations regarding her CPA status. Many of the pieces of mail were about Continuing Education classes that CPAs were required to attend to maintain their license. Of course, they would not be useful anymore to Sarah.

One of the envelopes in the pile of unopened mail contained a professional association membership renewal that was about due to expire. A payment would be needed to renew, it said, and it also went on to remind the member—in this case Sarah—what benefits they had from their membership. The one coming due, with a fairly healthy premium, had a $500,000 term life insurance policy as part of the benefit!

Russ was sure that he and Sarah would have discussed that policy, but he had completely forgotten about it. It hadn't seemed relevant to Russ at the time, probably. Dying was the farthest thing from the mind of either of them.

Mrs. McKenzie, a pretty sharp lady herself, made a call to the company. After a lot of conversation about who she was and confidentiality, she was told that the policy was in effect and that they would need to get a benefit request and a death certificate to them and a check would be sent to Mr. Russell Baker!

After finding this, they set out on a quest to see if there were any other policies. And indeed, Sarah also had a $250,000 whole life policy with Equitable plus one on Russ. It all came back to him, on those two policies, that they had taken them out when they bought the house to ensure they could stay there if something happened.

Russell Baker had suddenly gone from nearly broke to almost a millionaire in one afternoon! He would be able to pay all he owed and them some!

People started coming to look at the house once it was listed. They still owed almost $300,000 but had a lot of equity since the McKenzies had given them $150,000 as a down payment for a wedding present! Real estate values had gone up greatly in the eight years they had lived there. They were asking $650,000 and thought that was a reasonable price for the house and location.

Russ decided on what furniture and personal items he wanted to keep, offered the rest to the McKenzies, who did take a few things that Sarah had owned. They had a big yard sale and what was left they gave to a charity to come pick it up. The BMW that Sarah had driven was sold. Things were now coming to a head, and Russ had some more tough decisions to make, like where he was going to live. What was he going to do next? Was he going to try and get his job back at the Cobb Police Department? He had about four months left to decide before the decision would be made for him.

Russ sat down and was looking at the pictures of the life he'd had with Sarah. It had been a great life for as long as they'd had together. He missed her every minute of every day. He came across the pictures he had taken of her and her dad in Bozeman where they first met at the fly shop about ten years prior, and he knew what he had to do!

He called Dan McKenzie. It was while Dan McKenzie was in the Air Force that he had met and married Sarah's mother, Doris, and they had two girls. One was Sarah and one was a sister who died when about a year old of something like meningitis.

Dan retired from the Air Force and had accepted a position with Lockheed Marietta. He became a key person in their organization, and when not building airplanes, he spent all his time with Doris and Sarah. He loved fly-fishing and instilled that same passion into Sarah. Russ was not sure how to tell them of his plans but decided that he would just say what he had to say. He told Dan on the phone that he was coming over, if that was okay. And of course, it was.

"I have decided to go back to where I began as a person. I am going to travel out to Bozeman, Montana. I will not be in a hurry to get there, and my plan is to fish every spot I can on the way. My memorial to Sarah will be to do what I think she would have wanted me to do: trout fish and enjoy life. Trout fish, at least for a while, and enjoy life for as long as I live. I hope you understand. When and if I get settled, you can come and visit, and we will fish as often as you want. I will write and call to let you know how I am and where I am. I promise."

Dan and Doris embraced Russ as if he were their own son. Doris was crying.

Dan said, "I can't say I'm surprised. Doris and I kind of thought you might want to get away. We will await your calls and letters. We love you, and we appreciate what you had with Sarah and how you loved her. She would approve!"

Russ was very much relieved by their understanding.

The house had been sold, and Russ had written out a check to Dan and Doris for $150,000, the amount they had given to Sarah and him to pay down on the house. He said he felt he owed that to them. Characteristic of the kind of people they were, Dan McKenzie took the check and tore it up into many small pieces.

"Consider any debt you feel you owe to Doris and me as *paid in full*. We loved our daughter, and she told us time after time what a wonderful husband and companion you were to her. We more than got our money's worth!"

4

RUSSELL BAKER BOUGHT A SMALL trailer to haul the belongings he had decided to keep including Sarah's fishing gear and all her photos and much of her personal items. He put all of his fishing gear up front in the Tahoe so he could find it easily.

Russ left Marietta and Cobb County and headed to Memphis, Tennessee, and from there he was going to Jonesboro, Arkansas, and Heber Springs and the Little Red River. He planned to stay a few days at the Swinging Bridge Fish Camp and catch some giant trout at Cow Shoals. The White River would also be tested with the fly rod. This was home of world record trout and he wanted to give it a try. He was on his way!

With about a million dollars in the bank, no bills to pay, and his small disability pay from Cobb County, he would make out just fine. Financially, anyway. He still was uncertain about his mental state and his constant feeling of depression.

The trip to Heber Springs was uneventful, and the fishing was great! Russ used Sarah's fly rod to catch some fish that would have been considered trophies on many streams but are common to these big tailwater rivers in Arkansas. Sarah would have loved it.

From Arkansas, Russ planned to cut across through Oklahoma and make a stop for a few days in New Mexico at the Four Corners area on the San Juan. This is another stream of renowned fishing. He called Dan McKenzie and Doris on the way. They sounded fine and were glad to hear from him, and he gave Dan a fishing report. Dan said he might have to pack up for a few days and go to Arkansas!

Russ got a room at Abe's Motel and sprung for a guide and a drift boat trip. The water there is better fished from the river except at the Texas Hole. It was worth it, and the guide knew the water and knew how to handle a drift boat. He was not much of a talker, which Russ liked. He made short, understandable suggestions to Russ, and they caught a lot of good fish.

From Four Corners, Russ had decided he would head out toward Utah and the Park City area. He could do some lake trout fishing and catch the Provo River as well as enjoy Park City as he had not been there before. This, again, was a good decision. Russ had made up his mind about one thing. He was going to stop in Idaho Falls and buy a drift boat from Hyde. But after thinking about that, Russ realized he could not pull his trailer with the belongings and a boat trailer. The drift boat would have to wait until he decided if he would settle in one place for a while. But he could go by Henry's Fork and the Snake River. He would catch Wyoming and Colorado another time. He was going to Bozeman.

When Russ arrived in Bozeman, it was June. Water on the main rivers was coming down after the runoff, and the fishing should be good on the Madison and Gallatin. These were the rivers that he and Sarah had fished on their first meeting and on several trips that they made back there after they were married. They had used the River's Run Fly Shop every time to furnish them their guides and were never disappointed. Russ seemed to remember that the original owner of the River's Run may have been from Marietta. If so, that seems to bear out his meeting Sarah there as "fate."

Russ got signed up for a float at the shop and no one remembered him, but that was okay. Russ knew that he could not afford to have a guided float trip every day even with a million bucks in the bank. But he wanted to reacquaint himself with the Madison and the Gallatin before finding himself a drift boat of his own. He also needed a place to stay, but a cheap motel would be okay for a day or two. The least amount of details to tie him down the better. Trout fishing guides, like many other species, come from a wide range of backgrounds. There is the dentist that says he just plain got tired of being a dentist and decided to become a fishing guide because of his love for fishing. In truth, he lost his license for prescribing excessive amounts of painkillers to some folks addicted to prescription painkillers. The only other thing he knew to do, other than fixing teeth, was fly-fishing. And that would get him out of town. Then there is a former securities agent who says that he got tired of the rat race and was so taken by fly-fishing and drifting down the beautiful trout-filled streams that he moved out of his penthouse in New York and moved to a single-wide mobile home in Dutch John, Utah. Population 145. He left out the part about getting caught in some stock scheme and being booted out and given a hefty fine and narrowly escaping jail. So much for the idealist.

Then there are the ones that seem born to it. They fished when they should have been in class at some university their parents were scrimping to send them to. They fished when they were supposed to be working at the local feed and seed. They got a degree in biology and used it to help identify the insects that the fish are rising to in some spring creek. They have old trucks and flies stuck in their sweaty hats. They can roll cast in a wind and put a fly in a spot the size of a baseball cap. And when they are told they need to put "first things first," they tie some flies and go fishing. Fishing is first!

When the snow piles up in Montana, these guys and gals head to the Gulf Region in Louisiana or the Florida Keys or Belize. Wherever there is fishing that needs to be done, that's where you will find them. If you need to see them, look for their truck and boat trailer at some river takeout. They'll be along. Sometime!

Their best friend is the girl who shuttles the trucks and trailers for them. They trust her with the keys to their pickup. They prefer being alone, but to earn a living they have to put up with some hotshot novice straight out of the Cabela's catalog all day in their boat or raft. And some will even pretend they like you. That produces bigger tips. In truth, they would much prefer to be in the boat or raft alone, casting hoppers to the bank. And heaven help you if you marry one! They are used to traveling facing backward. They are not opposed to a longneck beer every once in a while.

Russ was not totally forgotten at the Cobb County Police Department. He got an occasional call from Schreiber, asking about a detail in a report or open case and testing his memory. Schreiber was also trying to see where Russ was in his head and if he was ready to come back to work. Russ wondered about the family at the last crime scene he visited and whether they caught the people responsible. For a while he watched no TV and read no newspapers, and then he left town. Hopefully they got the bad guys and put them away. Not his problem anymore. Or was it?

Russ stayed true to his promise to the McKenzies and called them occasionally. They seemed fine and truly seemed interested in what he was up to. The months were adding up since he left the force, and six months would be gone before you know it. Dan McKenzie was thinking about retiring himself and traveling some. They just might come to Montana for a while. Russ would really like that.

He started making a few casual friends in Bozeman at the local pool hall. His favorite place to eat was Montana Brew Works and he liked the Royale with cheese and fries. They had a good steak and great beer on tap.

But most evenings he got back from some riverbank or spring creek and grabbed a burger and went to the Super 8 Motel and watched ESPN or some old cowboy movie. Breakfast was usually a stop at McDonald's. He wished they had a Waffle House. He wasn't ready for the dating scene yet. He had Sarah's pictures on the little table and nightstand, and he talked to her every night. He had been talking to her about getting that drift boat.

Russ had not discussed with anyone in Bozeman about his previous job, and when anyone asked, he just said he was taking some time off from his job with the county. He had not talked to anyone about a job because he had not really considered a job at this point. Down deep, he really considered that he was still a detective with Cobb County, and as a technical matter that was true until the sand ran out in the hourglass.

He let it be known at the fly shop that he might like to buy a drift boat and had not had any offers yet. He had

33

in mind that he would buy a Hyde or a ClackaCraft but decided to go by the local RO boat plant in Bozeman. He really liked those boats too. He thought he would run it by Dan McKenzie who was, after all, an engineer and pilot who had fished from drift boats a lot. Dan was also helping Russ manage his finances.

After talking to Dan, he decided to buy a beautiful RO boat he had seen a couple of days before at the little plant there in town. It looked beautiful on the trailer hooked up to the Tahoe, but he could not wait to get to the river and give it a try. But first he needed to get set up with one of the several boat shuttle services.

Powerboating can be a solitary sport. Loading and unloading can be a hassle, but guys learn to launch the boats, park the trucks, and then reload them all by themselves. But with drift boats, there is the problem of "one way" fishing. You put the boat in upstream and take it out downstream, and your boat and trailer have to, somehow, find their way from the put-in ramp to the take-out ramp. You had to have someone shuttle the truck and trailer. Some of the guides had their wives or girlfriends helping them. Russ had neither. He had met a young lady that two of the guides at River's Run were using. Her name was Nancy Freeman, and he wasn't sure if she was single or married; it did not really matter. He got Nancy's number from River's Run guide that he had used and gave her a call. She agreed to help when she was available but suggested he might contact a couple more because she would give the regular guides priority and might not always be available. He took down some numbers she gave him.

Russ had seen a sign painter's truck at the Brew Works and got him to paint the name *Sassy* on both sides of the bow. The nickname for Sarah that no one used but him made the boat feel really special.

The guides around Bozeman had gotten to know Russ and saw him at the Brew Works, at River's Run, and at the river. The guides he had used recognized his skills at fly-fishing as much better than the typical tourist, and he had quickly won their respect. But he was surprised when he got a call one evening from one of the guides.

The guide had clients set up to fish the Madison early the next morning and had managed to hurt his foot rather badly on his motorcycle that evening. He had torn some tendons and cracked some bones in his foot. He wondered if Russ thought he could handle two out-of-town fishermen for a long float on the Madison in his new boat. There was one thing that was required by the fly shop and that was a first aid course certificate. And of course the boat had to be properly equipped with life jackets, etc. Russ told him he was a certified EMT. First aid courses were required part of his police training, including the recent training on defibrillators, but Russ had taken an EMT training program at the local vocational technical school on his own and carried a card in his wallet. The guide was very impressed.

He just told the guide he had the training as part of his job with the county, not wanting to get into the police story with him. He told he the guide he was willing to give guiding a shot and would not charge anything. Any payment the guide would have received for the day, including a tip, would still be his for the experience. That sealed the deal.

The guide was already set up with Nancy Freeman to do his shuttle in the morning, and he said he would figure out with her how to find Russ's truck and where for him to leave his keys. He was very surprised to hear that Russ was already set up with Nancy and all that was needed was a call to let her know she would be taking Russ's Tahoe down to the takeout instead of the other guide's truck. Russ had already provided Nancy with a set of keys to his Tahoe. Game on!

Russ did not sleep much that night. He checked and rechecked his boat. He made a list of stuff he needed for supplies for tomorrow. He went and filled up his truck with gas. He checked his fly box for leaders and tippets and flies for the float. Of course, the fishermen would pick up some at the fly shop too.

He stocked a few snacks and drinks in a new cooler for the trip. Soft drinks only. Too much beer could be a problem. And he made sure his phone was charged even though there were places the phones did not work.

5

M ORNING CAME QUICKLY, AND HE was supposed to
meet the clients at seven thirty since they had a drive
to get to the launch point. He was there at seven and the
guide who had called him, whose name was Chad, was there
on crutches to lend a hand and as a professional gesture to
the clients to let them know why he was not going with
them. It was also his way of retaining a client that might
slip away for future business.

The clients were brothers in their midthirties, and both
lived in Rhode Island. They had been fishing, according to
them, a number of times in Montana and fished extensively
in the eastern states. At least they were not beginners who
would have to have everything done for them. But as
experienced fishermen, they could be more critical of Russ's
performance. He needed to put his best foot forward.

In a few minutes, they were off. Russ had been this
nervous about twice before: on his first solo night patrol
as a Cobb County Police officer and the day he married
Sarah. The clients had rigged up with strike indicators and
nymphs that had been suggested by Chad. Their waders
and boots were not the usual, fresh out of the box look of
first-timers. Their rods and reels were top-of-the-line Sage

equipment, and their fishing vests showed much use. He believed this was not their first rodeo.

The launch went well, and no one would have known it was his first trip with a client. He had floated this section enough over the past few days to get a handle on the boat and the water. He made a few mistakes but probably were not too noticeable to the clients. But the fish weren't hitting the nymphs. Not good. It was now mid-July.

Russ looked at his fly box and dug out a stone fly. He asked that one of them tie that on and see if it made any difference. On the second cast toward the bank—*bam!* A big hit from a nice fish! They landed the nice brown, took a quick photo, and released it. Then they changed the other rod over to a stone fly, and the action was on! They had a quick shore break at one of the designated spots, and other than that, they fished hard to the take out.

They caught a ton of nice fish, and the clients were whooping it up. They arrived at the take-out about four o'clock, and the Tahoe and trailer were right where they were supposed to be.

"Thank you, Nancy," Russ said to himself.

When they got back to the fly shop, they gave him a $100 tip. They had paid the fly shop for the trip that morning.

This was his first-ever payment as a fly-fishing guide, and Russ was planning to give it to Chad, who probably really needed it. He went home across the street to the Super 8 exhausted but managed a few fist pumps on the way. He'd done good!

He called Chad and told him things went well but did not embellish just how well. He told him he had a $100 bill for him as well. He collapsed on the bed exhausted from no sleep the night before and a day on the river with the new RO and two clients. He was asleep almost instantly.

Russ was jolted awake by the phone about ten thirty. Who would be calling at this hour?

It was Chad, the guide from the fly shop. The client brothers from Rhode Island had just called him. They were supposed to do a spring creek wade-fishing trip tomorrow but had decided they would like to go back on the Madison again if they could book it this late and make the change. They said they had the best day on the river, any river, ever with Russ. Could he take them again? This time, he could keep the money for himself.

Russ was pooped and did not know if he was really up to going again but said yes, and he would still let Chad keep the money this time. Chad did not argue.

Russ jumped up and sat down at the small table to assess what he needed. And he would have to call Nancy, who might not appreciate being called so late. She did not seem to mind, though, and sounded super nice on the phone. She would do the shuttle for him again. The next day was a pretty good day, though not as good as the first trip.

The sky was overcast and gloomy, and the fish weren't hitting the stone fly as much. They rigged the nymphs that everyone had recommended for the day before and started getting more hits. While for some nymphing is not as much fun as topwater flies, catching is better than not catching. By the end of the day, they had done pretty well.

And Russ, now with two nights in a row with no sleep and two full days on the water, was ready for a beer at the Brew Works and a good-night's sleep! He dropped the brothers off and got another $100 tip. He put the $100 bill with the other one to give to Chad, headed to Super 8 for a shower, and then he would be off for that beer and a steak dinner.

Russ went by the shop the next day, but it wasn't early and all the guides were gone out. The shop was quiet, and he dropped off an envelope for Chad with the two $100s inside with a note saying that he appreciated the chance to get the experience. He was turning to leave when the owner stuck his head out of the office and said, "Russ. It is Russ, right? Could I talk to you for a moment?"

"Sure," Russ replied.

"Chad's clients were in here this morning on their way down to Missoula. They were raving about how your floats went and how well you did for them. Frankly, I did not know what they were talking about because Chad had not cleared that switch with me. They booked the trip with me, and I assigned that to Chad. You see, he shouldn't have booked that trip with you without discussing it with me. I have a list of guides that are on a standby list and one of them should have had the float. I don't want you taking any trips from my guide's for my shop. I have made promises to the regular guides, and I have liabilities."

His voice had a tinge of anger, seemingly directed to Russ.

"I can't just be having anyone taking out my clients, especially some drifter living in a motel who could be gone tomorrow."

Russ had been very low key around everyone. In fact, the events of the past few months had softened the cop in him so that he had avoided any confrontational situation, and no one had any idea of his background even though he had been a customer of the shop for years. He had held back a lot of anger since Sarah's illness and death. But the suggestion that he was a "drifter" and not a reliable person set off a suppressed anger.

"Sir, I am not a drifter. I booked two float trips with you and paid for them in the past two months. Prior to that, my wife and I booked six or eight trips with you in the past eight or nine years. Before that, my buddy and I booked four or five trips here. My father-in-law brought my wife here and booked trips eight or nine times himself. I am a longtime repeat customer here, and I don't believe you have missed being paid. I doubt you have a more loyal customer. It's not my fault that you did not know that. I just purchased a top-of-the-line, brand-new drift boat from a local company, and I believe he will confirm that I paid cash for it. I am here getting over the death of my wife who loved coming here, and I have several years of service to one of the finest police departments in the country. I may be a lot of things, but I am not a drifter."

The stance and the look and the tone, although he never raised his voice, stopped everyone in their tracks. They had not seen this side of Russ who had dealt with drunks, drug addicts, drug dealers, burglars, murderers, rapists, gang members, wreck victims, and wife beaters. At six foot two tall and two hundred muscular pounds, he was not someone to mess with. That was now obvious to everyone.

The Russell Baker that had been moping around with his head held low was suddenly standing up very straight, tall, and confident. His reaction even shocked himself.

The qualities that had made Russ a good cop, and excellent husband, and a good detective were still there. They had just been suppressed by sorrow and grief and self-pity. This was Sarah's husband and Dan's son-in-law

41

talking. This was the kick in the ass he had needed to get back to some level ground.

He turned and walked out to his truck and drove away. He stopped by the storage lot where he was storing his boat and started to hook it up and head to the river and then reconsidered. He would go get some lunch and he had a couple of phone calls to make. He headed for the Brew Works. He sat down at a table at the Brew Works where he usually sat at the bar, but this was a new day.

The waitress took his order, and he looked at some messages on his phone from Dan and a few old friends. "Not fishing or guiding today?" It was a female voice that sounded vaguely familiar. He looked up, and there was a striking young woman that he did not immediately recognize. She could tell he did not know who she was.

"I'm Nancy. I have been doing your shuttle service. I believe I have a set of keys to your Tahoe."

Russ could feel his face turning red. He had met Nancy briefly when he took her the keys to his truck. He had left an envelope in the glove compartment to pay for the shuttles and had not any further direct contact other than a phone call. When he saw her then, she was wearing blue jeans, a hat like the kayakers wear that covered her head and face and her hair pulled up under the hat, and glasses. He certainly had been walking around with his head down, apparently.

"Nancy, I am so sorry I did not recognize you. My head was somewhere else. I want to thank you for handling my shuttles. It's nice when people do what they say they will do. Would you like to sit down and have some lunch? My treat."

"I've ordered some takeout, and I am just here to pick it up. I have to get back to the shop. I can sit for a minute 'til it's ready."

She sat down on the edge of the chair looking for the world like she might run at any second.

"Is the shop a place you work? I figured you stayed busy with the shuttles."

"My mom and I own a ladies shop up the street. We sell women's outdoor wear, shoes, boots and nice dresses, cosmetics, and just about everything in that category. It's called—believe it or not—Nancy's.

"Mom opens the store for me at nine o'clock and stays until I finish the shuttles and comes back in the afternoon to stay until we close at six o'clock. We have two-part time ladies that help, so it works out fine. We also sell online and ship out a lot of stuff UPS. And when I get a day to go fishing, I have enough help to cover it."

"Wow. You are a busy entrepreneur, it sounds like," Russ stammered. "So you like to fish too?"

"Oh, sure. I grew up in this area, and my brother and I have been fishing since we were small. You know my brother. My brother is Chad. I thought he might have mentioned it. That's how I got into doing the shuttles."

"No. He did not. I never even knew his last name. But I am glad I only said nice things about you."

She laughed.

"I have to go. I have the store by myself today and had to put a sign on the door. Can't lose a customer, you know."

With that, she was gone. She paid at the register and walked out with every male in the place watching her as she left. Including Russ.

Russ finished his lunch and got in the Tahoe to go back to Super 8. He couldn't resist driving up the street and looking for Nancy's store. It was very nice, or so it appeared from the outside. His plan right now was to get on the bed,

43

turn on the air conditioner, the TV and take a long nap. He couldn't believe Chad had not told him about Nancy being his sister. But she could be married and have a house full of kids. He did not think to ask. No reason to know. It was none of his business.

The nap was going well. About one and one half hours into it, the phone rang. It was Chad.

"Well, I hear you talked to Nancy at lunch and the secret is out."

"I have to say I was caught off guard but was mostly embarrassed that I did not recognize her immediately," Russ responded.

Chad said, "She can dress herself down, that's for sure. It helps keep some of the wolves at bay, I think. A pretty, single woman can get hit on a lot around here."

Well, that had answered a couple of questions.

"I picked up the envelope at the shop. That is very nice, but I think you should keep the money."

Russ was firm about the money. "No. I feel that is like paying for a training course. I really enjoyed the clients and things worked out okay I think. Except that your boss is not happy at the shop. He and I had a few words."

"First of all, he is not my boss. I guide float trips for him when I am not booked on my own. I have a list of clients that I have guided for over the years and stay busy mostly with them. My website brings in all of the business I can handle most of the time."

Website? Well, Russ was now wondering if he had lost all of his observation and detective skills. There obviously was a lot he did not know about Chad than his last name, and he was becoming more impressed. But then, he did not think Chad knew a lot about him either.

Chad continued, "Sometimes schedules leave me a few days open, and I pick up some floats there and at another shop out of Butte."

That seemed odd that Chad would be taking bookings out of Butte as it was almost ninety miles away. But he did not ask any questions. Again, none of his business.

"And, Russ, you can expect a call from the fly shop. John was terribly embarrassed when he learned that you were not only a current customer but a longtime customer. He said he really got an earful and that you told him you were a cop. He is really a great guy, so I don't know why he was so upset. He is loyal to the guides and is a man of his word, and I guess he was afraid of being questioned about giving a float to someone who is not a regular there, even though it was me that gave you the float. I told him I thought you were an EMT since you showed me the card."

"I didn't say I was a cop. I told him I had worked for a police department. I am not really a cop. If you don't mind, I prefer not to go into that right now."

"Sure. Well, you made a hell of an impression on him today. And I think you have made an impression on Nancy. She asked a lot of questions. I know for a fact that you made an impression on the two clients. They went on and on when they called me. I think you may have made some clients for life."

Clients for life? Well, that was an idea that had not occurred to Russ. Being thought of as a professional guide was something he had not expected. It was a nice revelation.

He had not hung up from Chad more than a few minutes when the phone rang again. This time it was John from the fly shop. "Mr. Baker. This is John over at the fly shop."

So now it was "Mr. Baker" not "Mr. Drifter, thought Russ.

"I owe you an apology. I had totally misjudged you, and I should know when a client of long standing comes in our store. Especially someone who has been here so many times in the past."

There was a nice sound of sincerity in his voice.

"If you would have a moment, maybe you could stop by sometime tomorrow and let me tell you in person."

Russ thought about telling John where to stick his apology but realized that John had to be sucking it up to call and there was nothing to be gained by having a running feud when it wouldn't make or break either of them.

"I'll stop by tomorrow," said Russ.

6

MONTANA IS A BIG PLACE. It is, after all, Big Sky Country. Movie stars and athletes alike have chosen Montana for second homes, ski chalets, ranches and just a place to escape from the big city life and enjoy the wide open spaces. For all its size, Montana's population is just north of a million people.

Montana is 2.5 times bigger in area than Georgia and has a tenth of the population. Montana ranks fourth in overall size among the US states. All this space means freedom to roam, fish, hunt and hike, and do things that you really don't want people to see.

Ted Kaczynski, a graduate of Harvard University (he entered Harvard at sixteen) and a Berkley professor lived in Lincoln, Montana, and rode his bike around town while sending mail bombs to folks. He became known as the Unabomber and would probably still be there in Lincoln had his brother not recognized his FBI profile and turned him in. All traces of him were removed in the middle of the night by the FBI who loaded up his shack onto a flatbed truck and hauled it away for forensic analysis.

Outside of the major cities, there are numerous places where a person can land a small airplane. A lot are there so that ranchers can get around in the big space. Forest

Service, Montana Fish and Wildlife, and the Bureau of Land Management as well as numerous individuals use small, unlighted and unmanned landing areas. Many are grass strips where landings and takeoffs are largely unnoticed and unreported.

In bygone days, it was almost impossible to land on these strips at night because, first of all, you could not find them or see them and there are no beacons and no lights. In some cases, there are smaller public paved strips, also unmanned, that have a lighting system that can be turned on by the pilot using the plane's radio once you are in range.

But with today's GPS technology, even a small handheld GPS unit, any place can be located even in pitch-black darkness and with a degree of accuracy to within just a few feet. Using such services as Google Earth or Acme Mapper, a person can locate where they want to go online, get the GPS coordinates, plug them into their GPS, and away they go. Most registered airfields have their GPS coordinates listed as part of the airport information, and you don't even have to look for them. This has given rise to small, low-flying aircraft, which are hard to detect in the mountains, being used to transport illegal drugs and people and guns.

On the US southern borders, the flat terrain makes low-flying aircraft easier to spot crossing the border, thus they have resorted to tunnels and human "mules" to move a lot of drugs across into the United States. Apparently, tunnel building is a very big business in Mexico as they just dug a mile-long tunnel directly under a jail cell to allow a notorious criminal to escape.

Using STOL aircraft (short takeoff and landing planes), a few high-intensity LED-battery-powered lights or car lights, a GPS and a good and brave pilot, several hundred pounds of such drugs as cocaine can be delivered with pinpoint accuracy to one of these small, out-of-the-way strips to be picked up for local distribution. In other circumstances, the plane may not actually land on the field. Unbreakable items that can be wrapped in a big roll of bubble wrap packing material, that can be purchased at U-Haul stores or a big home center, are wrapped; and a couple of LED, long-lasting lights are wrapped in the roll. As the planes flies very low and slow over the chosen area, which may be just a field, a person simply drops them out the door of the plane to be picked up in a minute or so and thrown into a van, truck, ATV, or car. The whole process takes a couple of minutes, and the plane flies on and the people on the ground are gone. If someone heard and came to investigate, they would find nothing.

In a bar in Billings, Montana, Helen Potts (who knows if that's her real name) and Jeffery Bristol have ordered a burger, Cokes, and fries. They have just been driving for several hours to meet with some people they have never met before, but they have photos that were mailed to them. Making sure you are talking to the right people can make a difference in a successful venture or twenty years behind bars. They had them mailed to avoid having any computer trails or IP addresses that could be traced to them.

Many people have found that the speed of the Internet is great but also the speed at which people can find you when you are out there on the "Net" too much. Hector Martinez arrived at the bar and sat in the parking lot for a few minutes. He could call to see if the people he was here to meet had arrived, but he wanted no telephone connection records to them on his phone. If things went okay, he would get a throwaway phone later. Hector's father was Hispanic, and his mother was white woman from Oklahoma. His name was Hispanic and his father was Hispanic, but he looked and talked like a cowboy from Oklahoma. They had moved to Texas in recent years where his father worked as farm and ranch manager for a big outfit in Laredo, Texas. It was on the border where it was easy to find drugs and people with drugs.

He looked to see if there were any people sitting around in cars. People that might be local or federal law enforcement or drug cops. He was driving a Ram pickup that looked like about ten others sitting around in the lot. Nothing that attracted attention.

He got his small .45 caliber S&W automatic from under the seat and checked it and stuck it in the back of his pants under the fancy short-sleeved shirt that he did not tuck in. He was ready to go in and look for the people pictured in the photos in his hand. As soon as they met, the pictures were to be shredded. He had backed his truck into the parking spot to avoid his license plate being exposed and to allow for a fast exit should it become necessary. He had not had time to switch a Montana tag to cover his Texas tag that he now had on the truck.

Donny "Tap Tap" Bragg was in his Ford F-150 on the other side of the parking lot. He had been watching when the Ram truck came in and wondered why the lone driver was taking so long to get out and go in the bar. Was he watching or talking to someone on his cell? Donny decided to wait and see. He looked at the photos he had with a small penlight. He was to meet three people here tonight he had not met before. Too many people, he thought. But someone else was calling the shots on this deal and they were willing to pay well!

He wondered if he should take his gun but decided against it in case they were to be confronted by the cops. He had no record anywhere that they could connect him with, and carrying a concealed weapon with no permit might not be wise. Staying under the radar had its advantages.

The interior light in the Ram came on, and he could see who he thought was one of the people he was supposed to meet. He would wait a couple of minutes to let that guy find the others inside, and when he went in, he would not have to stand around and draw attention to himself looking for them.

When Donny finally went inside, Hector had already spotted Helen and Jeffery and pulled a chair up to their table, and the waitress was there asking for his order. Donny walked over to the table as if he were a long-lost friend, patting each on the back with a smile and a greeting for all the world to see. He pulled a chair up and said, "Hi. I'm Donny."

They each said hello and gave their names. Most of these jobs were done by men but there were times when a pretty woman could be very helpful playing the loving wife or girlfriend. Helen had played these roles several times and had proven herself reliable and resourceful. She had grown up in Chattanooga and tried over and over to be a country music singer, even going to Nashville for a while. She was a good singer but had never been able to get the big break.

They never knew her in Nashville as Helen Potts. She had used a lot of names in a lot of places by now. But she had a locker in the Amtrak station in Miami and a friend she trusted and paid well to maintain the fee. There were a couple of changes of clothes, fake IDs, a really well-done fake passport that cost a lot of money, and a bag full of cash. Lots of cash. She got paid well when she worked. If things were too hot, her friend could pick up the stuff and get it to her. For a fee, of course. When the bag of cash got big enough, she would quit this dangerous job and move to some nice place and just enjoy life and write music.

The four of them were there to figure out how to take a shipment of cocaine that was going to be brought in to some as yet unknown airstrip and get it to a distributor in Butte who could ship it out in smaller amounts on I-15 north and south and I-90 east and west. They knew from an informant on one of the local sheriff departments that the distributor was being watched and that the DEA had an informant inside the drug ring somewhere. The roads and airstrips and just about everything else were under surveillance. Five hundred pounds (226 kilos) of cocaine was worth about $4.5 million at wholesale and about $15–$20 million on the streets. Depending on what street you are on.

The shipment might be somewhere between five hundred and eight hundred pounds as that was about all they could haul on the small plane with two people on board. It involved lots of money, lots of risks, and a lot of danger. Standing in the way of these deals could be fatal.

They would each have a job and some looking around to do. They would do it without attracting attention. No speeding tickets, no drunk and disorderly, and no credit cards or cell phone contact at this time. They would meet at a local motel in Billings at a certain time on a certain date. Write this time, date and place down, if you want, but *no* names.

The person in charge of this operation was Donny because he had no record anywhere. He had earned the nickname Tap Tap because of his willingness to eliminate any potential threat. He was a dangerous man.

There were several tasks. They had to pick out two or three possible drop sites and take a visual of the location to confirm a plane could land or drop there. Get the exact GPS readings and then decide on the best one to use near the time of the drop to avoid anyone tipping off the cops. They then had to find a way to get the drugs from the Billings-area drop to Butte and bypass any roadblocks or traffic stops that might be out there.

They would have to second-guess, but if they could get the DEA informant the wrong information, then they might be able to find out where the intercept was planned and find a way to skirt it. The DEA informant could be to their advantage. Could be. And it also could be their informant and the DEA informant is the same person.

It would be Donny's and Hector's job to see that the drugs got to where they we supposed to. Helen and Jeffery would scout for airdrop sites and handle some transportation issues to get Donny and Hector where they needed to be. They also had to have their vehicles moved at some point, depending on how they set things up.

Russ got up, had a nice breakfast at the local home-style cooking place, and then went over to the fly shop. He had had a night to sleep on things and was not as uptight as he was yesterday. John was as nice as could be and repeated his apology. He invited Russ to come into his office and have coffee and just talk.

Russ learned that John had bought the business after guiding and working in the shop for a number of years. He had bet the farm, as they say, and he and his wife spent a lot of time building the in-house business, booking fishing trips locally and some destination trips. A lot of these tasks were online as many people thought of the Bozeman area as a destination area.

Their Internet sales had continued to grow and were a big contributor to the business.

He wanted to know more about Russ, but Russ was reluctant to tell John the whole story. But he did tell him that he had met his wife, who was from his own hometown, there at the shop. That they fished and did everything together and that she had died a few months ago now. And that it had hit him hard, and he was working through that loss now by doing the things they enjoyed doing together with only her memory now.

"I named my boat after her," Russ told John.

John asked a few more questions and then said he would be glad for Russ to guide for clients when he had overflow or was short of guides. He had commitments for this season with the current guides. Russ was not really looking for much work but did not tell John that bit of information.

The brothers had sung Russ's praises to John as they had to Chad. It turned out that John had a lot of respect for Chad and they had worked together a long time before Chad built a large following and went on his own. John knew Nancy very well too. That perked Russ's interest, somehow.

Nancy had gone to Montana State and gotten a degree in business as well as getting all the credits she needed for teaching and had taught at a local elementary school for a while. She then went to work for a local agricultural services company as a business manager. She fell in love with the owner's son, and they dated for a long time then became engaged.

He was in the National Guard and his unit was called up to go to Iraq. He and Nancy put their plans on hold until he returned. Some said he had insisted that they not get married in case something happened to him in Iraq. Something did happen in Iraq. Something bad. He was killed in a firefight, and Nancy was devastated for a long time. As a result, she had not really dated much since. She was considered one of the most eligible young ladies in Bozeman.

Russ confided in John that he had been a cop and a detective and that he still had a small, fast-closing window that he could go back but had not decided and time was running out to make the decision. He asked that John keep the info under his hat. He found that he liked John more and more and was ready to put the previous incident aside. Russ fished some days. Soon he began to get an occasional float trip as more people met him and heard about him and he got some calls from other fly shops asking him to take a float for them. He did not want to work every day, but it was nice to stay busy.

He loved being on the water and not being worried about the phone ringing day and night. He started getting invites to have a beer, go to dinner, play cards, and the normal stuff that people do in a community.

He was a little embarrassed about telling anyone he lived at the Super 8, but most knew it anyway. There probably weren't a lot of millionaires staying there. Dan had done a great job assisting Russ with his money, and he was very frugal in his spending. He was bringing in enough right now to cover his monthly bills, but his disability leave money would stop soon.

He still was using Nancy for his shuttles and spoke to her on the phone to set that up, but that was all the contact he had been having with her. Dating had been the farthest thing from his mind, but he was seeing the mental fog start to clear away. And when he thought of Sarah, it was a good thought, a memory, not just the bad stuff that had occurred. He was still going to the Brew Works often and was pretty much a regular in there now. He would see Nancy picking up her lunch once in a while and give her a wave, but she was usually in a rush, it seemed. He had been invited to a party by one of the married waitresses, just a friendly invite, and he had gone and enjoyed himself with the waitress and her husband and friends. It was nice to get out, but Nancy was not there, and he did not know if she had been invited. He had wished that he might see her there.

Russ had made a call to Schreiber that morning and had told him that he was not ready to come back right now and wasn't sure he was coming back. It was a pleasant conversation, and Schreiber said he understood. The six months was up, but Schreiber had not hired anyone yet to fill Russ's job and had not been pushed to do so by the chief. He told Russ that if he ever wanted to come back, he would try to make a place for him and would love to have him. That pressure of making a decision was over, and he felt a sense of relief. He then called his father-in-law, Dan, and he was not surprised but promised to come out soon. That chapter at the Cobb County Police Department was closed in his life, at least for now. He left for the Brew Works for lunch.

7

MOST OF THE GUIDES HE knew were always working this time of the year at lunch. Once in a while he ran in to John from the fly shop and his wife there having lunch and they would join him, but mostly he ate alone at the bar or at a table if the bar was full. He liked catching up on Fox News and ESPN on the Brew Works TVs that were always on.

Today he was at a table with his back to the front when there was a slight tap on the shoulder and a female voice. "Well, hello, stranger." It was Nancy.

Nancy was in her professional attire, and she looked beautiful. He had thought of her as attractive when he had seen her in there before, but today, she looked stunning. Not the shuttle driver attire she wore moving trucks and trailers around for Chad. She could have been in any fashion magazine and held her own. He invited her to join him for lunch, and to his surprise, she accepted.

"I have been doing a TV commercial in the store all morning, and I am pooped," she said.

"It's a lot of work to do a one-minute spot when you are not use to doing that sort of thing. I left Mom and one of the part-time people there and told them they would see me in one hour. I'm taking a real lunch hour today."

That suited Russ just fine!

"I thought you might have stopped by and checked out the store," she said.

"I have ridden by. It is very nice. I don't buy a lot of ladies' clothing, so I am not in too many ladies' clothing stores. But if I was going to, I would certainly come in there."

"Well, you could come by and say hello and not buy anything."

"I will take that as an invite," he said.

Then he added, "I wasn't sure if you were seeing anyone or in a relationship. Since my wife died, I have been living sort of like a recluse. Life's a little better now even though I miss her and think about her every day."

She leaned over the table and said softly, "I was never married, but someone I cared about and was engaged to died, and I have found myself doing the same thing. Working in the store and shuttling trucks for Chad is about all I have done."

A tear rolled down her face.

"I have just started to see daylight myself."

They seemed to have something in common. They had lunch and said good-bye, and she left. A nice lady, for sure. A very nice catch for someone, no doubt. But romance was not on his to-do list just yet. He did not yet feel single. He was married to a memory. All he had on his mind today was going by the courthouse to see about getting a concealed carry permit.

Since he was no longer officially on the Cobb Police Department, he might not be given a courtesy exemption if he was found with a gun. He did not need to get in any trouble with the law if he was ever going back as a cop again. He went and applied for the gun carry permit.

When they asked for his address, although he thought it might be a problem, he put down the street address for the Super 8 and his room number as the "apartment or unit number." He gave all of his previous addresses and job history, and he would be in the FBI database because of his police background checks. They got to the place that asked if he had a concealed carry permit from any other state, and he said yes, which meant he was covered in Montana and did not need a Montana permit.

The drug dealers had been busy. Using the Internet and good Montana maps, they had come up with several small airfields and landing strips that might serve to do the drop that was coming up and could be used in future drops. There were several near Big Timber and Billings with easy access to the interstate highway that went straight to Butte. The normal idea was that the stuff got dropped off, and some person or persons would make a beeline to deliver it to the distributor.

But the vibes were there that the main people were being watched by someone on the inside. They felt it unlikely that person knew who they were or where they were but would as soon as the drop information and delivery was set up.

Donny Bragg had maintained an air of invisibility so far in his career as a drug dealer by doing the unexpected, and he would find a way to keep that up. Helen Potts had used so many IDs and hairstyles that she was somewhat obscure. But this was a big payday, and a new drug stream being set up; and as badly as they wanted it to work, the Feds and locals wanted to bust them all. It was great to make a big bust near election time for the locals.

The plan being discussed was that Helen and Jeffery were to be the pickup people at the drop. Donny was the only one that was allowed contact with the headman, and he was not too sure who he really was although they had worked together on a number of deals.

Helen and Jeffery decided that they would use a specific strip for a rolling drop. It was near the highway and they could be in and out from the time the flyover took place in about two to three minutes. They had the GPS coordinates that would be eventually passed on to the people in Butte on a burn phone by Donny.

They would set up the plane, the pilot, and have the drugs on the plane somewhere, probably, in remote Idaho or Montana. Donny thought Idaho. He approved the landing strip near Billings and jotted down the GPS coordinates as they were too complex to safely remember. The drop would be taking place next week at about 2:00 AM.

Donny told them he would be out of town for the next two or three days and not to expect to hear from him. He would meet them back here in three days for lunch. With that, he was gone.

They paid for everything in cash; no credit cards and nothing bigger than a twenty—Donny's orders. No need to attract attention by throwing a lot of money around and especially big bills. And they somehow knew not to cross Donny.

Donny Bragg had been spending a lot of time at the Hampton Inn, mostly with a young attractive woman he had known and dated in college. Teresa Walker came to Bozeman a lot in her capacity with the State Division of Criminal Investigation and bumping into her at the Hampton had worked out very nicely for Donny in more ways than one. They were together a lot of evenings and nights at the Hampton.

Teresa's feelings for Donny had lasted since college, and she now had a business interest in providing him info on the operation of local law enforcement efforts, for which she got paid some cash and—she had a sexual interest. Just maybe, she was thinking, a love interest. There was a rush to it all!

Donny needed to go up to the Madison River and take care of a couple of things. He had found a small place with a few cabins and camper spots, and he wanted to go check it out. He also wanted to check out a landing strip he had found on the library's computer near Highway 87, close to the Wyoming and Idaho borders. He left Bozeman and turned south on US 191 that went alongside the Gallatin River. Beautiful Big Sky Country.

Donny used his GPS to find the strip off Highway 87. It was a grass strip, seldom used, and no houses right around. It had no lights. No buildings. No nothing. It did have a lake view. There were no trees to be clipped by a low-flying plane and no power lines. It was perfect for what he needed with a decent rural road access. He left and headed down US 287 to the roadside cabins. He was about 160 miles from the Billings airstrip that Helen and Jeffery had located for the drop as the crow flies.

He went in with his hat and sunglasses and cowboy boots. He looked right at home in that part of the world. He explained that he was meeting his sister and her kids up that way next week and he needed a cabin. They were going to do some trout fishing. The others would have a camper, so he wanted to pay for a camper space and a room to be sure they could all stay at the same place and he would pay in cash.

They asked for a credit card to hold the room and the space. He handed them ten twenty-dollar bills and asked if that would work. Surprisingly, they said, "You bet."

"I want to rent them for two nights," he said.

Donny's plan was simple. It was simple, and no one knew what it was but him. While the others were looking to do the drop in some place near Billings and that was the talk among them and the plans as far as they knew, he wasn't about to trust his freedom to someone like Helen and Jeffery. But their efforts would not be in vain. Their information would be fed to all the people involved, and that would be what the Feds and other law enforcement would get. If they were going to act, they would be acting on a set instructions that would be different than he was working on.

The drug task force would be preparing for an interdiction at an airstrip near Billings. They would have rolling roadblocks and pursuit vehicles. Heavily armed agents would swoop down on the drug dealers, and if they happened to make it away from the airstrip, the roads to Butte would be covered, and there would be no way to get through.

Donny had a different plan. One known only to him. He would handle the time, place, and transportation in his own fashion. He had it all worked out, but one small detail. He had to call the pilot on the burn phone, and he had already set up a trout fishing guide to handle a drift down the Madison next week. While the cops were shutting down the roads to Butte and dogs were sniffing the cars on I-90, Donny Bragg would be doing what a lot of people like to do in Montana: he was going to be in a drift boat trout fishing on the Madison. It might take the task force a few hours to realize that the drop did not take place as planned. He would give them time to call everything off while he was enjoying the day 160 miles away.

He called the pilot's number. If he did not answer, there would be no message left. He would only speak to him in person following a quick check to see if he was who he said he was.

"Yes."

"Who is this?" Was the answer on the other end.

"This is the angel of mercy."

"Do you have wings?"

"No. You have the wings."

"And I can fly."

"When you decide to fly again, call me at this number before you do. Got that?"

He rattled off his burn phone number.

"No birds will fly 'til I do."

Donny hit the End Call button.

Donny had been looking around for just the right fly-fishing guide to take him on a float down the Madison. He believed that the last place the Feds and locals would be looking for a few million dollars in cocaine the next day after a drop would be in a drift boat floating down the Madison River in broad daylight. A fast car, an interstate highway or an airplane, maybe. When they found they had been duped, they would be mad. He needed a way to stay right in front of them and yet completely out of sight as their circle widened from the drop site. They would be checking motels and airport control tower radar files and telephone calls and turning over all the regular suspects. They might

even find Helen and Jeffery if they have not been careful.
They probably would not be checking fly shops. He would
be sure that Teresa got the bad information to feed back to
the people in Helena. He trusted nobody.

Donny had looked up all the guides in the phone book
over the last several days. Some he could see were big
shops with lots of people, security cameras on all the time,
and people looking at trucks and cars in the parking lot.
He was looking for a lone operator without too much in
sophisticated business practices.

Donny had thought he could float the entire distance
from up near where he would be staying at the camp
on Highway 287 to Ennis Lake, not realizing that that
distance was too far for a one-day float. That distance is
pushing forty-five miles. This would turn out to be a flaw in
his plan but, in reality, did not affect anything as no one was
looking on the Madison for him after the drop took place
anyway. It was his intention for the authorities to assume
that the drop did not take place in the area, if possible, or
have them chasing their tails with roadblocks and random
truck inspections on all the routes around the Billings area
if they believed it had taken place at another location in
the area. He would be right there in the area in the most
unsuspected location.

There was a fly shop in a small building adjacent to a
house inside the city of Bozeman on a side street. He would
not have seen it except he saw an old Hyde drift boat being
pulled behind a rough-looking old Fleetside Chevrolet on
Main Street that had turned down S. Black Avenue as he
was passing by. He had followed it to see where it was going,
and it pulled up in front of a house with a small shop next
to the house. The shop looked as rough as the truck. There

was a small magnetic sign on the side of the truck that said, "Warren Cason, fly fishing guide" and a cell phone number and a small sign in the window had the same info but said, "Wade and float trips, 15 years' experience." As he drove by, Warren Cason, fly-fishing guide, was opening the door to the shop and turning on the lights. This looked like the one-man shop he had been looking for. Donny was looking for security cameras and did not see any.

He went up the street and called the guide's number on his burn phone.

"Hello. This is Warren," was the answer.

"Hi, Warren. I am looking for someone who could do a float for me and my friend next week on the Madison. My sister's family and I are spending some time up at the cabin and camping place near Quake Lake, and I wanted someone who could meet us at the put-in up there and do a float down to Ennis on Wednesday morning. I hear that is a good stretch. Are you available Wednesday?"

"Yes, I am available. I can do a twelve-mile float some days, but a float over that whole distance you're talking about could take two full days, depending on water flow. That's a haul, and you have to keep moving."

"I usually put in up at one of two places for eight-mile floats. If you are on a schedule, I suggest we stick to an eight-mile float. To get some good fishing and get out reasonably early, eight miles is enough. We can put in at Varney to Ennis or we can do the eight miles from a put-in on 287 up near Cheery Gulch down to Varney Bridge. Would that be okay? That's been fishing good and a little less crowded."

"The cost for that for two would be $425 and you will need a fishing license if you don't already have one. Do you want to set it up?"

65

"Yes. I suppose that will have to work then as I will only have the one day to fish. That sounds good. Let's do the float to Varney."

"How will you be paying?"

Donny always had the same answer about paying cash for everything.

"I had some identity theft issues, and I don't use credit cards anymore," said Donny. "How about I pay you in cash?"

"Cash would be great, but I need a deposit before I drive all the way up there and have a possible no-show."

"Tell you what, Warren, I will be down that way tomorrow sometime. Suppose I drop the money by and give it to someone there?" Donny was counting on no one being there to see him. He would soon find out.

"There is no one here but me, but you can leave it under the door—$100 will be enough. And leave your name and phone number."

"Warren, my name is Kile Davidson, and I'll leave the full amount. That way, we want have to have any money issues at the river. Is that okay?" Kile Davidson was one of Donny's phony IDs.

"Sure, Kile. Do you have your own rods, etc.?"

"I do not have any equipment with me on this trip, so bring what we need, if you don't mind. We both fly-fished some but had not counted on having a day to fish. We will meet you at the put-in. Which one do you want us at?"

They got the logistics worked out, and Donny hung up and gave a little, "Yea." The plan was coming together. He and Hector would meet Warren down the road from the cabin camp. No one would likely see them together up close. He had done some good work and thought he would go back to Bozeman and get himself a good meal and a cold beer.

As Russ was pulling into the Brew Works parking lot, the sharp, black Ford F-150 pulled in just ahead of him. What he noticed was the fact that the truck was immaculate. No mud or dirt anywhere. It pulled in a space just down from where Russ was putting his Tahoe in, and he noticed the Ford had what looked like an unusual custom-made, rear bumper. It was chrome, and the trailer hitch was the type that rotated to provide a variety of sizes for trailer balls. But it did not look like a work truck to Russ.

The fellow getting out was a clean-cut, nicely dressed guy with cowboy boots and hat and a nice Western-style denim shirt. The cop in Russ was interested, but he did not know why and had no reason to give it a second thought. When the fellow finished his meal at the Brew Works, he paid cash and left.

Russ finished dinner and started out Main Street toward the Super 8. The Super 8 was actually just across the street from the fly shop, and there were a number of motels at that exit off Interstate 90.

To his surprise, the black Ford F-150 with the bright chrome bumper was turning onto Main Street from a side street just ahead of him and headed in the same direction as he was going. That appeared to be a residential neighborhood. Maybe the guy lived down that street. The same guy with the cowboy hat. He stayed behind the truck until it turned off onto the access road that went by the Hampton Inn, which was not too far from the Super 8. Just another coincidence that meant nothing to Russ. How many black F-150s were there in Montana?

8

RUSS HAD FINALLY GOTTEN A visit from Dan, his former father-in-law, and he took him on a float trip in the boat. Dan spent two more days in town and met John at the fly shop, Chad, and they bumped into Nancy at the Brew Works. When she walked away, Dan, a pretty astute guy, mentioned how pretty she was.

Russ explained her situation and that she had been the one that shuttled the truck and trailer a couple of days before. Dan put his chin in his hands and looked at Russ.

"You know that Sarah loved you, and she would want you to find another person that you could love and be happy with. I know that we do and you would have our blessing to do just that."

His former (he guessed that was the right relationship) father-in-law had just released him from any further obligation to them or his late wife. He did not realize until later how liberating that had been for him. Dan left for Atlanta, and Russ decided to go to the gun range. He had not fired his guns since he did not know when. His main gun was a Beretta M9, 9 mm. Not a small compact gun but a military and cop standard that had been around for a while. With a fifteen-round magazine, you could pump out some serious firepower in close-combat situations.

Then he also had an S&W M&P .45 cal. It was small and carried eight rounds. It fit easily into his jacket or pants, and he carried it more often just for that reason. It felt good to have the chance to shoot again. Maybe he was clawing his way back from the hole he had crawled into almost a year ago.

Tuesday was a beautiful day in Bozeman. The sun was coming up in grand fashion. Russ did not have a float trip today, so he came up with this idea out of the blue: why not call Nancy and invite her to lunch? He called the number and got her cell voice mail. "Please leave a message at the tone." Now that was original!

"Hi, Nancy. This is Russ Baker. Two things: I need a shuttle in the morning, but it is all the way up above Cherry Gulch put-in and I will be taking out at Varney Bridge. Are you available to handle that for me? Secondly, are you available for lunch today or, maybe, dinner tonight? It will be an early night since I have to get up early in the morning. Thanks"

It was a while before the phone rang and Nancy returned his call. "Yes, I can do your shuttle tomorrow. I will be up that way anyway at the 287 put-in and taking them down to Varney Bridge. Milly Cason, she's Warren Cason's mother, called me to do one for Warren tomorrow. She normally does them for him, but she is having a bad time with her emphysema, so I agreed to help them out."

They worked out the logistics as to where he was taking out and the put-in. Nancy would be busy but would have plenty of time. Russ did not know who Warren was and had not heard his name before.

"As far as lunch today, I have a sales rep in town, and he has invited us to lunch, so I will not be able to meet you for lunch today, and I also have something planned for tonight. Thanks for the invitation though."

Darn! he thought. *I was really a day late in this one.*

In some small way, he felt a pang of jealousy for whoever she was going out with tonight. That caught him by surprise.

The big day was here. Helen Potts and Jeffrey Bristol were bored out of their minds, but they would be meeting the drop plane in a few hours, and there would be an adrenaline rush getting to the drop area over near Billings, checking for the bad guys, who were really the good guys, and making sure the coast was clear.

They would set out a number of high-brightness LED lights to mark the area for the plane's pilot to be able to drop the cushioned packages on a flyover. They would chase down the packages, probably about five, and should be able to see them with the lights on inside the clear packaging. They would get them into the trunk of their Camaro with the big engine and haul ass out to Butte.

They would not be taking the interstate as the word was there would be a chance of road checks between Billings and Butte. Jeffery Bristol was along for one reason: he could drive an automobile! Although they were talking about a fast trip on I-90, they were actually going up Highway 3 to US 12 and going west through Helena and dropping down from the north to Butte. A longer way but safer since they were concerned about a possible informant. They would get a call from Donny as to when to go, and they were not to leave until they got his call in case there was a problem.

No one felt safe in crossing Donny, so they would wait. They got some fast food and went to their hotel, where they were registered as Mr. and Mrs. Phillips, to wait.

Somewhere at a small private hangar in Idaho, there was a beautiful Maule M-7 airplane. It was taildragger with 235 HP engine and a state-of-the-art Garmin Seven 50 series avionics system. It could carry about 895 pounds, and the rear seats had been removed and were carefully sitting out of the way in the single roll-up-door hangar.

This was to reduce weight and create spaces for five round and glowing packages wrapped in bubble wrap and duct tape. Lots of both.

Someone had taken colored duct tape to modify the aircraft's N-number so as not to be recognized, but it would still look legal if spotted from the ground. The owner had spent about $350,000 for this baby, but he would not be flying it tonight. He was on vacation in Hawaii. His plane was being "borrowed" for some special business tonight and would be returned in fine condition, hopefully in a few hours. Hopefully.

It was about four in the afternoon, and Donny had called the pilot at about 3:00 PM. The pilot was told to be loaded early and be prepared for a change in plans.

At four o'clock, Donny set the new plan in motion. He was already at the Camp Inn and checked in. He got in his truck and found a high place where he had a signal on the burn phone. Hector was in the truck now with Donny, having driven down from town right behind Donny. He had no idea what was happening. Donny called Helen.

"Are you guys all packed up and ready to move out?"

"Yes," she said.

"Good. I want you to come to near Quake Lake on Highway 287 to the Cabin Inn. Here is the GPS." Donny rattled off the GPS location for the Cabin Inn.

"I have a cabin here that we can all stay in tonight. Get here as fast as you can without raising suspicion. Pay for your room over there as you won't be using it after today. Hector and I will not be here when you arrive, so just go inside and wait. If anyone asks, you are my sister."

"Okay," she said.

She told Jeffery they were clearing out and leaving for some place over past Ennis, and he was confused and concerned. Why the change in plans? But Jeffery and Helen got in the Camaro and headed for Highway 287 and the cabins, making sure they weren't followed.

Donny then made another call. This time to the pilot.

"Are you ready?"

"Yes."

"Here are the new GPS coordinates." He gave them, and the pilot read them back to confirm. "How long to replot?"

"About fifteen minutes."

"Leave in fifteen minutes and we will have lights in case you need them. I anticipate it being about 150 miles."

"Okay. Dropping five totaling two hundred."

So there would be five wrapped packs totaling two hundred kilograms or 440 pounds of merchandise worth about $14,000,000 in street value. This was about half of the original shipment, and it had apparently been split.

Donny hung up and they drove south on 287 toward Highway 87 and the drop site. They got a drink and a sandwich to go at a bar and grill. They did not want to be too early or too late. They had a handheld FMS radio with a range of about twenty miles that the pilot would call them on when he was ten minutes out or so.

Helen and Jeffery were on the way, and Jeffery had put his gun handy because he did not like the sudden changes. But they were closing in on the Camp Inn.

In Billings, a task force was being mobilized based upon the information they had from the informant. The local sheriff's drug unit, a state police team, agents from the state's Department of Criminal Investigation unit, and the DEA were assembled. Sharpshooters had been concealed near the drop site so they could get a view of the field and cars would be situated to block any exit. Since they were told this was a rolling drop, the DEA's King Air, with sophisticated tracking equipment, was in place to follow the plane and arrest its occupants when they landed. No normal single-engine light plane could outrun the twin turboprop.

Landing could be a problem for the King if the runway was too short or the strip was dirt, but they would know where the plane was to alert people on the ground. Everything was set and checked. They would all go to dinner and be ready for the drop to take place at 2:00 AM. The Butte Police were ready. The Bozeman Police were ready. These drug dealers would be in for a surprise.

Donny's radio came to life at about five forty-five. There was a lot of daylight left.

"The bird with wings is ten minutes out."

"Lights are coming on." Donny waved for Hector to start turning on the six lights on his side of the field, and he had to run do the ones on his side. They showed the width of the target, and the guy onboard with the pilot would have the door latched back and roll the rolls out at about fifty feet off the ground and about seventy miles per hour.

73

"Five minutes ETA."

"Two minutes."

"Field and lights in sight."

Donny could see the beautiful Maule with full flaps dropping in and was down not much higher than twenty-five feet.

One roll out. Two rolls. Three. Four. And five. They hit, bounced, and rolled for several feet. Before the last roll stopped rolling, the Ford F-150 was moving down the strip with Donny driving and Hector putting the rolls in the back. On the radio he said, "Perfect."

"Of course," was the reply.

They stopped long enough to cut the duct tape and remove the bubble wrap. They would put that in a roadside dumpster they had seen on the way up. When they stopped there, they would put the merchandise into four duffel bags they had for the purpose. Donny slowly drove to the road and headed to the highway while Hector spread a tarp over the duffel bags and put the several small bales of hay they had picked up at a feed and seed store in Bozeman over the tarp to look like a local guy going to feed some livestock. He got in the cab when they got to Highway 87 and started back to the Camp Inn.

When they got there, Helen and Jeffery were there. They were done for the day about seven thirty, and they sat down with some beer and watched TV. Donny made one more call to someone, "All is well," and hung up. He sat down at the table and cleaned his gun.

About 4:00 AM, a group of very angry and frustrated law enforcement people up near Billings, Montana, came to the realization that they had been fed bad information or that the drop was called off. They would learn later that the drop had been successful, but no one knew that now and no one knew where. If there was a drop tonight, it wasn't in Billings, and the informant had no explanation.

Even the people expecting the drugs in Butte did not know where they were. That's exactly the way Donny Bragg had planned it.

Wednesday morning found Nancy and the young lady that she had help her on the shuttles up having breakfast. From the time the guide put his boat in on the long floats, she had a large window of time to make the transfer of the truck and trailer from the put-in location to the take-out point. Several hours on the floats like today. But she had a clothing store to run, so she liked to get the shuttles out of the way so she could devote her time to the store. She had thought about stopping the shuttles, but she did enjoy the contact with the guides, helping her brother, and she had needed the extra money when she first started the store with her mother.

On these long drives, today was about seventy-five miles one way; she got paid more and the guides were happy to pay her more than some others because she was reliable and accurate. The fact that she was a beautiful woman did not hurt. And today, as was usual for her, she had two shuttles to do at the same place. Russ had called about doing his up near Cherry Gulch, and her old-time, occasional customer, Warren Cason was going to need a shuttle there too.

Warren was a hard worker who lived with his mother and looked after her financially since his dad died at an early age of a heart attack and his mother's emphysema kept her from a full-time job as a bookkeeper. She kept up with Warren's bills and made sure the taxes were filed and money went in the bank on time. Warren was a great guide and a wonderful person but a lousy businessman.

Russ picked up his boat at the storage facility on N Rouse, which was just around the corner from the Super 8 and the fly shop, and was headed to the shop to pick up a father-and-son from Knoxville, Tennessee. They were making their first fly-fishing trip to Montana and were waiting at the fly shop with their gear. It turned out they fished a lot on the Holston River in drift boats in Tennessee. That would make it easier on Russ since they were accustomed to fishing from a drift boat and were not greenhorns.

Donny Bragg and Hector Martinez were putting some clothing and fishing gear on top of the drugs in the four duffel bags. At fifty pounds each, they still were manageable. They would go in the boat with them when they went downstream with Warren. If he asked questions, they would say it was some personal stuff, clothes, and valuables they wanted with them since they were not going back to the motel when they left the river that this afternoon. That wasn't really true, but by then it wouldn't matter.

A quick look would not reveal anything. They would sweeten the deal by offering Warren a couple of hundred dollars extra "for his trouble." Offering too much would only arouse his suspicion.

Helen and Jeffery would take them to meet Warren, drop them off, and go back to the cabins or just ding around until the anticipated arrival down near Varney Bridge. This was all part of an elaborate scheme to not be seen by any inquisitive Feds.

They would bring Donny's truck and their Camaro. Donny would later drop off Hector to pick up his truck and then drive Highway 2 over to Butte with the hay and drugs in the back. Helen and Jeffery would be leaving the area, going probably to Idaho or Washington State. A job well done by drug dealer standards.

Donny and Hector would go back to their daily routine in Bozeman, at least for a few days, and wait for the next deal to come along. It was a beautiful day in the Madison River Valley.

Russ reached the put in and as he was turning in, to his amazement, there was a beautiful and spotless black Ford F-150 with a chrome bumper leaving the boat launch area. It appeared to be a woman driving. He glanced over and thought the woman looked vaguely familiar. His three years in a police cruiser made him decide quickly that this was the same Ford F-150 he had seemed to run into several times the past few days.

A boat with a guide and two clients was already starting their float and were down river from the boat ramp. They were quite a distance away and not where Russ could see the people clearly.

As Russ made the turn into the lot, the sidewall of the right trailer tire hit a broken edge of the asphalt, and there was a jolt to the Tahoe as the asphalt ripped the trailer tire open and the tire was destroyed. Russ did not know exactly what had happened until he got out and looked, and he and his two Tennessee clients saw the problem.

Had Russ not been distracted by the Ford F-150, he might have seen the pothole and avoided it. But that was history now.

The trailer tire would have to be changed so that Nancy could transfer the rig to the take-out when she got there. Not a great way to start a float trip or anything else for that matter.

The trailer had a spare mounted and locked on the trailer, so that was not a problem. He would use the Tahoe's jack to raise up the trailer and take the old wheel off and put the new one on. The trailer tire lock key was on his Tahoe key ring, and this shouldn't delay them over fifteen or twenty minutes. The clients seemed willing to assist.

Russ found the jack in the Tahoe, although he had never had occasion to use it, but it worked fine in raising the trailer. He then got the lug wrench, which had been attached to the jack, and bent down to loosen the lug nuts of the trailer. He then discovered a real problem. The lug wrench for the Chevy Tahoe was for bigger lug nuts than were on the trailer. He could not take the wheel off with this wrench!

There was no one around, and he was in a bind now. He knew Nancy would be coming along, but when?

He hit her number on the speed dial. In spite of the somewhat spotty service, luckily, she answered.

"Hi, Russ. What's up?"

"I have a bit of a problem. I was pulling in here at the put-in and hit a bad place in the pavement with my trailer tire. Now I have a flat tire on my trailer and my lug wrench won't fit the lugs on the trailer wheel. I was wondering when you might be here and if you might have a wrench that would fit my trailer."

"As a matter of fact, I think I will have one that fits. I ran into that problem once and Chad got me a four-sided wrench with different sizes. I haven't needed it since, but it is in with my spare tire on the 4Runner. I will be there in fifteen to twenty minutes.

It ended up being more like twenty-five before she arrived, looking for all the world like a female trout bum in jeans and baggy shirt and hat. She worked hard at hiding the beautiful lady that she was.

She did, indeed, have a wrench. She told Russ to just leave it in his truck and she would get it when she came back to get his rig in a few minutes. It worked great, and they got the tire changed. As she pulled out in Warren Cason's truck to move it to the Varney Bridge take-out with a wave, he noticed the older Chevy Fleetside pickup with a magnetic sign on the side: Warren Cason, Fly Fishing Guide. Russ had not ever met him.

While they were changing the tire, Russ thought he might have heard a gunshot, but he wasn't sure. This was an area with a lot of open land, so it could have been someone taking a shot at a coyote, a tin can, or about anything. He did not have time or any reason to investigate.

Russ finally got the tire changed, and they were at last ready to get under way. They were now about an hour and a half later than expected. The clients had been very helpful and patient but were anxious to get fishing.

There were no boats in sight on the river, and that was unusual as the river usually had a lot of fishermen. They would get in some wade-fishing in a few spots as well as working from the boat and would not have to work around other boats.

There was a spot about a mile downstream with a little island at Cherry Gulch where a lot of boats would stop, have coffee, use the rest room and wade out to cast some. Russ had that in mind if it wasn't too crowded there, and it did not seem likely it would be.

Warren had asked about the four bags when Donny and Hector arrived and was suspicious from the start, but as Donny had suspected, the extra $200 in cash was enough to put the matter to rest. At least, that was the way it seemed. Warren seemed to understand they were transferring from one ride to another this afternoon. And he could use the $200.

Donny and Hector were not experts at fly-fishing, but both made respectable casts and had gotten off to a good start right away with both landing a few nice fish and missing some too. They were both actually enjoying the fishing and Warren was now focused on handling the drift boat. Things were going well. There was the little island at Cherry Gulch that most of the guides would stop at and allow the clients to wade, use the trees as a rest room area, and grab a coffee from the thermos. There was no one in sight, so he told the guys he was pulling in.

Donny said, "Great. I was about to ask if I could run behind a tree? I need to go bad. Do you have a roll of toilet paper I could use?"

There weren't a lot of trees along the river to get behind, but there were a few here.

"Sure. No problem," said Warren, and he headed to the gravel spot to beach the boat. He jumped out and pulled the boat up and got his thermos.

"This is a good spot to wade out and cast when you get back, and I will help you if you want or leave you alone to do your own thing. We just need to release the fish unharmed, but I can take some pictures if you want some."

9

DONNY RAN ACROSS TO THE Island and disappeared behind a tree. Hector walked away and turned his back to relieve himself, leaving Warren standing close to the boat with his coffee. Standing there, he took notice of the four duffels, all just alike, in the floor of the boat. He couldn't help but wonder what they contained. Glancing back, no one was looking, so Warren thought he would take a quick peek inside one of the duffels. He unzipped it and saw some T-shirts and shorts. Then he reached to see what else was in the bag, moving the underwear aside, and he saw the bags of powder. He'd been duped!

Someone grabbed Warren by the arm and yelled, "What the hell are you doing? Get your hands off of that!" It was Hector, and he was trying to drag Warren away from the boat. Warren was a quiet, unassuming guy, but he had been rowing drift boats, kayaks, and rubber rafts his whole life and was tremendously strong. Nobody was going to snatch him around like that and he grabbed Hector's arm and spun him around, and the shocked Hector was in a headlock before he knew it, and Warren had him locked up so he could not move.

Hector was yelling for Donny. "The guy has been in our bags!" Warren had his back to the river and was about to turn him around when Donny ran up behind him, his 9 mm in his hand. He shot Warren in the back of the, head and the shot took out Warren's right eye as it exited. Warren fell dead at his feet.

"Shit!" said Donny.

Hector was startled and horrified that Donny would just walk up and shoot the guy! He wanted to tell him what a stupid thing he'd done, but Donny was standing there with the 9 mm in his hand and a dead man at his feet. Maybe this was not the time for Hector to say too much or he would be lying beside the fishing guide! Up to now, Donny had been cool, calm, collected, and in charge. Now he lost it for a minute. The plan had just hit a royal snag. He had a dead guy on his hands and was seven miles from the take-out with no way to get there with the drugs but the dead guy's drift boat. This was not the low-profile day he had planned on.

He was sure he had seen a boat coming in as they were leaving the put-in. They should have already come into sight, and he ran out past the island to look, but he still did not see the boat. Forgetting about his own danger for a moment, Hector completely lost it and was yelling, "Why did you do that? Now what in the hell are we going to do? Why didn't we just buy him off?"

"Shut up and let's get him over to the little island and cover him up as best we can and get the hell out of here! We have to get this boat to the take-out where Helen can meet us. I'm not real positive which one it is for sure and if we will recognize it from the river. We will have to hope his truck has been moved down and we can see it." They dragged Warren across the small, shallow channel and put some tree limbs and sticks over him to hide him as best they could.

83

They did not see anyone in either direction as they pulled the boat out and jumped in. Hector, full of adrenaline and fear, started rowing the boat in the moderate water as fast as he could. This was a real mess!

Russ jumped in the Tahoe and backed the trailer down the ramp, released the boat, and pulled the boat up on the ramp. He parked the truck in a spot in the parking area. His clients could at last get in the boat, and they pushed off.

They had lost water time, but there was nothing he could do now but make the best of it. They were finally in the water, rods in hand, and fishing. These Southern guys were good, and their experience back on the Holston was paying off. They needed little instruction and started getting some hits quickly. They fished slowly, and the guys wanted to wade some, so he was dragging along at a slow rate, and he would be pushed to finish on time. But they were enjoying themselves and catching fish, so he would let it ride. He had no place to be, himself.

They finally made it to the island at Cherry Gulch where he also usually stopped for coffee, bathroom break, and wade fishing. So he pulled in on the gravel bar where about an hour and a half before, Warren Cason had pulled in and never left. The clients were focused on fishing and went out in the river to wade and cast and catch. They needed little help so Russ had a cup of coffee and relaxed. In a few minutes, he would gather them up to continue the seven miles of float to Varney Bridge.

He noticed something on the edge of the gravel bar at the back, and he walked over to see what it was. What he saw looked like blood, and it appeared that some dirt and rocks had been kicked over it too try and conceal it. That caused the cop in him to be awakened. There was no way to know what it was. Maybe some joker had shot a rabbit or gutted a fish here. It looked very fresh. But time was getting by, and they had been here far longer than he intended. Over two hours had passed since they pulled in the lot at the put in. It was time to move.

"Let's go, fellows," he yelled across the sound of the water and waved to the father-son clients. They would have stayed a while longer as they were getting some hits, but they understood the need to go. They splashed back to the boat. The father got in, but the son said, "I really need to make a trip over behind the bushes for a minute before we go." He grabbed his roll of toilet paper from his boat bag and ran across the shallows to the island to take care of his urge. He was gone for a few minutes when they heard him yelling,

"There is a guy lying over here! I think he's dead!"

Russ and the guy's father ran across to see what the son was talking about. The body was pretty well concealed, but his feet were not well covered, and that was what had caught the younger man's attention.

Russ, suddenly thinking like a cop, said, "You fellows need to step back and let's not disturb anything. I want to look at this guy and see if he is actually dead." The father started over toward Russ, and Russ took a firm tone. "Sir, if this guy is dead, we probably have a crime scene here. We need to leave it undisturbed, and we have to get some help here. I have some experience with this sort of thing. I was a cop for several years."

The father complied, and the younger man was visibly shaken. Russ bent down carefully to remove the limbs from over his head and torso. What he saw was bad. The bullet had entered from the back of Warren's head and exited the front around the right eye, doing serious damage to his face. Russ felt for a pulse, and there was none. There was little doubt the man was dead.

Russ had no idea who he was. He moved his clients away and back to the boat. He got his cell out and looked to see if he had a signal, but he had no bars showing.

"Fellows, would you check your phones and see if you have a signal? We need to call someone." He punched in 911 as he was asking and got a "No signal" message. His clients did not have a signal on their phones either. Checking upstream, he could not see anybody coming. Any other day there would have been a steady stream of drift boats, but they were late getting started, so that might account for it.

Russ decided to take a quick look over the scene and take some good-quality pictures with his Nikon digital camera. He carried it for those clients that wanted some better pictures than they usually got from a cell phone. He took pictures around the boat and where he had seen the blood. He would mark that in case the authorities were late in coming so they could find it easier.

Taking a stick and some heavy tippet, he tied a pink streamer he had to it. Where that fly came from he did not remember, but it may have been one Sarah had used somewhere. He pushed the stick in the ground near the bloodstain. Russ figured this was where the guy was shot.

Russ went over to the body and took a number of shots and some of the shoe tracks that he could find. A lot of the tracks were his and his clients, he knew. He asked them to hold up their boots and took pictures and took some of his also. This would help separate their tracks for any investigator.

While he was taking the last photo, the younger of his clients called out to him across the water. "I think I see something in the grass that looks like a cartridge shell. It is almost hidden under the stuff here."

Russ saw the 9 mm shell casing and took some photos. He then marked the spot as he had done the blood. He couldn't resist taking his hemostats and picking up the shell and taking a couple of pictures. He then put it back where it was, being careful not to touch the metal casing.

"We have to go. Sorry about the fishing, but we have to get where we can call this in."

He got no argument from the clients; they were more than ready to get the hell out of there! They climbed onto the boat, and Russ started pulling the oars as hard as he could and as fast as he could. The take-out was about seven miles. He had at least an hour of hard rowing in the slow water.

Donny and Hector had dropped the boat's anchor and stopped to wait for a boat that had just reached the Varney ramp ahead of them to clear out. It seemed like forever for them to get the truck and back down and load their boat. Donny did not want to be seen. He had a big enough mess now because he had been so trigger-happy. As they moved on down to the ramp, he did see something in the parking lot as they came by: an old Fleetside Chevrolet truck with a trailer and a sign that said, "Warren Cason, Fly-Fishing Guide." He had seen that, and he knew that was the one he needed to get the boat trailered and out of the water. He did not see his black Ford.

They were here much earlier than expected, and Helen and Jeffery had not dropped off his truck. Donny had to make a decision about the boat: abandon it at the ramp and get Helen there as soon as possible with his truck or go ahead and put it on the trailer and park it at the edge of the lot so that it would not attract any attention any sooner than necessary. She would not get there any sooner, so he decided to get the boat on the trailer, tie it down, and park it and hope no one came while they were getting it done.

Then he realized he did not have a key to Warren's truck! Was it in Warren's pockets, the truck, or was it on the boat? This could be a serious problem if the key was still in Warren Cason's pockets.

"Hector, do you know where the key to the guy's truck is?"

Hector reached down to a small storage where he had seen Warren putting some things and pulled out a Ziploc bag. As with most boats, you need a place to keep your valuables accessible, safe, and dry. There were the keys, Warren's wallet and cell phone, and the two hundred dollars that Donny had given him that morning. He threw the bag back in the compartment and handed the money to Donny and took the keys and ran to get the truck. Donny called Helen while Hector was getting Warren's truck. He got no answer on her cell, and he knew there was little coverage at the camp. He had the camp's number in his phone, and he tried that. They finally answered on about the fifth ring and he asked for his cabin.

Helen answered. "Where are you?" she asked. "Are you still fishing?"

"We are here at the Varney boat ramp where we planned to meet, but we got here early. I need you to get my truck and get here fast! Bring all your stuff with you because you won't be going back up there!"

"What's wrong, Donny?" she asked.

"Never mind that! Just step on it! There is nothing for you to worry about. Just get here with my truck. Now!" Helen did not like the sound of that, but they threw everything in the Camaro, and she got in Donny's truck and headed to Varney with Jeffery Bristol following in the Camaro. She had dropped her fake IDs in the mailbox earlier today to an address in Miami. She did not want to be picked up with fake IDs in the car. She would have them mailed to her next assignment when she needed them.

Jeffery was worried about the urgent call and wondered what was going on to change the plans as they sped toward Varney. But it wasn't a problem for him in the Camaro. There weren't too many cars and too many drivers that could leave him. That was what he did best: drive.

Helen eventually pulled in the Varney parking lot and ramp area. At first she did not see Donny, but he stepped out from behind a Chevy Tahoe with a boat trailer attached and Georgia license plates.

Odd, she thought.

Donny and Hector had moved away from Warren's truck in case someone came into the lot. They were two guys from Georgia about to load up in their Tahoe as far as anyone was concerned. Helen pulled into a parking spot and before she could get the door open, Hector was putting the four duffel bags under the tarp and placing the bales of pine straw on top.

"You guys hit the road and get out of the area, fast!" was the only thing Donny said to Helen. She and Jeffery had been paid. They did not need to know anything else. Donny needed to get himself and Hector the hell out of there and get back to the cabin camp and think about what to do next. They did not want to be around when the shit hits the fan. If it hadn't already happened.

Helen got in the Camaro with Jeffery and said, "Drive. Fast."

"What's wrong," Jeffery asked.

"I don't know, but Donny said get out fast, so let's get out fast!"

Jeffery pulled out of the lot without throwing gravel or burning rubber on the road. He would not be leaving any tire tread marks for some smart cop to figure out. This wasn't his first getaway. He eased the car up to about thirty-five and then pushed the pedal all the way down and the powerful V8 was up to a hundred in a few seconds. If Helen wanted fast, she would get fast. They were headed toward Ennis, and they would jump over to the Western-movie-sounding towns of Virginia City and Nevada City and on to Sheridan and Twin Bridges. He would swing across to Dillion and then back roads, at the speed limit, to Missoula where they would get a motel, some rest, and then on to Idaho. They may or may not ever see Hector and Donny again. Donny and Hector had the black Ford F-150 heading back toward Hebgen Lake and the cabin camp. They needed to pick up Hector's truck and decide their next move. Luck was with them at the take-out. No one came or went, and they weren't seen there. Donny thought if he should he stay up here in the cabin tonight or get back to Bozeman? He needed a shower, some food, and a beer, and then he would decide. He had all those things in the refrigerator at the cabin. Except for the right decision, he would have to come up with that. He had made a mess of things today, and he had to find a way to clean it up.

All the way to Varney, Russ and his clients were trying their phones. Finally, Russ got a signal.

"Nine-one-one, what is your emergency," the operator answered.

"My name is Russell Baker. My clients and I were fishing on the Madison today just north of the put-in at 287 near Cherry Gulch. It about eight or nine miles from Varney Bridge. We found a body there of a man who has been shot at that location, and the body is on the small island. That was some time ago, and we have just gotten to an area we could call from in our drift boat. We are at Varney Bridge now."

It took a lot of back-and-forth to get them to understand exactly where the body was, and he finally got them to write down the GPS coordinates for the spot where the body was. Russ had made a waypoint on his phone GPS.

"You will need a helicopter to get there the quickest, and they will need to come prepared to get the body and process the crime scene. I don't know how to get there by truck or car. If they want to get to the scene by boat, they would do best by launching at the 287 put-in."

"They will know how to do that, sir." The reply seemed a little sharp.

"I need to ask you to stay where you are, sir, till the sheriff or state police arrive."

"I will be at the put-in at 287. That's where your people need to come to," Russ replied. "They can land a helicopter or get boats in easier there. The lot is big enough for that. Where I am is over seven miles away. That put-in is a little over a mile away from where the body is." Russ and his clients got the boat on the trailer and headed back to where they had put in. It was about thirty minutes before they heard the first siren, and soon a state trooper pulled in the lot.

"Are you the guys that called in a dead body?"

"Yes, Officer, I called it in," said Russ.

"The sheriff will be here in a few minutes. Where is the body?" he asked.

"It's about a mile and a quarter downstream in that direction," Russ said as he pointed north.

"How do I get there?" the trooper asked.

"You have to go by boat or come in from the ranch side. I don't know how to get there by car. I told them to send a helicopter and gave them the GPS location," Russ added.

A Madison County Sheriff's car pulled into the lot behind the state trooper. He looked over the situation for a minute and got out of his car and walked up to where they all were.

"What's the story here? Who called this in?" he asked.

Russ gave him the short version. No, he did not know the guy. They had not seen anyone. They had no idea who did this. They may have heard the shot.

Then a game warden with the Montana Fish and Wildlife service pulled in, and he was pulling a shallow-water boat with a jet outboard. After a quick discussion with the sheriff, he asked Russ for the exact location, and he knew right where Russ was talking about. He backed his boat into the water and was ready to go in quick order. The three officers had a brief conversation. The game warden and the sheriff's deputy would go down to the site, and the trooper would stay with them until another person for the sheriff's office arrived to take their statements. Russ knew the trooper was to keep them there in case they wanted to leave.

A medivac helicopter from Bozeman was coming to assist and remove the body when they were ready. The jet boat roared off. A second car appeared from Madison County. It was the sheriff and not a deputy this time. He was businesslike and asked for their IDs. He walked back to his car, and the clients who were now tired, hungry, and scared as it was getting to be a long day asked, "What's he doing?" The State trooper was still there with them.

Russ answered, "He's running our IDs through the computers to see if we have any outstanding warrants and if we are wanted for anything. Standard procedure in this type of situation where we are possible witnesses to a murder."

The state trooper gave an inquiring glance at Russ.

"I hope you paid all your parking tickets and child support," Russ said, trying to lighten the mood.

In a minute, the Sheriff came back and handed them their licenses. "What's a big-city police detective doing guiding a drift boat, Mr. Baker?"

"Well, officially, I am retired from the detective job as of last week. My wife died, and I needed a break."

The sheriff wanted a full rundown, and they told him everything they could including how they marked the bloodstain on the gravel and the shell casing. And then the sheriff's radio crackled. The deputy and the Fish and Wildlife game warden had found the body, and there was no ID on him. A helicopter from Bozeman landed in the lot to pick up the sheriff to go to the scene. The afternoon dragged on and on, and they could only sit there and wait. It had started to get late, and by now, the day was shot.

The sheriff finally made it back with the Fish and Wildlife officer in the jet boat. "You guys can go, for now. Here is my card and cell if you think of anything else. I'll be in touch tomorrow."

Russ and his clients were dead tired. They'd had no lunch and were drained from the experiences of the day.

"Fellows, when you get ready, I will take you on another float trip. You will get a refund for today. And I will buy you a steak dinner if you will do me the honor on the way back. We can stop in Ennis at Sportsman's Lodge. I hear it's pretty good, or we can wait till we get back to Bozeman."

The father protested mildly about the payment, but Russ would not back down. As far as stopping in Ennis, well, that was just fine with them! So they pulled into Ennis for dinner. They all were starved, and they took a long time to eat, and it was almost 9:00 PM when they got on the road to Bozeman. But they had rehashed the day, and they did catch a few fish that first hour or so, and they had a story to tell when they got back to Knoxville! But right now, they had the sixty-five miles back to town. Russ would drop them off at the fly shop and leave his boat there in the yard tonight instead of taking it to the storage building. When they got to Norris, Russ took Highway 84 to Bozeman. At Anceney, a vehicle came up behind them, and when the road was clear, it passed Russ, who was slower pulling the boat. The driver of the passing vehicle had seen Russ's Tahoe with the Georgia plates earlier that day and had stood right beside it in the Varney Bridge lot. Russ saw the black Ford F-150 with the chrome bumper as it passed, and he knew he had seen it before too.

After getting some food, showering, and getting his mind in focus at the camp/cabins, Donny knew that he should get back to Bozeman, and Hector could take his own truck and go back whenever he wanted, or he could leave town if he wanted to. Donny could get the duffel bags over to Butte tomorrow before they sent someone looking for him. They would go back to Bozeman tonight. After all, the task force had been focused all along in the Billings/Big Timber area, anticipating the drugs and would not likely be looking for anything coming in to Bozeman from the south.

He made one last call on the burn phone. "Tomorrow, 4:00 PM." He hung up.

He would dispose the burn phone in a dumpster after wiping it clean in the morning. He and Hector headed for Bozeman and took Highway 84 at Norris. This was the shortest way but now, he came up behind the Tahoe pulling a drift boat. He recognized the Tahoe with the Georgia plates as having been at the Varney boat ramp earlier today, but they had not seen him. All he wanted to do was get around this slower vehicle and go home.

When Russ finally got to his little room at Super 8, he collapsed on the bed. He did not turn over until the next morning. What a day he had! He thought he had seen his last murder victim and crime scene. Now, he wasn't safe from them even on the beautiful Madison River. He was awakened by his phone at 7:45 AM. It was Madison County sheriff, whose name was Barry Steinbrenner.

"Hope I didn't wake you, Mr. Baker. This is Sheriff Steinbrenner."

"Well, I think you did, but that's okay. What's up?"

"Well, we still don't have an ID on the victim. We have his body at the state crime lab as a John Doe right now. I was hoping you might have thought of something else."

"To tell you the truth, I was dead tired when we got back here last night and I went right to bed. I have just gotten awake this minute. Let me shower, get some coffee and breakfast, and I'll call you back in about an hour and a half. How's that?"

Russ called the sheriff back in about one hour and twenty minutes.

"Sheriff, there was one thing that puzzled me, but it didn't hit me until this morning. When we got to Varney bridge and got my boat out, I was preoccupied with calling the murder in and getting back up there to be there when all of you got there at the put in. But when we got to Varney, there was a boat and trailer parked off down at the end of the lot. I recognized the name on the side because I had seen it that morning when the people doing the shuttle were leaving the lot with it. Those same people did my shuttle. That boat left ahead of me, but the rig was still at Varney when I got there. The truck is an old Fleetside Chevy with a sign on the side that says, "Warren Cason, Fly Fishing Guide." I did not see anything of him, and he may have been wade fishing with the clients. I don't have a number for him, but I can probably get it from the person who did the shuttle. And the number of his cell is on the truck, I believe."

THE DRIFT BOAT DETECTIVE

"Okay. My deputy is back down that way to go over the crime scene again. I'll get him to swing in there at Varney and see if the truck is still there. Anything else?"

"Sheriff, I did fail to mention that I took some photos of the scene, the tracks around the area that were visible, and the bloodstain and the shell casing in the grass. I also took pictures of my boots and my clients' boots for elimination. I can upload those and get them to you if you want."

"I'll let you know if I need them, Mr. Baker."

With that, he was gone.

Deputy Wayne Dunkin was new to the case, not having been on duty the night before. He got a call on the radio from the office, which was in Virginia City where they had the sheriff, the undersheriff, and six deputies and two sergeants. Deputy Dunkin served the role of undersheriff. There were about eight people working in administrative jobs. And fortunately, they worked very few murders. Zero murders in a normal year! The sheriff wanted the deputy to go by the Varney take out and see if the fly-fishing guide's boat was still there from yesterday.

The boat was still there when the deputy arrived. He called the sheriff. "Yes, sir, the boat and rig is still sitting here. What do you want me to do?"

"Stand by the boat and use your cell phone to call the number on the boat. See what happens. Maybe we can contact the guy. He may have had problems with his truck and gone home with someone else."

The deputy entered the number and waited. To his surprise, he could hear the phone ringing, and it was somewhere in the boat.

"I can hear the phone ringing in the boat, boss."

"Try to locate the phone without disturbing anything. Use your latex gloves."

By then, the phone had gone to voice mail, so the deputy hung up, crawled onto the boat, and redialed. He could hear the phone ringing and found it in a small storage compartment along with a wallet, camera, photo ID, and a small knife. They were in a plastic Ziploc bag.

"I found the phone and his wallet, camera, and driver's license. He lives in Bozeman."

"Check and see if the truck is locked and if there is a key."

"The door is not locked and the key is in the ignition."

"Stay with the truck and listen out for his phone. I will send the guys down to process the boat and truck. I will call the sheriff over in Gallatin County and get them to check on this guy's house and see if anything is wrong there since he lives in their county."

The Gallatin sheriff's deputies were dispatched and went to the shop in Bozeman on S. Black Avenue, and no one was there. They then went to the house and rang the bell. A tired lady, breathing hard, came to the door. She was frightened when she saw the officers.

"Has something happened to Warren?" she asked.

"Why would you ask that, ma'am?" the officer replied.

"He did not come home last night, and his truck and boat are still gone, and he did not call me. He never fails to call if he is not going to be here for supper or be gone overnight. And he did not answer his phone. Do you know something about Warren?"

"We are looking into his whereabouts, Mrs. Cason, that's all we can say at this point. They found his truck and boat parked at Varney Bridge, and we are just making sure if he is okay."

They called the sheriff in Virginia City. Population 190 (give or take) and told him the news. By now he had scanned in the photo ID and sent it to the crime lab, which could also look it up on the state's system. A preliminary conclusion was that the body was that of Warren Cason. A few more tests would be needed and some further investigation. They would also need Mrs. Cason to identify the body, if possible.

Russ called the sheriff about noon to see what they had found, and he was told that indeed it appeared to be Warren Cason. Who would want to kill this guy? And so far, there were no leads other than a shell casing and a body. Russ called Nancy to tell her the news and asked if she had seen the clients Warren was guiding. She had not as Warren had already left the put-in when she arrived. Of course, Russ knew that. She did not have a clue and was very upset that Warren might be dead. A state Department of Criminal Investigations agent called Russ and asked that Russ meet with her to give a statement. They could meet at the sheriff's office in Virginia City and include the Fish and Wildlife person as they all had an interest in the case since it was on the Madison River. Russ agreed to meet with them that afternoon in Virginia City. They also would like to talk to Nancy since she was involved in moving the truck that morning.

Russ was hoping to go back over and nose around, and maybe this would get him a chance. His suppressed detective personality was trying to break free from the shackles he had placed on it for the past few months. Fighting a lot of emotions and against his better judgment, he felt somehow connected to the dead fishing guide. Russ did not know the victim but knew of him through Chad and Nancy. Their opinions of him were that he was a straitlaced guy, a great fishing guide, a devoted son, and someone who would not likely have an enemy that wanted to blow his brains out on a gravel bar in the Madison River. But someone had done just that. The big questions now: who and why?

Russ called Nancy and asked if she would like to ride over to Virginia City with him, if she was going. The two clients from Chattanooga had gotten the first flight out of Bozeman that morning. They just might do all their drift boat fishing in the Holston from now on!

"The lady did call me and I said I would come over too. I will do anything to help find who did this!" she said.

Russ agreed to pick her up at the store. This might be considered their first real date, he thought.

Sheriff Steinbrenner was looking beat. He had obviously gotten a tough case, lots of publicity, and little in the way of clues. He had limited resources, and his people had very little major investigation skills. They usually did not need them, for the types of cases they handled and road patrol activities. If you had a wreck or hit a deer, they knew what to do. If some unknown person blew the front of a fishing guide's head off, that was somewhat tougher.

It was also tough for the state investigator, who in this case was a very-nice-looking lady with a steely eyed stare and no-nonsense style named Teresa Walker. She too was not used to dealing with murder cases. The game warden was about the male version of the state lady. Then there was the Deputy Wayne Dunkin, who Russ felt did not appear to care for Russ too much. But no one was paying Russ much attention when he walked in with someone who looked more like she was at home in *Vogue* magazine or in a Wall Street office. Nancy did not look at all like a drift boat shuttle operator!

From the surface, it looked like this fishing guide took some people fishing, an argument or disagreement took place, and one of the clients shot him. They took his boat down to the Varney take-out and left. But why was their car at that take-out? Did they call someone to come get them? Was it all preplanned to kill the guide? Why risk leaving the guide in the river? Why plan a murder on a river that was usually full of potential witnesses? And why a guy like Warren who spent his time on the river or at home looking after his mother? Plenty of questions. No answers.

After many questions and going over the details several times, Russ asked, "What did you find in the boat? Was there anything there that that could help?"

Before anyone could answer, Deputy Sheriff Wayne Dunkin, who was not too fond of Russ, it appeared, responded, "We can't talk to you about any evidence on this case. You are not a Cobb County Georgia Police detective anymore and you are in Montana. For all I know, you may have shot the guy."

"As to the possibility of my having shot the guy, I have witnesses who will attest that I did not. I can assure you that had I shot him, I would not have called you guys, and I would not have been hanging around waiting for all of you to show up and arrest me."

Russ's steel-eyed glare at the deputy made it clear that Russ was more than pissed!

"I am certainly aware that I am not a policeman and am quite aware that I am not in Cobb County, *sir!*"

The way he said *sir* removed any doubt from those in the room that Russell Baker was seriously offended!

Was this the same guy who has been moping around Bozeman? thought Nancy.

Russ had to hold his temper because he knew that, technically, the guy was right on all counts.

"I knew that when we found the body yesterday and when I stayed here all evening last evening. I also remembered this morning that I took crime scene photos, which I have on this SD card from my camera for you. I apologize for not giving them to you last night, but with all the stuff going on, I did not remember that I had done them. You will see all the tracks and also the boot treads on my clients and me so you can separate them. I don't know how much the investigators corrupted the scene last night and these may be of no value."

Russ did not tell them he made a copy and loaded them on his computer.

"The bloodstain where the man was probably shot and the shell casing are also on there."

He had deleted those of the shell casing when he held it up with his forceps. Probably best to keep that to himself.

"I know that the man was shot for some reason that was not obvious at the crime scene. But if you look at the photos, you will see that there was some type of scuffle. There are also signs where he was dragged across the gravel bar to the island. Those signs are probably obliterated by now, especially if the crime scene has been left unattended or not roped off.

"I would also respectfully suggest that the boat or his truck probably hold the only clues as to why he was killed. Say, for example, did you let your drug dog check them out?

I know you have one because he's on your list of officers on the internet."

By the time Russ stopped, talking the deputy was red hot, the sheriff was leaning over his notepad writing notes, the state investigator was tapping notes into her iPad, and the game warden was listening but not doing anything. Nancy was a startled spectator. Nancy sat in amazement! Russ had taken over the entire meeting with his formidable personality, keen observations, and grasp of the facts. She had not seen this side of Russ before in the brief amount of time she had been around him. She really liked what she saw, but she was waiting for the other shoe to drop. The deputy was now furious that his investigation was being questioned and leaned across the table and started to say something in response. The sheriff raised his hand in a "Hold it just a minute" sort of way.

"Are you suggesting that the guide was dealing drugs? Do you know something we don't?"

"Not at all, Sheriff, but I would suggest that people don't normally shoot their fly-fishing guide in the river because the rainbows are not hitting top-water flies. Women, money, or drugs are more often the root problem. I did not know this guy, but Nancy, her brother, and most of the fishing community around Bozeman seemed to have been quite familiar with him. Most seem to think he was a good guy. He was killed by a 'not-so-good guy.' Where are the clues as to why? His boat, his office, his truck, his pockets, his cell phone, and maybe his bank account. Those are where someone needs to be looking. There weren't too many clues at the scene."

The sheriff looked at his deputy, "Did we sniff the truck and the boat?"

"No, sir, we did not," the deputy responded. "No one considered doing that."

"Let's get that done, *now*." There was a big emphasis on *now*.

"Yes, sir," he responded, and with that, he left the room and slammed the door.

The state investigator seemed to have some other place to be. "Sheriff, I have to go over to Billings to a meeting with the drug task force, so I have to leave now. I will check back on your findings after I'm finished over there." With that, she left the room.

The Fish and Wildlife warden asked if the sheriff needed him further, and the sheriff shook his hand and thanked him for coming. He left as well.

The press now was having a field day. This was the biggest thing in Ennis, Virginia City, Bozeman, and the Madison Valley in a long time. Headlines and lead stories: "Madison County Sheriff Baffled by Guide's Murder," read the Bozeman paper. Another read, "No Clues in Death of Fishing Guide." Another said, "Local Authorities Not Experienced in Handling Major Cases." The sheriff and his department were bombarded by calls, and reporters coming in, wanting an interview. He was not a happy man.

"Sheriff," said Russ, "how about we go and look at the boat and truck when your guy gets through? Nancy, can you give me thirty minutes more?"

Nancy was certainly okay with it. The sheriff was reluctant. "We have a chain of custody problem if we have a nonapproved person involved. Also, there is an image problem."

Russ understood and knew it would have been a rare instance when a civilian was invited to look at crime scene material and potential evidence. He told the sheriff he would he would call him if he thought of anything else, shook the sheriff's hand, stood up, and he and Nancy walked out toward his truck. Russ had gained a lot of respect for the sheriff for his desire to solve the crime was bigger than his ego.

Russ and Nancy were backing out of the parking spot to head back to Bozeman when Russ's cell phone rang. "Mr. Baker, have you left the area yet? This is Sheriff Steinbrenner."

"We are just pulling out of the parking space. What's up?"

"My deputy and the dog handler just called me from the impound area over in Ennis. The dog has gotten a positive scent on the boat. Can you come back in for a minute?" Nancy was listening on the speaker in the Tahoe, and she nodded okay. So Russ pulled back in, and they went back inside.

They were met by the Sheriff, and he took them back to his office and shut the door. He asked Russ if it was okay for Nancy to be there, and Russ said yes. The sheriff looked at the two of them and said, "This is got to be kept confidential, especially from the press. Is that understood?"

"Of course," said Russ and Nancy almost in unison.

"I have six great deputies here, and we cover a lot of ground, but none of them—and I guess you have to include me—are very experienced in forensics and intricate cases. If you need a bar fight stopped, my guys can hang with the best of them. Traffic accidents and domestic disputes, well, we are pretty good. It is obvious that this case is far from routine, and we have no witnesses, no nothing. And to top it off, the state investigator that was in here is up to her eyeballs trying to find a drug ring operating somewhere over around Bozeman and Billings. As important as this case is to me and the family and everyone, that situation is occupying everyone around. She doesn't know I know that, but some of us sheriffs talk to one another, maybe when we shouldn't. They all have egg on their face, and everyone from the governor down is very upset. They thought they were going to make a big drug bust the other night and they came away empty."

Russ was wondering what this all had to do with him. He quickly got his answer.

"Mr. Baker, when we did a background check on you—that's routine in these cases as you know—I got a pile of information. You were a highly decorated policeman as a patrolman in Cobb County Georgia and a very successful homicide detective. Your former boss, Alan Schreiber, told me this morning that you were his ace out of over a hundred-man detective pool."

Russ was flabbergasted at the comments. The sheriff had really done some homework. Nancy was staring at him with something of a smile and a questioning look. He could feel his face turning red.

"By the way, I guess you knew about the clients you had yesterday: the old guy owns two Ford dealerships around Bristol and Knoxville, Tennessee, and his son runs the Lincoln dealership. They are old money, and lots of it. Probably rules them out as someone who would murder a good ole boy from Bozeman. And we kind of ruled you out too."

This guy is more than he seems too, Russ thought. Now he was really impressed. The sheriff had eliminated the three potential witnesses right away.

"Well, Sheriff, I'm glad to know that I am not a suspect and the guys from Knoxville are probably happy too, even though they may not know it."

"Now. Here's what I would like to propose: I will offer you a position as Madison County special investigator. You would report directly to me and have no authority over any of the personnel here. You would work only on the assigned case, not meddle in anything else. You would do everything possible to help me make these guys better as investigators and to feel better about their jobs."

"The pay would not be very much, but from what Alan Schreiber told me, you probably are doing more than okay financially."

Russ did not like him saying that, and he caught a glance from Nancy. He had not talked about having a good deal of money or anything about his finances.

"You would have a badge and a gun issued by the department and full arrest powers. I will make the people in Bozeman aware of your status, and you would be plainclothes. After this case is decided one way or the other, you can turn in your badge if you want. These people are all kind of friends of yours, and it appears you want to help. What do you say?"

Russ thought about it for a half minute. "Okay, Sheriff, but I hope you aren't expecting a miracle. We have our work cut out for us. And your deputy already doesn't like me."

Russ's quick acceptance of the sheriff's offer surprised even him.

"My deputy likes being a deputy. I'll explain things to him. Once you get to know him, he's a great guy, just a little insecure and inexperienced. I hired him when he got back from Iraq, and I can assure you he is a man to be reckoned with and a good man to have on your side in a tough situation. No one wants him shooting at them. He is a crack shot. You can make it work."

"I need to get Nancy home, Sheriff. I'll be back in the morning or whenever you want me to start."

Nancy interrupted. "Aren't we going look at the boat and truck?"

"Let's go," said the sheriff.

Russ was back in police work. At least for now. He hoped he would not regret it.

They went to the impound lot. The sheriff asked that Nancy stay in the car for now. She did not like it, but she understood. Two deputies and a police dog were going over the boat and truck and cataloging everything they found. The sheriff had gotten their attention.

No drugs were found on the boat or the truck, but the dog was giving all the signs of drugs present. They had opened every storage area, taken out every scrap, and made a list before putting the piece in the plastic bag. There was no sign of blood in the boat, confirming what they already knew: Warren was not killed on the boat. But it was likely from the dog's reaction that there had been drugs in Warren's boat at some time.

Dusting for prints was somewhat hopeless, but they lifted as many as they could for analysis by the Montana DCI or the FBI. Russ was not too hopeful about getting any useful prints, but it was worth a try. The oars, which would have certainly been used, produced no usable prints, which indicated they had been wiped down. There was a thing full of moist wipes that Warren probably used for wiping fish blood off when they had a problem releasing the fish and got a bleeder. Usually, the fish was not harmed and swam away grateful and mad, but sometimes a fish gets a hook a little too deep and bleeds, and fishing guides are funny about keeping blood cleaned up in their boat. The wipes would have been perfect for wiping down the boat to get rid of fingerprints.

Russ looked in the truck while the sheriff had called the two deputies aside to explain that Russ would be helping them, at least temporarily. The deputy that had been so unpleasant walked over, extended his hand, and said, "Welcome aboard."

"Thank you," replied Russ.

It was really getting to be an infringement on Nancy's time. "Sheriff, I have to take Nancy home. I will be back early tomorrow, and I will help go through the items from the boat if you don't run across something before I get back. Please don't discard even the simplest piece of paper." He and Nancy left for Bozeman.

10

DONNY BRAGG HAD GOTTEN DRESSED in a suit and tie. He looked like a banker or a lawyer. If anyone asked what he was doing, he was going to Butte on a job interview. The duffle bags were now under a full load of hay in the back of the truck. He had several bales covering the $14,000,000 of cocaine. He had screwed up on the river, and he knew it. He had gotten a little carried away, but he had avoided being busted at the drop by changing it. But now it was put up or shut up. He had to deliver the goods to Butte. Failure to do so would be the end...of him.

He would take Highway 2 to Butte but would go to great lengths to make sure he was not followed, which was why he had done all the stuff with the drift boat and the float trip. Maybe it had been a dumb idea. There was an informant somewhere. Until he could find that informant and eliminate him or her, he had to do a lot of looking over his shoulder. There were about ninety miles to cover, but he would drive a few more miles for safety. Once the drugs were delivered, he would not have any worries for a while, even if they were still looking out in Bozeman. He had no drugs on him usually, and he felt he could not be directly linked to anything.

Helen and Jeffery were gone, and Hector was the only witness to the shooting. He would think about how to handle that situation later, but there couldn't be any more bodies floating around in the Madison right now. Today, he was Kile Davidson. He had all the credentials to prove it. The license plate and registration papers on the truck were beautiful. There was a difference in the VIN, but most license checks would not catch that. The license plates on his trucks were for a black Ford F-150; everything would look legit, and the owner was Kile Davidson.

Kile was really a paraplegic who lived in Missoula and who received cash from Donny every month to use his name. If it was ever revealed that Donny was using his name, Davidson would simply say he had no idea that his identity had been stolen! The $500 per month in cash came in real handy to pay for his specially equipped black Ford F-150 sitting under his carport that he never drove much either. It did not currently have a license plate on it. The real Kile Davidson liked cash. It was not traceable.

Donny, alias Kile, made the run to Butte and parked his truck at a place that did hand carwashes. They gave him a ticket and he walked across the street to get a soda and a candy bar. Looking like a million dollars. When he came back, a few minutes later, the truck was spotless. The bales of hay were gone, and so was the $14,000,000 in drugs. He climbed in the shiny black truck and turned on some good music and headed back to Bozeman! He was finally done!

He made a call. "Hello there! I was in town and just wanted to say hello. Are you feeling better?"

"Much better, today. I was feeling a little sick for a day or two, but I got some prescriptions sent over and I am feeling a lot better."

111

"Glad to hear. I have to go. I was just in town for a job interview, and I needed to have a clean vehicle, and I stopped and got my truck washed. Need to make a good impression, you know."

"Sure. I hope to hear you have a job soon."

Donny touched End Call. This was all a lot of mumbo jumbo to be sure the boss knew the delivery had been made and all the shipment was there. He would have some more work for him soon. If the Feds were listening or recording, they did not get too much to go on, and the burn phone went into a trash bin without a battery. The drugs had left the carwash before Donny had walked back across the street.

Russ had a hard time sleeping. He had dropped Nancy off at the store and waited until she was safely in her 4Runner and headed home. They had grabbed a fast-food burger on the way to Bozeman, and they really had not talked too much. When he got to his room at the hotel, he got out some clothes from the closet he had not worn since he arrived in Bozeman. Some nice khaki slacks, a solid-blue button-down shirt, and a sports jacket.

Most of the folks in this area did not "dress up" too much, but he wanted to look professional for his photo that would go on his new ID. He took out a yellow pad that he always used to do planning and problem solving and began to write down what he knew, and that wasn't much.

Nancy was really conflicted now about Russ. She had thought he was handsome from the first time she met him but had not really been attracted that much to him. He did not seem to be what she saw as an *ideal* man. He was an out-of-work, down-on-his-luck, sometime fishing guide living in a cheap hotel. She did shuttles for him when he called and she was available, and he had always paid a little more than she told him. He had never appeared to have a lot of ambition, as far as she could see.

He seemed to mope around the time or two they had lunch together, and he had not really expressed a lot of interest in her personally and certainly not romantically. "He had been in a shell" was the best way she could describe it to herself. So a time or two when he had called her about going out to dinner, she had been conveniently busy.

Today, the cocoon had opened, and a new creature had emerged. She saw him in the meeting with a high-level state law enforcement officer, and he was not intimidated. He had a big brute of a deputy ready to chew him up and spit him out and had skillfully handled the situation so that the deputy, before the day was out, was shaking his hand. He had a pretty sharp country sheriff asking for his help. And the down-on-his-luck, out-of-work, sometimes fishing guide was apparently very well off financially from the comments the sheriff had made. And now, the most eligible single woman in Bozeman was paying attention too. What a day this had been! Now what?

Donny got back to Bozeman, got himself some dinner, and called Hector to let him know they were in the good graces of the folks in Butte. Then he clicked on the local news. They had a quick interview with the sheriff in Virginia City who did not have any new leads to report and seemed unlikely to find any, in Donny's view. This would be old news in a few days, and they would be talking about something else.

Russ saw the local news too. The sheriff did not come across as overly confident about finding the killer of the local fishing guide. He did not seem at all like the man Russ had been dealing with all day. Russ decided that was the way the sheriff wanted it. Let the bad guys think he was Barney Fife. He was probably closer to Matt Dillon, Russ figured.

Nancy thought the sheriff was smart in not saying on TV that he had hired a special, handsome, rich, and self-confident investigator from Georgia to assist in the investigation. They would all find out soon enough. The next morning, Russ was sworn in, given a badge and a Glock 9 mm. His ID would be ready before the end of the day as the laminating machine had to be repaired. They had some cards being done by a printer in Bozeman, and he could go by tomorrow and pick them up. He was now officially "back in business." It, somehow, felt really good.

He was impressed with the professional manner with which the tiny sheriff's office was run. There was more here than met the eye. Somehow, to his surprise, he was happy about this new development. He called Dan McKenzie when he got a moment, and Dan was happy that Russ was back doing some law enforcement work because he knew how much Russ had loved it.

He did not articulate how concerned he was that his first case was a cold-blooded murder. But the Russ that Dan had known over the years was quite capable of taking care of himself. A man who was gentle and kind to Dan's daughter but tough enough to stop a suspected burglar or drug dealer on I-285 in the middle of the night and who could be tough when he needed to be.

Russ and the deputy sheriff Dunkin gathered in the back conference room at the Madison County Courthouse and started laying out and studying every piece of paper and trash from the boat and truck. Candy wrappers, pop cans, and all manner of matches and matchbooks. It seemed that Warren liked to smoke cigars and would have one when he was driving sometimes or working in his shop tying flies. But one matchbook seemed new and out of place to Russ. It was from the cabin/camp on Highway 287 up near the Quake Lake. He laid that one aside for now.

Russ requested that they get some pictures of Warren, his truck and boat, and give each deputy a set. They could ask around on their shifts if anyone had seen Warren and his rig around the day he was killed or the day before. One of the staff in the office scanned some pictures in and ran copies on the color copier and put them in a notebook for each deputy and himself. A nice job. Nothing was jumping out at them. The crime lab had sent a report back on the shell casing, and there were no prints or even partials on the casing. What that told Russ was this was no amateur that shot Warren. This guy had worn gloves to load his gun or wiped the cartridges with a rag while loading.

He left early and drove by the impound lot and just sat and looked through the fence. He could visualize Warren in the older-model truck with a cigar and hat driving out to the river in the cool of the morning for the last time. "I'll find these guys, Warren." Russ made a promise, and now he had to keep it. He left for Bozeman for a little dinner and a phone call or two.

The new Glock, holster, and cartridges were on the seat. He might go by the range in the morning and try it out. He might, however, stick with his trusty old Beretta. He hoped he did not have to use either one. Russ called Warren's number and got no answer. Not on his cell but on his home number. Russ thought that Warren's mother might pick up, but it may have been too late to call. Then he called Nancy.

"Hello, Russ. How was the first day in Virginia City?"

"Very uneventful. I did get a gun, a badge, and a very striking picture ID."

Was that an attempt at some humor from Russ? Now, things are looking up, she thought.

"Nancy, do you know Warren's mother? I tried to call her tonight, but I did not get an answer."

"Oh yes. I know her. I met her several times doing shuttles, and she used to come in the store a lot buying gifts for birthdays and the like. Warren did not grow up here, so I haven't exactly known him all my life or anything."

"Do you think sometime tomorrow, on your schedule, you could ride over there with me? Having you along might make it easier to get her to answer some questions. You could follow me over and then leave or ride with me, whichever."

"Sure. I have a shuttle for Chad and need to be in the store a while in the morning. How about we go after lunch? You could buy my lunch at Brew Works." *Oh crap,* she thought. *Did I just ask him out on a date?*

"You have a date. See you at the Brew Works, say eleven forty-five?"

Yep, I have just asked him for a date, she thought.

"Eleven forty-five it is," she said.

Russ got up and shaved and did all the things a working man does and went to pick up his business cards. He then drove over to the Rifle and Pistol Club. Russ wanted to get a little practice with his Beretta, his compact .45 S&W,

and his brand-new Glock 9 mm. This should be interesting since he had not fired a gun in some time.

When he arrived, the place was not too busy that early on a week day. He noticed a nice-looking red Ram pickup at the end of the spaces with a Texas tag. Then the usual assortment of BMWs and Range Rovers and four-wheel-drive pickups. He went in and went to the end away from the five or six active shooters in the range area. He had brought the guns in cases and did not exhibit a police holster. He could have gotten a discount, according to the sign, as a law enforcement officer, but he chose to not ask for that.

Two guys were on the end, and he thought one looked familiar. He was sure he had seen him a couple of times at the Brew Works. He went about shooting at his targets, and it was not long before the guys finished and left. After he finished, he left, and the red Ram truck was gone. The two guys were likely riding in that truck he thought, but it was not a big deal.

He had lunch with Nancy, and they went to see Mrs. Cason. She had been questioned and requestioned but had been of no help in finding Warren's killers. She had become very emotional each time the investigators talked to her, and every day that went by without finding the killer, the less likely that they would. In fact, he could be long gone from here.

Nancy knew exactly where to go and rode with Russ, giving him instructions. The street he was driving down was familiar, and when they got to the intersection to turn down Mrs. Cason's street, he was sure he had taken notice of that house on the corner of S. Black and Main Street with the ugly green shutters before but he couldn't think when. They arrived at the house, and it looked very dark from the front, and no one appeared to be home. The little fly shop was dark also. No lights were on inside, but it was the middle of the day. Russ thought there was a chance they would not be on again in the shop with Warren dead. Russ rang the doorbell at the house, and they could hear it ring inside. There seemed to be no one home. Russ rang the bell again and was turning to walk away when they heard, "I'm coming. Just give me a minute. I can't move very fast."

Finally, the door opened, and there stood a very frail-looking old lady wearing a breathing apparatus. She was out of breath with her emphysema.

She recognized Nancy immediately. Nancy had gone to the funeral as had hundreds of others in the area out of respect to her and to Warren. Russ could not bring himself to go.

"Hello, Nancy. Won't you come in? Who is the handsome young man?"

"Thank you, Miss Milly. This is a friend of mine and Chad's. He is working with the Madison County Sheriff's Office on Warren's case. This is Russell Baker."

"I have told everyone all I know." Tears welled up in her eyes. "I don't know who killed my Warren. I just don't know."

Nancy was wonderful with Miss Milly Cason. She held her hand and spoke to her with kindness and compassion.

"I know this is hard for you. But Russ really wants to catch the person responsible. It was Russ that reported the crime to the authorities. He was on the river that day."

Russ asked a number of questions, and she answered as best she could. He wanted to know several things:

"Who booked the appointment?"

"It was Warren."

118

"Was he paid for the trip?"

"Yes, the money was dropped off under the door of the office."

"Was this paid by check or cash?"

"It was cash."

"How much was it?"

"It was $525 in cash."

"Did he mention anyone by name?"

"No, not that I recall."

"Was that the normally what he charged for a two-person or a one-person float?"

"Warren only charged $325 for a one-person float and $425 for a two person float. But I remember Warren saying the guy had already included a tip."

That would explain $525—$425 plus a $100 tip.

"Did you happen to see who put the money under the door?"

"No. But I did see a red truck backing out of the yard that afternoon, but I can't say for sure that was who put the money under the door. It could have been someone turning around."

"Do you know what kind of truck it was?"

"I am not sure. All I know is it was red."

"Can I look in the shop?"

"Yes. The key is on the desk there with the wooden thing on it because we kept losing it."

"Is there any alarm system or security cameras on your house or the fly shop?"

"No, we couldn't afford it, and no one has ever bothered anything here."

Nancy stayed with Milly while Russ went over and looked in the shop. There was a pretty messy desk and office area. But there was a neat fly-tying station on the back wall with nice lights. The trash can had not been emptied, and he looked to see if there was anything interesting without actually touching anything in the small can.

He saw a scrap of paper that caught his eye. It said, "Kile, Wed, 425." He put that into the jacket of his notebook but did not know what it meant. He found a trash bag and poured all the stuff from the can into it and put all of the junk on the desk in it as well. He would tell Miss Milly and would bring back anything that looked like something she needed tomorrow. He would go through it all tonight and wondered if any of the other investigators had bothered to do so.

He went back over and told Nancy he was ready. "I have one last question. Does the name Kile mean anything to either of you?"

They both shook their heads.

"We will leave now, Mrs. Cason, but I may want to come back. Here is my card, if you think of anything, call me. Anything at all. And I will make you this promise: I have been hired to find out who did this, and that is all I am doing. I will do everything I can to get the people who did this to Warren."

"Did we learn anything, Russ?" asked Nancy when they got in the car.

"Yes. How valuable at this point, I don't know. We confirmed that there were two paid clients. We confirmed they paid cash that was in an envelope and slipped under the door by someone, possibly driving a red truck, and his name may be Kile. Lots of maybes. I am hoping the envelope is in the trash can, but that is probably wishful thinking. We also know that this shop was probably chosen because it is isolated, has no one there during the day, has no security cameras, and they probably thought there was no one home looking from the house. They could bring the money that he insisted on to make the float, and no one would see them. There was some amount of preplanning, but whether they planned on killing Warren, I don't know. The major question is, was this all to get him to the river to kill him or some other reason? Going to all this trouble to kill Warren seems far-fetched."

"If Kile was the name of the person, Warren either did not know him or he thought him to be friendly. Not someone with a grudge. By all accounts, there is not likely anyone with a grudge against Warren."

"I'll drop you off and go dig through some trash."

"Russ. Thank you for letting me come along. I am impressed with how you piece things together. I think you will get them."

Surprisingly, Nancy halfway believed what she had just said. Russ could only offer a smile in acknowledgement.

Russ dropped off Nancy and went to the Super 8. So far, Russ was more and more convinced that Warren's murder was not about him or his job as a fly-fishing guide as such. Warren must have gotten caught in the middle of something that was big enough to kill someone over. But what?

Russ dumped the contents of the trash can and the stuff from the desk from Warren's shop on the floor of his room. He put on some latex gloves he had picked up at the drugstore and started going through each scrap of paper, receipt, and candy wrapper piece by piece. All the DNA equipment in the world was no good unless a good detective found the evidence first. This was a long shot.

But if someone had left Warren $525 under his door, there should be an envelope somewhere.

It might have some handwriting or other info he could use. There were several likely places that such an envelope could be, as he thought about it. The trash on the floor he was going through from the shop was one place. The house trash cans, which had now been emptied, as best he could observe, would have been another. The other might be the truck, and that trash was at the sheriff's office in Virginia City, and he would go through that again tomorrow.

Or the envelope could still be with Warren at the crime lab. You would think that they went through his pockets, though, before he was sent over there.

Teresa Walker was headed from her task force meeting in Billings in her Montana DCI Ford Taurus. It was a plain car with no writing on it. It was assigned to her to travel and work cases in the southern jurisdiction, and she loved driving the car with the big tires and a more-than-capable engine. Growing up in Butte, she had always wanted a nice car, but her family could not afford one. They had to scrape to get her through college in an old pickup.

There were a couple of very small antennas on the trunk and the roof that put her in communication with all the major law enforcement agencies along with her highly secure computer and her clearance, which gave her access to facts and people and crime statistics.

This made her a valuable asset for anyone wanting information about internal activities at DCI. She was working the Warren Cason case to assist the Madison County Sheriff's Office and had been in an interview with

Russell Baker and a woman from Bozeman named Nancy Freeman. She had to leave that interview and still had a few questions. Maybe she would try to call them and meet with them individually and get this case closed if possible. She had more important things to do on the drug task force.

The drug dealers had just made a big delivery in this area in spite of the task force's best efforts. Those were cases that got you promoted if you solved them or froze you in time if you didn't. She did not want to be riding around all over Montana in a Ford Taurus when she was sixty! But getting promoted at DCI was not the way she envisioned herself getting rich. She had other ways in mind that would pay more money and a lot faster!

She had thousands in student loans to pay off, and so she would have to work for a long time at DCI just to pay them. No time for a love life or anything else; she was a woman in a *man's job*, and she had to prove herself every day.

11

RUSS WAS CHECKING SCRAPS OF paper from Warren's trash when his phone rang. He did not recognize the number on the screen of his phone.

"Hello. This is Russ."

"Mr. Baker, this is Agent Walker for Montana DCI. You should remember me from our meeting at the sheriff's office in Virginia City regarding the murder of Warren Cason."

"Of course, Ms. Walker. What can I do for you?"

"I am coming through Bozeman in a few minutes, and I wanted to finish asking you a few questions regarding what you saw regarding this case. Would you be available?"

"I can make myself available. I'm not sure I have anything else to add to what I have already told you."

"I will call the Gallatin County Sheriff's Office and get them to make a room available where we can meet in private. I won't keep you long. Say in thirty minutes?"

"Sure, see you in thirty minutes."

Russ decided to put a Do Not Disturb sign out so the maid would not come in and throw away his potential evidence. They did not exactly overwork themselves cleaning, but he could not take a chance. He wondered if the DCI agent was aware of his new status as special investigator. The sheriff had told him to hold it close to the vest so if the sheriff wanted her to know, he could inform her himself.

Russ would answer any questions he could, but he was not going to volunteer anything right now since he really did not have any real leads.

Under most conditions, Ms. Walker might have found Russ Baker attractive, but she had no time for an unemployed, down-on-his-luck, ex-cop who was living in a Super 8 Motel. She had her sights on bigger things, but she would get this interview done and she would be through with him. The fashion model, Nancy Freeman, did not have much to add to the investigation, so she would not be bothering with her.

Russ walked in to the Gallatin Sheriff's Office and told them he had an appointment with Ms. Walker from State DCI. They showed him back to the office she had borrowed, and she was sitting behind the desk.

"A gentleman to see you, Ms. Walker," the staff person said.

Ms. Walker looked up and, for a second, was taken back. There was a very handsome, well-dressed guy in khakis and a solid-blue button-down and a sports coat looking like a million bucks! This couldn't be the guy in the fishing shirt and pants she had seen a few days back in Virginia City! There was something different about him.

She asked a few questions that Russ thought were repetitive and irrelevant, but sometimes cops did that to get past the defenses of a suspect or witness. The interview lasted about twenty minutes, and she made a few notes in the iPad. Russ thought she was just going through the motions and did not see this case as a high-profile case to

125

tie up the time of a State DCI officer. After all, it was not some prominent citizen that was killed.

But if she were to try, she could be an attractive woman. It was her personality that was the problem, and that might be a work face. She might be entirely different outside of work. Russ did not bring up his special investigator job. He was just a witness in a murder investigation. And he needed to get back to his own investigation that was spread out on the Super 8 Motel floor. The interview ended, and Russ was walking out to his Tahoe where he had parked at the edge of the lot in the only available slot. Ms. Walker had parked in an Official Use Only spot right outside the door. Naturally.

Ms. Walker got to her car, tossed her briefcase in the trunk like most cops would do, and got in and drove off in a hurry in a sharp, unmarked, Ford Taurus police vehicle. Russ made it to his Tahoe and saw her turning out of the lot to the right and then another right on N 3rd Avenue. She flipped her right blinker on again to turn right on W Main Street. She was probably going out to I-90.

Russ pulled out and went left on W. Mendenhall. He would go down two blocks and then go right on North 7th Avenue and head out to I-90 also since the Super 8 was just on the other side of 90. As he got to North 7th, he saw the unmarked Ford Taurus police cruiser going past. He had to wait for another car or two, and he turned right. He could still see the Taurus and the State DCI agent up ahead a few cars.

North 7th becomes a divided four-lane, and at I-90, there are a number of fast-food places, motels, and shopping centers. Very convenient for anyone staying in town as everything is right there about a mile from the county courthouse. Just before the I-90 interchange, Ms. Walker turned into on E Baxter Lane, which runs almost parallel to I-90 before turning west and going by the Hampton Inn, Homewood Suites, and on to open ranch and farm country and a private, secret river access he had come across where one could wade-fish. He did not take any clients to that place!

Russ saw the Taurus make the curve to the west on E Baxter and wondered where she was going. It was none of his business, of course, but he just wondered. Hopefully, he would not be seeing her again unless it was to see them booking the guy who killed Warren. He had trash to go through right now.

The Taurus pulled into the Hampton Inn where it had been many times before. Ms. Walker had chosen the Hampton as a place to stay on several trips to the Bozeman/Billings area. She often parked her car in the Homewood Suites lot and walked across to her room at the Hampton. For a while, there had been a handsome fellow at the Hampton that drove a black Ford F-150 truck with a chrome step bumper. He had moved out to a double-wide with a business associate now, but he might drop by later. They had some business to discuss, and it might require him spending the night.

As Russ pulled in to the Super 8 he noticed something he had not really noticed before: the Hampton Inn was directly across the street from him on E Baxter. He had passed it several times without realizing that. No matter.

Russ spent the evening going through the trash, and he did not find much. The note on Kile and the $425 he had found when he was at Warren's place was so far the only clue. Where were the envelope that the money had been left in and the deposit slip?

The next morning he was back down to Virginia City to meet with Deputy Dunkin and finish processing the stuff they found in the truck and the boat. After a brief meeting with the sheriff and a free cup of coffee from the break room, they set about looking at what they had and the pictures Russ had taken.

The sheriff stuck his head in a couple of times, and once, while Dunkin had stepped out, he mentioned that he had met with the DCI agent and did not mention the new arrangement. Was that the right thing to do? The sheriff was fine with that.

Russell felt they were missing something. Where were Warren's clothes that he had on the day he was killed?

His body had been sent to Kalispell to the State Crime Lab. Other than a quick examination, not much had been done as the lab was backed up for months. One crime lab for the state and it's in Kalispell, and some stuff was taking six to nine months.

It's 319 miles from Virginia City to Kalispell. A little more than a casual drive. But Russ wanted to be sure there was nothing in the clothes and vest that Warren had on that would be useful. And he did not feel he could wait six months. Maybe everything had been removed, but no one could identify anything that was on him at the time of his death. And maybe there was nothing.

Russ asked the sheriff if he could get some help getting him to Kalispell and back and help get him into the crime lab to examine the clothing. The sheriff said he would make a few calls. In a few minutes, the sheriff had it set up. He asked Russ to meet him at the Ennis-Big Sky Airport, which was not far from where the murder took place. He would meet Russ there and they would fly up together to Kalispell and give him two or three hours at the lab with a supervisor to examine Warren's effects. The sheriff had connections, it seemed.

There was a knock on the door at the Hampton Inn. Teresa Walker looked through the peephole and saw Donny there. She opened the door and ushered him in quickly. A long embrace and a kiss were next. They had actually known each other for several years but recently had been working together in a strictly business arrangement. But they could not resist rekindling an old romance. They had not let Hector know about how serious that part was. They did not want word getting around. Donny would not be telling her about the Madison River incident, no matter what. And he had advised Hector that if anyone found out, it would not be good for Hector. Donny did not really like it that Hector could hold this over his head at some point, but he knew that Hector was afraid to cross him too. Hector had seen more than once Donny's willingness to use his 9 mm. Teresa had not seen that side of Donny, who could really be a charmer. He was handsome, exciting, and brought out something in her that no one else did.

"How did you do it?" asked Teresa. "You had the whole bunch looking like idiots. They were mad as hell!"

"Tess, it's better that you don't know everything. Then you can deny everything. Had it not been for your info, we would not have been able to pull it off."

Donny really liked having some fun with Teresa at the Hampton. They did takeout, drank Jack Daniels, smoked a joint now and then, and spent a lot of time in bed and watching movies. A few times he had talked her into taking out her contacts, putting on her glasses and baseball cap and going out to a dance club or a pool hall, but she was always nervous about being seen and especially when the heat was being turned up. She liked the danger of it all and the idea that they were socking away a nest egg of big money and someday she would not be worried about student loans or a new car. Fun, profitable, exciting, and romantic. What else? And it would not be for too much longer. Someday soon they would make a big score!

Donny knew that all good things must end. That might include Teresa with the Montana DCI and Hector with the red Ram truck. But for right now, he'd just enjoy the ride. As long as they did what they were told and did not pose him a threat, they could hang around. Pretty girls were everywhere, and being tied down to one was not really his style. He wasn't sure that Tess, as he called her, would ever see any of the money he had been putting away. But for now, the night was young. And he really did enjoy her company!

Donny and Teresa had met in Butte at Montana Tech where she was enrolled in the liberal studies and he was taking a mining and engineering path. The school is top rated and had been around for a hundred years. They dated a few times and were starting to get serious when he announced one day that he was dropping out. He called her one evening to say good-bye and was gone. Just like that. He had put in two years at Montana Tech, home of the Orediggers.

Teresa's family had moved to Butte with the oil and gas exploration business that her father worked for, and they never left. She went on to get her BS degree, and in her senior year, the state of Montana had a small booth at a job fair, career-day event. She stopped by the booth and picked up some papers and filled in an application for a career in state law enforcement. She was eventually accepted by the Criminal Investigation Division and worked inside for a time and took various law enforcement courses. She was finally moved into the agent slot, given a gun, badge, and car and she started working cases with city and county sheriffs and police departments who often needed help. She would spend three or four nights on the road due to the vast distances of driving required, and she started staying at the Hampton Inn in Bozeman, which was in her per-diem price range. She was checking in at the desk one evening when there was a tap on her shoulder.

"Tess, is that you?" said Donny

"Yes, sir, that's me."

She was startled to see Donny. As handsome as ever! They went to dinner and caught up, and she showed him her business card from the DCI, and he showed her his business card from a real estate and land company based in Butte. He was back there and working on buying and selling land, big ranches, and farms. At least that's what he had said. He was staying at the Hampton Inn when in Bozeman, and they started meeting there on a somewhat regular basis. After a while she started expressing the desire to make some real money. One thing led to another, and he finally asked her about helping him in his real job:

managing drug trafficking. It was a risk, but he knew how to manage risks if necessary.

He was now a hardened criminal in nice-guy clothes. She did not hesitate, however, and he tested her several times before really letting her in on any significant deals. Donny needed her to keep them advised on the drug task force and what they knew and did not know. And some cash found its way to her that she was putting in an old chest at her mom and dad's home under lock and key. They had no idea it was there. And now, they were planning to make a big score and sail off into the sunset together. Only, Donny might be sailing alone.

Russ was putting a lot of miles on his Tahoe back and forth, and no one had said how he was going to get paid for his expenses. But he had to meet the sheriff at the airport at seven thirty and he would be on time. His fishing and guiding was now on hold. For how long, he wasn't sure.

Russ got to the small airport, which was busier during ski season, and parked and went inside with his laptop and small briefcase. The sheriff was standing there in the lobby area with two cups of coffee and some fixings.

"I didn't know how you like your coffee, so here's some of everything."

"Thank you, sir. Is our plane here?"

"Yes. It stays here most of the time. It's sitting right out there on the loading ramp."

A beautiful Cirrus SR22T was sitting there with the door open.

"Are you ready to go?" asked the sheriff.

"Sure," said Russ, and they started walking toward the plane. "Where is the pilot?"

"That would be me, Russell," and with that, he walked around to the left side and climbed in, and Russ went to the other side and did the same. This was no stripped-down plane but had a big array of avionic and GPS stuff. Russ did not fly himself, but his father-in-law knew airplanes and would fly him and Sarah around to places. They flew out of McCollum Field in Marietta. Russ knew that this airplane was not cheap. There was a headset on the wheel, and Russ put it on.

The sheriff was settling in to pilot mode and starting the engine, so Russ withheld any comment.

"I've already done a preflight and got her warmed up, so we will be out of here in a minute," he said to Russ.

There was no tower at Ennis-Big Sky, but the Salt Lake City airport handles approach and landings. The sheriff was given the okay to roll and to take off. He gave a careful look in all directions and rolled the Cirrus into the wind and turned up the power. It was clear to Russ that this guy was not an amateur pilot. They came around on direction and reported in to the Salt Lake tower, who would be monitoring them while in their airspace. They gave some altitude and heading instructions to the sheriff, and he brought it up to altitude.

"So, Sheriff, this is a pretty nice ride. My father-in-law is a pilot and Air Force veteran who works now for Lockheed. So I have flown with him a lot on trips to Florida and a few fishing trips. Is this your plane?"

"I own a third of it. I couldn't afford it by myself, and we bought it used.

"I was lucky and my father knew some people and got me an appointment to the Air Force Academy. I got my wings and stayed in for twenty-two years, and I retired as a colonel a few years back and settled in Ennis. I actually grew up in Missoula, and my dad was sheriff there for many years and now my brother has that job.

"The former sheriff and his son in Madison County got into some trouble and they had a special election, and some people talked me into running. I thought it would be nice to have the extra money, some benefits, and so I did. The reputations of my father and brother in Missoula were helpful, and I won. This county is big but has an average murder and armed robbery rate of zero. It has been mostly an eight-to-six job, and I rotate weekends and an occasional night shift with the deputies so they don't get stuck there every weekend. I was doing fine 'til you and Warren Cason came along. Remind me to get your father-in-law's name, and I will look him up and see if I ever served with him."

Russ now understood some things. This guy had been around and was used to running the show. He had the office shipshape for a small town, and he had the respect of his people. He was way overqualified for this job but was happy doing it after those years in the Air Force and probably a nice retirement check coming in too. There were probably already too many Steinbrenners on the Missoula Sheriff's Department. He wasn't used to much back talk, and the deputies knew it, and they also knew he was a straight shooter. Russ was liking him more and more. They were speeding along at about 150 to Kalispell.

The sheriff reached into his shirt pocket and said, "By the way, Russ, here is a county credit card for expenses and gas related to your work. You will turn in an expense report to the office, and we will match it up to your card expenses."

Now Russ liked him even more. A perceptive guy, this sheriff.

"We *will* match it up." And Russ knew that was right!

When they arrived in Kalispell, they were under control of the Glacier Park International Airport tower, the busiest airport in Montana. But the sheriff was not bothered by the traffic or all the chatter and put the little Cirrus down with hardly a bump and taxied to a stop in front of a local FBO. Russ and the sheriff caught a taxi, one of the few in town, to the Montana State Crime Laboratory.

It took a few minutes of signing in and getting past the security, but they seemed to know their business, and Russ and the sheriff were ushered in to a room with lots of light and windows. In a few minutes, a staff member appeared rolling a cart with all of Warren Cason's stuff and some latex gloves. They were not to handle anything without the gloves, and they were to list any items they found. Anything that was deemed investigative evidence could be gathered and taken by the sheriff if he wanted. The staff member was there to oversee the process. They took out Warren's pants and wading shoes. He did not wear waders this time of year when it was hot and the water was warmer. They found nothing in the pants or shoes. Russ used his cell phone to take a picture of the wading shoes and the tread to compare to those pictures he had of the crime scene.

There are a lot of "fishing" shirts. Some with more pockets than a fly vest. That was the kind that Warren had been wearing. Russ carefully checked each pocket before he finally found something. It was a small, plain white envelope like you find at any office supply store. It was just big enough for a check to fit inside and it had been folded and mashed down as flat as possible and was in a pocket inside a pocket. The lab staff member and Russ and she Sheriff were paying close attention as Russ carefully unfolded the envelope and on the front was written "Warren Cason, S. Black Ave. $525 from Kile." Inside was a deposit slip from the bank for the $525 and the date. All this was not too useful except to confirm the name Kile. It was when Russ turned over the envelope that their luck began to change.

In lead pencil and very faintly written were a few words. "Tess Hampton 212." This was obviously written by a different person than the note on the front. Who was Tess Hampton? A friend of Warren's? Was 212 a time or address? They needed more to go on. The envelope had been wet, and the staff member said he could do a quick check for fingerprints but not to expect much. He came back in a few minutes and had found a couple of usable prints, but they were Warren's. The people had been careful not to leave any prints, and Russ believed that meant they were dealing with pros. Russ had seen enough of Warren's scribbling to think that the writing on the envelope was not his. They could compare to a suspect later if they had something to compare with. They concluded they had seen everything, signed for the envelope and contents to ensure chain of custody requirements, and left for the airport and home.

Russ spent most of the flight writing on his yellow pad, and they did not talk a lot coming back. When they got to the airport at Ennis, Russ shook the sheriff's hand and said, "Thank you for doing this. I promised Warren I would find his killer, and tomorrow I will be trying to find out what this means. I will call you."

With that, he was off to the Tahoe and gone. The sheriff liked his new special investigator. He thought Russ just might pull it off. He realized that with all of his own Air Force Academy training and his long career, Russ was better prepared and more experienced at this part of the job: murder investigation.

12

RUSS GOT UP THE NEXT morning and gave a call to Nancy, but she did not answer her phone. She may have been doing a shuttle. He called Chad, and he could not reach him either, and he may have been on the water with clients. So he drove over to see Mrs. Cason again.

Mrs. Cason finally made it to the door as she was having a breathing problem more severe than usual. She brightened up when she saw Russ and invited him in. She had made a fresh pot of coffee, and she poured Russ one and told him to sit at the table with her. Russ took out the plastic wrapper bag and asked Mrs. Cason if she knew anyone named Tess Hampton, and of course, she did not. He showed Miss Milly the note and asked if that looked like anything Warren would have written. Miss Milly produced some items written by Warren, and they truly looked like hen scratching. Nothing like the note.

Then she said, "I want to thank you for restoring my faith in people."

Russ asked her what she meant by that, and she explained that all the other investigators had contacted her once and nothing since. To know that someone was actually dealing with Warren's murder was at least comforting.

THE DRIFT BOAT DETECTIVE

"If there is anything else that comes to mind, Miss Milly, you have my card."

As he was getting his car turned around, his phone rang, and he could see it was Nancy. "Hello, Nancy."

"I saw where you called."

"Yes, I was going to let you look at something and get an opinion. I have just visited again with Miss Milly, but she wasn't feeling well and wasn't any more help."

"Well, Mom is preparing some lunch at home and I was going to eat with her. Why don't you come by at about eleven forty-five and eat with us, and I will introduce you to her and look at whatever it is you have."

Sassy had now been dead now a few days past one year. Nancy was asking him to her house. That might be nice. Then he called Deputy Dunkin in Madison County and asked if he could meet him at the sheriff's office at about three thirty to look at the stuff from the boat again. He felt they had to try to find another clue to go on.

Nancy lived in a fashionable part of town in an old renovated house from the late 1800s. Bozeman was founded in 1864. Like Nancy, the house was beautiful. Likewise for Nancy's mother, for an older woman, she was a very pretty lady. If Russ were to bet, Nancy would look just like her when she made it to her mom's age.

Lunch was great, and he could hear some whispering in the kitchen. Was it about him? After dessert of macaroon pie, he asked them to look at the note on the envelope and asked if either knew someone named Tess Hampton. They did not remember anyone by that name, but they would look at the store's customer list and see if there was a person like that there.

He was pushing it to get to Virginia City and his meeting with Dunkin, so he thanked them for the lunch and gave a little hug to Nancy's mother. Nancy walked him to the door, and as he started out, Nancy said, "What is this? My mother gets a hug and I get nothing!"

He turned and gave her a hug and a kiss on the cheek, and he saw Nancy's mother give him a thumbs-up as he was turning to walk out! Had Nancy's mom just given him her passing grade?

When Russ got to the courthouse in Virginia City, the sheriff was in his office on a conference call. Russ and Dunkin started looking through the stuff from the boat and truck again. Something stood out from the rest of the trash in the truck: there was a matchbook from the cabin/camp place up the road, and it looked new. Not like something that had been in the boat or truck a long time. Not a lot of places bothered with matches anymore since fewer people use them, but a camping place might need lots of matches for campfires, etc.

It wasn't much of a clue, but then it was about all they had to work on right now. Dunkin volunteered to go up to the place in the morning, take the photo they had of Warren, and see if he had been there. If he had not been there, then someone had been there and left the matches in Warren's boat. If he was there, did he have someone with him? The sheriff was off his call and came in and closed the door.

"The drug task force was supposed to have a big drug bust a few nights back and had all these people in place, and the people did not show up even though they were supposed to have had very credible information. It was supposed to have happened up near Big Timber near

Billings. Now reports are it may have taken place up near Cliff Lake in our county. Some people reported seeing a plane flying very low up there."

"What night would that have been, Barry?" asked Russ.

"That would have been the night before the murder of Warren Cason."

"Is anyone going to check on that?" asked Dunkin.

"I think the DEA and DCI and who knows who else is involved, but I do not know who's doing what," said the sheriff.

"Are there any airstrips up that way?" asked Russ.

"We were all looking on the computers, and there are two or three grass strips associated with some ranches, but my guess is they did not take off and land but rolled it out at very low altitude."

Russ's cell rang, and he started to let it go to voice mail since he did not know the number. The sheriff motioned for him to go ahead and take it. It was Miss Milly.

"Mr. Russell, I saw a truck on TV that looks a lot like the red truck that was at the shop that day. It's called a Ram and has a ram's head on it. I remembered the ram's head. Does that help?"

"Well, it sure might. That gives us something to look for and eliminates a whole lot of possible red trucks. Thank you so much for calling, and I am here right now with the sheriff and deputy sheriff in Madison County and we are working on Warren's case. Please call if you remember anything else."

With that, he hung up.

Speaking to the deputy, he said, "Would you mind if I went with you tomorrow? We can take Warren's picture, pictures of his rig, and pictures of a red Ram truck with us.

141

We will ask also if anyone was there named Tess Hampton. I want to look tonight and see if there is an airstrip close to that cabin/camp place, and maybe we can check it out."

"Sure, Russ. Let's get started about eight o'clock. Do you think that the drug deal and Warren's death are connected in some way?"

"That would certainly be a motive for murder, and we currently don't have one. If Warren stumbled into this deal somehow, it could have gotten him killed. I don't believe Warren was a drug dealer. If he was, he wasn't very good at it and wasn't making any money, as best I can see. Anyway, if we are close by, we won't be out much."

Sheriff Steinbrenner said, "I'll drive us up in my four-wheel-drive SUV, and we can all ride over to the field together. I would love to get the jump on the Feds on this one."

"Do you want to call that DCI lady?" said Dunkin.

"No," said the sheriff.

Russ left for Bozeman and decided to just stay in the area and not have to keep running back and forth. He spotted a hotel sign called Reel 'Em Inn Cabins, and that caught his eye. He pulled in and asked about a cabin, and they had one vacancy; but he didn't have enough cash for the room and he had not been carrying his credit cards, but he had the Madison Sheriff's Department card. They took that and were quick to give him a discount. He went in and really was glad he stopped. This was almost like an apartment. He set about getting logged on their wireless and looking up airstrips and GPS coordinates.

When Donny Bragg and Teresa Walker started meeting and she was getting involved in providing information to

Donny on the drug task force, they needed to be careful and not get caught by her DCI people, especially if a deal was going down. The drug network felt that the Feds may have a mole planted in their organization, so elaborate schemes were used to throw off the Feds' efforts. So far they had worked. Donny had stayed quite often at the Hampton Inn and sometimes next door at Homewood Suites. When he was going to meet Teresa, she would call his cell and simply leave her room number, which he often wrote out on a piece of scratch paper as a reminder if he was busy with a lot of details. It might look like "Tess Hampton 212," meaning that Tess, as he called Teresa, was at the Hampton Inn in room 212. He could then place a call to the hotel and have them ring her room, and she would simply say to him that he had the wrong number if there was a reason for him not to come. That's what he did on the night before the money was taken to Warren. Teresa had called and left the info while Donny was in the shower. He grabbed an envelope from his little box that he kept to mail money to Kile Davidson and to his confidant that put some cash in a lock box for him at a UPS Store mailbox. He jotted the note down with a pencil. Later when he saw he was not going to make it back to the hotel to see Teresa, he called Hector, who had a key to his room, and told him the name and address of Warren Cason.

"Go to my room and get $525 from on top of the closet and put it in one of those plain envelopes and carry it and slide it under the fishing guide's shop door. There should be no one there, but drive by and check before you pull in. Leave it and get going. There is no security stuff there."

Hector had picked up the envelope with the dimly written note on the back with Teresa's room number on it, put the money in it, and put it under Warren's door. No one, including, Warren had noticed the note but Russ. "Tess Hampton 212."

The next morning, the three Madison County Sheriff's Department personnel started up to the head of the Madison River Valley in Montana. They would be a few miles from Idaho and the Yellowstone Park in Wyoming.

They stopped at the cabin/camp and showed the pictures of Warren and his rig. Everyone was positive that neither it nor Warren had been there. None had ever heard of Tess Hampton. But they were pretty sure that a red Ram truck had been there, but that was not too unusual as those were pretty popular. But the one that was here had Texas plates though, and that made a couple of the workers think about the Dallas Cowboys. The truck was not registered with one of the cabins, but they believed he was visiting one of the units, and that happened a lot. Which one they weren't sure. There was one thing: someone had left a plastic bag with some rags and gun-cleaning items and gun oil. They were wondering what they should do with it.

"We'll take that off your hands," said Barry Steinbrenner.

Russ had spent quite a bit of time looking at the Google Earth maps on the computer. He believed that there was one place very close by but isolated where a plane could fly low safely and make a drug drop without trees and with no houses nearby. They headed over to Highway 87 and followed the GPS. There was the airstrip with the lake view, and the three of them got out to walk it from one end to the other and each had a plastic trash bag that Russ had taken from the Reel 'Em Inn Cabin. At first look, there wasn't much to see. Then they saw them: several pieces of bubble wrap and duct tape that had been torn off the rolled-up drugs were down the length of the grass strip. None were very big but large enough to tell it was a piece of bubble wrap. They had indeed done a drop here recently. It was difficult to estimate how many packages because they each hit multiple times as they bounced to a stop. They collected the small pieces and put them in the trash bags. Fingerprints, who knows? There was no sign of the vehicle that picked up the drop on the grass. The plane apparently did not land.

13

SHERIFF STEINBRENNER HAD WANTED TO upgrade the tiny department in as many areas as he could and had managed, in a town of about 200 people, and a county of 7,700, give or take, to do that with some really good people. And when he could, he had taken advantage of free training to make the staff there better and to make them feel better about the department and their jobs.

Madison County, Montana, covers 3,603 square miles— 2.14 people per square mile in density. By comparison, Russell Baker came from Cobb County Georgia that is only 345 square miles in area but has 688,000 people—1,994.2 people per square mile!

New York City has 27,839.6 people per square mile. Not much elbow room there!

The town of Virginia City has a courthouse built in 1875 and was territorial capital of Montana from 1865 to 1875. And Big Sky, known for skiing, lies in large part in Madison County.

One of the things he had done was have one of the staff attend the FBI Criminal Justice Information Services Division class to learn fingerprinting, among other things, and she had taken the IAI Tenprint Certification test and passed. He felt that this would help with burglaries and identifying possible true identities of an offender trying to pass themselves off as someone else for whatever reason. Having the certification also helped get a conviction to stick in court.

Miriam Alexander was married and had two kids just starting college. She had attended the University of Utah and married a local fellow there who was a building contractor. He built homes of all sizes in and around Salt Lake County where they both were from, and she worked for the Salt Lake County Sheriff's Office, and that was a department in one of the major metro areas in that part of the United States. She had worked as an assistant in the criminal investigation division there, but when her husband wanted to move; she was all for the change. Her husband had heard from a local architect that she was doing some nice homes in that area and that Madison County, Montana, was having a building boom. It turns out that new home construction was the largest industry in Madison County. People buying ranchettes and building permanent and vacation-type home in the Big Sky Country. The architect liked Alexander's work and promised him a lot of business if he moved there.

It wasn't long before Miriam was really bored in the small town and wanted something to do. A new sheriff had just been elected and there had been some major housecleaning at the department. An ad was being run for some replacement staff. She applied, and Barry had jumped at the chance to get her. She had now become his "right-hand man" so to speak. In no time he could tell this tiny department was not going to be able to keep her interest. When he saw a bulletin about some law enforcement grant money, he enlisted the county clerk and the commissioners to help him apply. They got a $50,000 grant to upgrade the communications and other equipment, and he used part of the money to send Miriam to the FBI course and got her to sit for the certification exam, which she passed. He used the rest of the money to buy the fingerprinting kits and the scanner. This kept her happy for a while, but she had not had a lot of interesting work. An occasional burglary was about it.

Using a federal grant, he had acquired a state-of-the-art Suprema RealScan-F Live Scan device from Fulcrum Biometrics and some onsite dusting and retrieval kits. He was about to put this to the test.

They could scan and send fingerprints to any government agency and the FBI for quick analysis. If they could find any. He probably had not mentioned all this to Russ Baker.

They got back to Virginia City, and Russ left for the Reel 'Em Inn and made a couple of calls. One to his father-in-law and told him about the sheriff. His father-in-law did not think he had served with him but was impressed that the sheriff had a Cirrus SR22T. "And, by the way, Russ, your investment portfolio is doing great. Do you want me to mail you the statements?"

"I'll get with you once I get done with this case. I may come home for a few days then. As long as it's plus, I guess I am okay."

"It's a lot more than plus. You will be pleased." Well, at least Russ wasn't going broke. He then called Nancy. He wasn't real sure at this point what to call their relationship. There had been very little contact, and he did kiss her on the cheek. Once. He was at about the second-grade level in this relationship, by his calculation.

Nancy had been asking herself the same thing.

"What is my relationship with Russ?" It had been mostly arm's length, business, and somewhat standoffish. The kiss on the cheek she had to ask for. But for some reason, the last few days, she kept thinking about him and worried about him getting involved with some bad people who had already killed one person she knew. For a moment, when her phone rang, she felt a sense of real excitement! Russ was calling!

"Hi, Russ. How are things going?"

"Not too much to report, yet. I got to ride up to Kalispell yesterday with Barry in his plane and found out a lot about him. He's quite impressive for a small-town sheriff."

"I remember when he was running for that office that a lot of people felt he was a real catch for the county. His family has been in law enforcement for a long time, I believe. Maybe over in Missoula, I think."

"That's right. If I only knew as much about the case as I know about him, I'd be cooking."

"How are things at the Super 8?"

"Well, now that you mention it, I have me a cabin in Ennis at the Reel 'Em Inn and it's cool! All the comforts of home, and I don't have to drive so much. I'll be down here tonight and maybe longer, depending on where the leads take us."

"I've seen that place when passing, I'm sure it's better than the cramped quarters you've been used to," she said.

"Like being in the Ritz Carlton in Buckhead compared to the place I've been staying." He was fumbling for what to say. "On the case, we have picked up very little in the way of concrete evidence, but we haven't thrown in the towel just yet."

"Well, that's something, anyway."

149

"I just wanted to say hello, Nancy. Be careful moving the trucks and doing the shuttles until we find this guy. And by the way, when you moved Warren's truck, was it locked when you came to pick it up and did you lock it when you parked it at Varney?"

"You know, Russ, I don't shuttle for many guys, but for the ones I do, I insist that I have a set of keys. If you drive fifty to seventy-five miles to do a shuttle and the guide took the keys with him on the float, that can make you pretty upset, and he will be upset when he gets to the take-out and the truck is not there. That happened to me a couple of times. I am not breaking into anyone's truck.

"When I got there, the truck was locked, and I used my keys to get in and move the truck. I locked it at Varney and took my keys. Warren had his keys with him, I'm sure. I would guess that they would have been with his wallet and phone in a waterproof plastic container or his boat bag. Just a guess. Why do you ask?"

"They loaded the boat on the trailer at Varney and parked it in the farthest-away place from the ramp. They had to use the key, and if what you say is correct, they probably had to take them out of the bag the wallet and phone were in. We are going to take a close look at that bag in the morning and see if it tells us anything."

Russ was trying to cover all the bases. "I'll let you go, Nancy. Have a good evening, and I'll catch you later."

"Good night, Russ," she said as she hung up and the doorbell rang.

My God, she thought, *I may as well have been talking to my brother!* Nancy opened the door, and she looked like a movie star silhouetted in the light of the room. At the door was her date for the evening, and she had not been on a real date in a long, long time.

Dr. Stephen Carter, PhD, was at the door. Dr. Carter had recently moved to Bozeman to take a professorship at Montana State in the math department. He was a Rhode Islander, and she loved the way he talked. He was not a bad-looking guy either and had the poise of a cultured person from, say Newport. Dr. Carter had been in the shop buying presents to send to his mother, aunt, and sister at different times and had introduced himself to Nancy. He finally got around to asking her out, and they were going to a faculty dinner affair at the school to welcome a new dean. This was a big social affair in Bozeman, and Dr. Carter was certain that he would have the most beautiful date there.

Sitting around waiting for somebody like a Russ Baker wasn't going to get it. If she was ever going to move forward after the death of her fiancé, now was the time to do it. She might not get a better chance. There was no reason to have mentioned it to Russ, as far as she could see, and had not even considered it worth mentioning. She wished him well and would be his friend if he wanted her to be.

Back at the sheriff's office, they had a meeting in Barry's office. Russ had a list of things he would like for them to do. Most of it involved testing for fingerprints and comparing the results to see if there was any match. "Barry, can we get some help from someone on doing some print analysis on some of these small items to see if there is any linkage? Maybe Bozeman or Gallatin County could help. Sending this stuff off may take forever."

"Miriam Alexander, whom you met I believe, is FBI certified. I will call her in here, and she can probably do what

151

you need." He called Miriam from the doorway, and Russ was pleasantly surprised to find he had a resource right there.

"I would like to check the Ziploc bag that we have that had the wallet, knife, and cell phone inside. Warren had keys to his truck somewhere that the killer had to use to move the truck, load the boat, and put it back. The keys were in the truck when we found it, I believe. I know that the keys were not left in the truck by the person who did the shuttle. Nancy Freeman did the shuttle, and she used her own keys and locked the truck when she left it at Varney Bridge.

"I want to check the matchbook from the cabin/camp. While Warren apparently was not there, the killer may have been.

"I want to check the bag with the gun-cleaning oil and rags and barrel-cleaning brush. That bag may well have an oily fingerprint.

"I want to see if we can get a test on the shell cartridge found at the scene. It may be a stretch, but a good lab may can tell us if that shell has any traces of gun oil. We already know it has no prints on it. I know the state crime lab is way behind, but they have a biochemistry and chemistry program at Montana State. They could test it, or some independent lab may be available. Maybe if someone in Missoula could help. I would like to try to see if we can connect the shell to the oil and rags in the cabin/camp.

"Finally, there are the tape and bubble wrap fragments we found at the drop site. The tape would be the best bet for having a print, and it's a long shot. Anything that I can do to help, let me know.

"Wayne and I need to go over the truck and boat one more time just to be sure we have not missed anything. I think we can move on from those after that.

152

"Then there is the note on the envelope. *Tess Hampton 212*. What is that about? There doesn't seem to be a lead on who this Tess Hampton might be."

Miriam had just been given more police work to do than she had the entire time she had been there. She couldn't wait. But she was interested in the comment on the note.

"Can I look at the note?"

Russ handed her the plastic bag containing the envelope, and she looked at both sides and handed it back to Russ.

"That doesn't look like a name to me. That looks like someone was talking on the phone and taking down a message."

"What do you think the message is, Miriam?" asked Barry.

"Tess—whoever Tess is—is at the Hampton Inn in room 212," was her response.

They all were dumfounded! That made perfect sense! "Of course," she said, "it's possible that the person who used the envelope had nothing to do with the other note. They just happened to use a piece of paper that someone else had left behind. It's happened to all of us at one time or another."

Russ thought she was right. He had often used a scrap of paper that was handy that someone else had also used. Sometimes he would just scratch through the old note. When you are on the phone sometimes, you even write on your hand if you can find a pen.

"Would you think that Tess is a name or a nickname, Miriam?"

"I have known a few girls called Tess, and they were usually a Teresa or Theresa, or something like that." she said. "I knew one girl called Contessa, and she never wanted to be called anything but Tess."

"Then, Barry," said Russ, "we have here a mention of a red Ram truck and there are several instances where a red

Ram come to my mind. Miss Milly Cason says there was a red Ram truck in her yard the day before her son was killed. She's not certain. The folks at the cabin/camp say there was a red Ram truck with Texas plates up there the night before the murder, and it stayed there most of the day. It was gone later that evening. I saw a red Ram at the gun range in Bozeman with Texas plates. There were two guys inside that I think were driving that truck but I actually did not see them in the vehicle. It was gone when I came out of the gun range. But we definitely need to have an area-wide 'be on the lookout and advise' status on that truck. Probably don't want to rattle them just yet with no more than we have. I can follow up if it's spotted."

"On it," said Barry and he walked into the radio room to get the BOLO out on the truck, and then he came back in.

"There is another thing that has been bugging me," said Russ. "Several times around Bozeman, I spotted this very fancy black Ford F-150, and it has a distinctive-looking, possibly custom-made, chrome step bumper. It has Montana plates. I am pretty sure I saw it in passing turning down the street that Warren lived on a couple of days before the shooting. I did not see the driver, but he had on a cowboy hat. There certainly are a few of those in Montana, so that is not much of a lead. But here is the curious thing: I saw that truck, I'd bet my last dollar on it, coming out of the Highway 287 put-in and a woman was driving it when I arrived for my float with my clients that morning. There may have been a man in there with her. That same evening of the day that Warren Cason died, after being hung up with you guys all day, my clients and I stopped in Ennis and ate. We were late going up the Highway 84 to Bozeman. A vehicle came up behind us, and as soon as they could, they passed us. It was the same black F-150 with that fancy bumper. It had some hay bales in the back. That's a lot of times to see the same vehicle and particularly at the put-in."

"That is a long shot too," said Barry. "Do you want me to do a BOLO on that?"

"Let me see what I can come up with. Maybe we can do that tomorrow," said Russ.

"If I spot it, we can do a follow-up on the plates. I may go up to Bozeman this afternoon and follow up on Tess at the Hampton. I'll see if they will tell me anything without us getting a warrant. A judge may think our case is too weak to back us with a search warrant just yet."

"I agree," said Barry. Barry looked at Miriam.

"How long do you think it will take to process the items here that Russ is asking for?"

"To do it right, possibly four or five hours. I will work as late as I can tonight if you will approve the overtime," she responded.

"I will approve it. Do you need me or someone to stay to help?"

"I think I would like to work on it alone so I can control the process. It's been a while since I've done this work, so I may have to regroup."

"I will make a few calls on the oil and shell casing idea. There may be someone that can test that for us."

"Miriam, if you get anything you feel is very significant, call me and I'll run down here," said Barry.

14

Donny Bragg and Hector Martinez had found a double-wide for rent in a mobile home park out of Huffine Lane in Bozeman. This was not more than about three miles from downtown. Huffine Lane changed to Main Street about 19th Avenue. It was about four miles to the Hampton and the Super 8 from their place as they were hiding in plain sight.

The drug drop had gone very well as far as the people in control knew, and they were not aware of the Warren Cason murder mess that Donny had been involved in. While they weren't necessarily opposed to murder, they did not want to have one that threatened their business. As far as that went, Donny Bragg was a hero because he had thwarted the Feds' attempts to interdict the last shipment and, from all accounts, did it very well. The only person who knew differently at this point was Hector, and Donny wanted him where he could keep an eye on him in case he started falling apart.

Donny and Hector would cool their heels for a while until things calmed down and the task force moved somewhere else. Tess would be able to let him know when the heat was off.

Things were pretty hot and heavy between Donny and Tess, but Donny was pretty sure that Hector was not in on all of that. Hector had a job at a local trucking company working in the cross-docking of trucks. Big trucks came in and were reloaded onto smaller delivery trucks to be delivered. The job did not pay a lot, but it gave an air of legitimacy to Hector when someone asked if he had a job because he always seemed to have money for beer and pool and the occasional woman friend. Donny's friends in Butte had arranged the job as they had some trucking connections as well. Donny had business cards that said he was a real estate salesperson, and if someone called the Butte number, they sounded pretty legit and did occasionally sell some property or an occasional house. He kept some actual sales flyers and did have a real estate license. So Donny was doing okay in "real estate sales." They looked somewhat normal on the surface.

Russ went to Bozeman and decided to cruise around for a few minutes. He did not see the Ford truck with the special rear bumper, and he saw about one hundred red Ram trucks; but when he got close to them, none had a Texas tag. He headed out to the Super 8 and decided to try out his new badge and ID on the front desk people at the Hampton Inn. He first drove around the entire lot to see if there was a vehicle he recognized, and finding none, he went inside.

Russ asked for the manager and was told that the manager would not be in for a couple of hours as his kid was in something at the school he attended. And no, they could not answer any questions about who might have stayed there and when. They had the privacy of their guests to consider. He would have to see the manager.

So much for the badge and ID. Maybe he should have shown them his gun, he thought.

When he got to his room, he decided to call Nancy and see if she was free to join him for coffee or dinner some place. She did not answer her cell phone. She had it off while in the movie with her new friend, Stephen.

Russ decided that paying rent in two places was dumb, so he loaded up all his stuff in the Tahoe (threw it in the Tahoe is more like it) and settled up with the Super 8 Motel on his bill and headed for Ennis and the Reel 'Em Inn. That place was a lot nicer and was closer to his base of operation for now. The running back and forth was putting a lot of miles on the Tahoe. Not to mention his behind.

Nancy's date with Stephen did not last too long as they both had to work the next day. He brought her home about nine o'clock and there was a brief and awkward kiss good-night at the door. It was awkward but nice, she thought. She put her purse and phone down and realized she had not turned her cell back on. When she did, she saw a "missed call" indication and saw that it was Russ.

At first she was going to ignore it but decided that it might be important and redialed his number, and it went to voice mail. She had the Super 8 number in her phone from previous contact there with Russ, so she dialed it and the front desk answered. When she asked to speak to Mr. Russell Baker, the person said, "I'm sorry, but Mr. Baker has checked out."

For some reason, that news caused her to feel hurt and sad. Why, she did not know. He had probably been calling to tell her he was leaving.

When Russ got to Ennis and got all of his stuff in the room, he was suddenly tired and lay down across the bed and fell asleep for a few minutes. When he woke up, he looked at his cell and he saw Nancy had called at some point and he did not hear it or he missed it in the dead zone along the way. He thought it was too late to call her tonight and turned on the news.

There was only a quick comment about there being "no new developments in the Madison River Murder" as it was being called. In a few days, they would forget the case entirely.

Miriam had worked very late into the night and had not gotten in to the office in Virginia City when Russ pulled into a spot beside the old courthouse building on the dirt street. There was no parking lot as such although a lot of people would park across the street, but a new building was probably going to put an end to that.

This part of town looked a lot like it did one hundred years ago. A lot different from the urban sprawl that had hit Cobb County, Georgia, with multiple fire stations and police precincts and ever-widening interstate highways, flyover bridges, and plants that built the F-22 Raptors and cargo planes. The Marietta Town Square, where he and Sarah used to listen to music and see parades and eat ice cream, was always alive and bustling, bringing back the small, old-hometown flavor to an otherwise big county. Antique stores and pizza and live theaters were at every corner.

But times were changing, and more and more people seemed destined to be coming to Madison County, for good or evil. For now, the entire length of Wallace Street, the main street through town, was one half of a mile long with no traffic light. The Vacancy sign was always out at the Fairweather Inn. There was not much ever going on at the Wells Fargo & Company Overland Mail and Express Office either. Today, in a building built in 1875, some people were hoping that with old-fashioned police work and some modern technology, they could catch a murderer. That would be just fine with Russ. He had a promise to keep.

Russ found the coffee pot, and everyone started coming in, and there seemed to be a commotion on the street so he went to the window to see. There was a rollback wrecker-type truck from the Dodge Chrysler Jeep dealer in Bozeman unloading a dark-gray, almost-black, Dodge Charger Pursuit vehicle. It was unmarked but unmistakable as to what it was. It looked like someone was getting a new car at the courthouse today. He saw Barry looking on with Deputy Dunkin.

Russ saw Miriam coming in and walked back to say good morning and to see what progress she had made. She looked tired, and he assumed she had stayed late. Barry and Wayne came in, and they all met in the conference room. Miriam had laid out several stacks of the evidence material, and there was a report for each of them on what she had done so far.

Barry said, "You must have worked late last night, Miriam. What time did you leave?"

"I left about twenty minutes ago and went down to Nevada City to the restaurant and got some coffee and something to eat. I haven't been home all night. My husband was out of town, so I just kept working, and before I knew it, it was 5:00 AM."

Everyone's mouths dropped open in unbelief. Barry leaned against the wall and just shook his head.

"I want us to catch the SOB that killed that man in our jurisdiction. I'm new here, but we can't let someone get away with that," she said. "All this is in the report that each of you have. Please excuse any typos. I'll correct those after I get some sleep."

"We have a usable print on the matchbook. And as you thought, Russ, we have a print on the gun oil bottle. Those two match. Same thumb and index fingerprints. That puts our person who was in the cabin also in the boat, or at least it would seem that way.

"I have a print on the Ziploc bag that the wallet and phone were in. It is right in the corner, and they tried to hold it where they would not leave a print, I believe. They probably did have to get the keys out of that bag. That also was a thumb and index finger, but a different person than the others, and they are not the victim's.

"The oil bottle and the matchbook were from some *safe* activities," said Russ. "Those were done when the perpetrators were doing something away from the crime scene and they were not concerned about being found.

"The zip bag was after the crime had been committed, and that was a result of being in a hurry and getting careless."

"All we have to do now," said Wayne Dunkin, "is find the people the prints go with."

"Wayne, if you can, we will go take one more look at the truck and boat. Then, if it's okay with Barry, we can get them back to Miss Milly. Then, Sheriff, I will try again to locate the manager of the Hampton Inn and see if I can get line on Tess.

"Miriam, can someone scan those prints in and check them with the DCI or the FBI? I know you are worn out."

She said she would send them and go home for a while and rest. Barry suggested that one of the other ladies take his SUV and carry her home so she wouldn't fall asleep, and she did not argue.

Barry said, "Russ, I need to talk to you a minute. I got another grant from Uncle Sam to buy a police cruiser. It came in last week, and I was supposed to get the lettering done over in Bozeman. I was going to give my SUV to Wayne and use the new car myself. But we agreed that you should not be using your vehicle on the job, so we will keep what we have right now and we are assigning you the unmarked Dodge Police Interceptor, for the moment. If that is okay."

"Of course it's okay with me, Barry. That is very nice of you. I will try to not get it full of bullet holes or anything."

"Wayne will show you the radio set up, and we have repeaters so we can cover the area, and the service is more reliable than cell phones at present. You can reach here from Bozeman."

After the car orientation, they took one last look at the truck and boat. There appeared to be nothing left to find. Wayne drove the new car out to the Reel 'Em Inn, and they left the Tahoe there. Russ got behind the wheel of his new ride! He dropped Wayne off at the courthouse and headed for Bozeman.

Russ hoped they would get a break on the prints in the National Crime Information Center database, part of the FBI. He was going to give Miriam a hug when she woke up! They had now taken up most of the day already.

Russ drove to the Hampton Inn and went in to the desk and asked for the manager. The clerk said that the manager was in and he would be right back with him, and the clerk disappeared and was gone for several minutes.

Russ was getting impatient, and as he was pacing the floor, he saw a familiar face going through the lobby holding a cup of coffee and a chocolate chip cookie, that had the lobby smelling wonderful, and carrying a laptop. It was Agent Teresa Walker from DCI. He almost called out to her but caught himself. He did not want to discuss the case with her anymore. She had officially put it on the back burner due to "high priority" cases that needed her attention. It was an "open" case, but "inactive awaiting new evidence" was how she had put it in her report. He watched her get in her car and drive up the access road, and in a few minutes, he could see her car going down the ramp on the interstate and headed out of town.

A chill went down Russ's back! The names Teresa and Tess! Could this be his Tess! Surely, not.

The manager appeared and asked Russ what his business was, and Russ asked that they talk in private, so they went back in the manager's office where Russ showed his credentials and told him what he needed. The manager said he would not release any information about guests without a court order. It was company policy. Russ tried to appeal to him on the grounds that a Bozeman citizen had been murdered, but the manager would not budge.

Russ went down Main Street, and it was getting close to five o'clock, and he might try to run up on Nancy at the shop and see if she was free for dinner. He would surprise her.

It was Russ who got the surprise. He drove by the dress shop just as Nancy and a nice-looking guy came out of the store and started walking to a car. Had Russ been in his Tahoe, she would have probably noticed him, but she did not recognize him in the Dodge Cruiser.

Russ was really feeling down. He had to keep moving but saw the car pull out, and he wondered where they were going. He was surprised that he would have such a reaction and knew he had no right to feel that way. She hardly knew Russ. Russ pulled in to a spot and waited until they passed and then pulled out to see where they were headed. They had gone a couple of blocks when there it was, going in the other direction: the black Ford F-150 with the chrome step bumper!

Russ did not want to spook the driver, and he did not have probable cause to do anything with this guy yet. The guy had the cowboy hat, as usual, and was driving within the speed limit. Russ had to try to get turned around in the busy street and get behind the truck to get a license number. The traffic and the lights were not working in Russ's favor, and by the time he could go down a side street and make a U-turn and come back, the truck was gone! Russ went all the way out Main Street to where the name changed to Huffine, and there were several turnoffs and a number of mobile home parks, but he wasn't even sure the truck had come this far.

Now, in one evening, he had not gotten any cooperation from the motel manager, he had lost sight of the F-150 and the BMW that Nancy was riding in. This had become a real shitty afternoon!

Russ made a quick trip back to the Brew Works to grab some dinner before he went back to Reel 'Em Inn. He parked at the end of the lot to avoid any attention and went inside to head to the bar and watch some news. On the way, he walked right by the table where Nancy and Stephen were sitting, and they made eye contact and, she said, "Hello, Russ."

"Hello, Nancy, so nice to see you." And with a nod and a little wave toward Stephen Carter, PhD, he said, "And hello to you, sir."

He had been very cordial and polite, but he kept on walking to the bar and got up on a stool, and the waiter was there immediately, taking his order. Russ could not be upset with Nancy as she did not owe him anything. They had barely been more than casual acquaintances, but for some reason, he had a knot in his stomach and a feeling that he had just struck out in the bottom of the ninth in the World Series. He did not look back over toward the table again and was looking at some news from Georgia on the TV when there was a touch on his shoulder. He turned around, and Nancy was there alone. The guy she was with was walking toward the men's room.

"Is everything okay, Russ? I haven't heard anything on how the project is going." She was referring to the case, as far as he knew. "Any luck yet?"

"We haven't had a breakthrough, yet but we have a few leads we are working on. We aren't dead yet, so to speak."

165

"Well, I hope you have some good luck soon. I guess I'll talk to you another time."

"Sure, Nancy. Good-bye."

As she walked away, she thought the way Russ said *good-bye* did not sound like a "See ya later" good-bye. It sounded like a "forever" good-bye.

Russ left the restaurant and wasted no time in getting to his little cabin in Ennis where he would spend the evening alone, like most evenings. He had ended up having a rotten day after a great start that morning.

15

THE MORNING COFFEE WAS GOOD at the old courthouse. Miriam looked unusually nice and appeared to have gotten some rest. There had been a technical glitch with the fingerprint scanner, and the service guy was coming from somewhere sometime today. That made it a certainty: the day before was just plain crap!

Miriam came in where Russ was, and he said, "I owe you a hug for all the hard work you put in if Mr. Alexander won't be too upset."

She pushed the door closed and tears were in her eyes. "Mr. Alexander has a girlfriend somewhere and is not staying home much these days. I'm not sure he is coming back. I could use that hug!"

She seemed to just blurt it out. Then she said, "My God, I'm sorry to dump that on you. I don't think anyone knows the situation yet, so just keep that to yourself, if you don't mind."

About that time, Barry came in. "Sorry about the scanner problem. Apparently, a light is not working, and it requires some special thing."

"I understand, Barry. I have something very sensitive to ask you," Russ began.

Miriam looked startled and hoped he wasn't about to say something about what she had said.

"Barry, I went by the Hampton Inn last night and, as we suspected, they said no info without a judge saying so. I could have threatened to call in some fake 911 calls, but I decided to wait on that. But while I was in the lobby, Teresa Walker from DCI walked out. She did not see me. However, I had a really bad thought, though: could she be our Tess?"

"The day we had that short follow-up meeting in Bozeman and we left, I went out and fell in behind her, and she turned into the road that goes to the Hampton. She did not see me then either, and I did not think anything about it, but I'll be willing to bet she stays there every time she comes to town."

"Oh my," said Barry. "We would have to really handle that right! To accuse a DCI agent of being involved in something, and we don't know yet what that something is…that would cause some big rumblings!"

"Could we at least get a background on her, Barry?"

"That stuff is very closely held, I'm sure. I thought getting the oil testing done was tough, but that's nothing compared to this!"

"Barry, this is one of those deals where you call in a favor. Does anyone owe you a favor in the DCI?"

"Not me. But I know someone that they might owe some to. My brother in Missoula is both a good sheriff and a good politician. Let me see if he can help us on that. And by the way, Russ, we do have someone who can examine the rags and cartridge to see if they are connected. It's a company called Intertek. They are a worldwide company, and we are sending the stuff to Seattle, Washington, to get it done. It may take a week."

Barry was a "get it done" guy, and he had gotten Russ new wheels. Pretty good. Russ's cell phone rang, and he looked and saw it was Nancy. He decided to let it go to voice mail. He couldn't deal with this right now.

The radio operator stepped in the room. "We have a hit on the BOLO for the red Ram pickup. The Gallatin sheriff is on line 1."

Barry picked up and put the speaker on. "High, Charlie. They say you have something for me."

"Yeah, Barry, we think so. One of my deputies was serving a garnishment on a guy at a truck line facility up here and spotted the truck parked in the employee parking lot. Here is the license number on that Texas license. Anything else you want us to do?"

"Right now, no. My investigator that I told you about may come up and observe this guy to get a line on who he is hanging out with. If we need to make an arrest, of course, I will ask for your assistance. And let me ask you about a couple of other things while you are in such a generous mood."

"Dare I say anything, Colonel?" Russ could tell these guys had an Air Force connection.

"I need a background personnel check on a DCI agent, and I need some help with the Hampton Inn management there to find out about who may have stayed in one of their rooms. They are saying a court order is going to be required to get the info I need, Charlie."

Charlie Neilson had not served with Barry Steinbrenner but had also been in the Air Force, and their paths had crossed a few times. He had been a captain in the military police. When he left the Air Force, Neilson had come back home to work in his family's hardware business but eventually ran for sheriff with his father's blessing and won. He was now in his second term and well liked in the county. He was a friend and supporter of Barry's and had urged Barry to run for the Madison County sheriff's job when the old sheriff was ousted for misconduct. Their Air Force careers had been a strong link that helped them form a great relationship.

"Man! You don't ask easy ones, do you? Are you by chance wanting a background on our darling Teresa Walker?"

"Yes. That's the one, Charlie."

"You know she is considered an ace employee!"

"Yes, I realize that, Charlie, and to make matters worse, without the Hampton's help, it's just a hunch."

"So, Barry, if I could get the Hampton to go along on the info request you might not need that inquiry. Is that right?" Russ nodded his head.

"That's right, Charlie. We need to know if someone named Tess, possibly a nickname for Teresa, stayed in the room 212 at the Hampton on or around the time of the murder of your Warren Cason."

"So this is about Cason?"

"At the very least. But it may be a lot bigger than Cason. We don't think his getting killed was anything related to him. He just happened to get in somebody's way on something bigger."

"Bigger, as in 'drug task force and organized crime' bigger?"

"I see why they keep electing you sheriff and talk about you being governor, Charlie."

"Well, that did it, Barry! Flattery may get the info you need from the Hampton. I'd really like to not have to ask for that DCI background info unless we have more than a hunch. I think a Gallatin County Sheriff's Department meeting out there at the Hampton about five in the afternoon in a bunch of patrol cars might be enough, don't you?"

Russ did a double thumbs-up at Barry.

"That would do it for me, Charlie," Barry replied.

"Why don't you have your guy there at about five o'clock today, Colonel?"

"Well, if you insist," Barry said with a laugh. "But he doesn't have a marked car! He's traveling incognito."

"Colonel, you always did use big words in those briefings! See him at five. My note here says he is Secret Special Agent Russell Baker who speaks with a Southern drawl."

"Right. That's how you will recognize him. His password will be, 'How are y'all doing.'" Barry hung up.

Russ gained more and more respect for this *tiny-town* sheriff every day. He could see why he did well in the Air Force and wondered why he did not stay for a general spot.

"Russ, Montana does not have a reciprocal computer interchange with Texas on auto license registration. Since we do not connect, we use National Motor Vehicle Title Information System. I'll go get this done now."

Barry walked out and left Russ and Miriam in the room. She made a quick move and gave Russ the hug they had talked about earlier and left the room with no more said. In a couple of minutes, Barry walked back in. "How's that new car?"

"Fast! It handles great and sounds great."

"I wanted one of those 707 HP jobs, but I couldn't get it in the four-door. You'll have to get by with 375. It did not have any dents on it, so try to give it back to me the same way." Then he added, "What's the problem with Miriam?"

"Barry, I'm sworn to secrecy. She has some personal problems at home."

"Yeah, her husband can't keep it in his pants and has been cheating on her for months. It's too bad. She is a great person and very attractive. My wife has been telling me not to get carried away. Since my wife is an expert marksman, I try not to make her mad, you see. And of course, you are a single man with a hot girlfriend in Bozeman."

Russ was amazed. Barry had picked up on a lot of things and really had his hand on the pulse of his people.

"That hot girlfriend in Bozeman is just a friend and has a new boyfriend in a BMW these days, Barry. And I can't handle my own stuff, so I won't be trying to solve Miriam's problems. But I like her and wish her the best."

Miriam walked back in. "We have a reply on the red Ram pickup."

At last! Something! Russ started getting over being depressed about Nancy and the case.

"The truck belongs to one Hector Rafael Martinez of Laredo, Texas. We did a quick check on the FBI database, and there is nothing on him there. Here is the address for him that they have."

"It doesn't surprise me that there is nothing on him," said Russ. "If he is in with some big organization, they want some people that have clean records. Some of those people have kept themselves clean with aliases and by doing away with people that know them. Also, we know not to go to Laredo looking for him as he is right up the road in Bozeman!"

"I will need to get a bead on him and see where he goes and see if the black Ford truck is at the same place. If so, we have a real solid start on these guys."

And Miriam said, "Sheriff, you did not ask me to, but I also put agent Teresa Walker's name in the database, and she is there with quite a bit of info. She grew up in Butte and went to school there. Obviously, no criminal background. Hope that helps."

Barry was impressed and went to take a call in his office from his wife. Russ looked at Miriam and said, "Barry is a great guy and is a sharp individual. He knows all about your problems at home too. I didn't tell him."

"Well, damn!" she said and walked out.

Russ had something to go on now. He would be at the Hampton Inn in Bozeman at five o'clock and then see if he could pick up the trail of Hector. If he got to town a little early, he might go by the truck terminal where Hector was working. He could be a dangerous guy, and Russ was aware that he may be Warren's killer. The fact that Hector was working seemed to mean that this had become his base of operation. If he was with some drug ring, the job was just a cover. For now, Russ would cruise up to Bozeman and maybe get some lunch at Brew Works or the hot dog joint. Really, it was a deli called Betty's, and the hot dogs would make a rabbit hug a hound!

Like everything else in Bozeman, it seemed, Betty's was on Main Street. He might see what was happening at the dress shop too. But that horse may have left the barn.

Betty's was very busy, and he was pretty sure that Nancy would not be there. But as he walked in, there was her brother Chad and an attractive lady seated with a table full of hot dogs, fries, and drinks, and they were going at it! Chad motioned for him to join them. Chad introduced Russ to his wife.

"First open day I have had in a while from the river. So I thought I would ask my beautiful bride out and little did she know it was for hot dogs!"

His wife said, "They are good hot dogs though!" with a chuckle.

They chatted for a few minutes, and Chad told him how he missed him at the shop and taking some of his floats. He then mentioned something else.

"Nancy misses you too. She's probably too bullheaded to admit it. I know you guys never got going, but I sure thought there was a chance there. She's seeing that guy from the college some, and he seems like a nice-enough guy, but that won't ever work out unless he learns to handle a drift boat and a fly rod. I guess we'll see."

"Nancy is a wonderful person, Chad," Russ replied. "She deserves a good guy and a happy life with whomever she can find it. I was in a big hole emotionally when I arrived, and I have just about clawed my way out. But I can understand no one would want to take on that baggage.

"As far as the fishing is concerned, maybe I can get back to it sometime soon. I really miss it. But I plan to find the people who killed Warren. I did not know him, but I made him a promise and his mom a promise. I am convinced of one thing at this point: Warren Cason was not involved in anything that should have gotten him killed. He got in the way of a cold-blooded killer. Who and why, we are still trying to figure out. I have to go now, Chad. It was so nice running in to you two here."

"We'll tell Nancy we saw you. Be careful out there."

Chad looked at his wife as Russ walked out. "When I first met him, he was a depressed and uncertain fly fisherman. That guy that just left, he is a tough-minded, no-nonsense cop, and I would not want him after me!" She nodded in agreement.

Russ had some time to kill, and he had a brand-new car to ride around in, so he started by driving out to Warren's house. He stopped and rang the bell and waited until Miss Milly finally got there. "Mr. Baker. It is so good of you to stop by. Won't you come in?"

"No, I just wanted to check on you and see if anything unusual had turned up that might help our case. I am in town following up on some leads today."

"I'm sorry, but I haven't thought of anything since I called you on the red truck. Was that helpful?"

"Very helpful. I will know just how helpful in a day or so. But one thing that I wanted you to be sure of is that Warren did not do anything wrong as far as I can see. He was truly a good guy."

Miss Milly reached and gave Russ a hug, fighting back the tears, and said, "Thank you for saying that because a lot of the news had been trying to dig up what he was mixed up in."

Russ headed for the truck terminal where Hector Rafael Martinez worked. He pulled in the lot into a visitor's spot in the very-official-looking Dodge. He walked to the back of the car and popped the trunk. Looking around, he saw a red Ram pickup on the side of the building. For the first time in a long time, Russ took out his 9 mm that had been issued by Madison County and slipped the magazine out to confirm the weapon was loaded and put the Glock into a slip-on paddle holster. He put on a shoulder holster for the S&W M&P .45 cal and then put his sports coat on over everything to cover the shoulder and most of the gun on the side holster. He did not know if this guy was the shooter, but he did not intend to have his face blown off like Warren's.

With a notepad binder and some pictures of Hector from his driver's license, he went inside. There was a man sitting at a rather-beaten-up desk with clipboards full of shipping waybills. He was moving them around and entering some information into the computer terminal on his desk and did not like the intrusion. "What do you need? We don't see salesmen or anyone this time of day! We have trucks to get loaded and unloaded!"

"I'm here to see a Hector Rafael Martinez," said Russ as he put a photo in front of the guy.

"I'm not sure that we have anyone working here by that name. Check back in the morning," he said, ignoring the picture.

Russ took the photo and put it on the computer screen so the guy could not see anything on the screen. "Look. Don't try this bullshit stuff with me. We both know he is here and his truck is sitting out there by the building! If you are trying to cover for him, it makes me wonder if maybe I need to run a background check on you and maybe call immigration while I'm at it. Maybe we should do a drug sweep of the entire damn place and really shut things down for a couple of hours."

Normally Russ wasn't this aggressive, but he wasn't usually tracking down a killer that shot people in the back of the head. This guy just didn't want to be bothered or he had an interest in protecting Martinez.

"I am here on a criminal investigation, and you can stonewall me and make it tougher on both of us, or you can call him up here so I can talk to him for fifteen or twenty minutes and I'll be on my way." Russ did not sound like a guy you run off easily. The guy looked at Russ, and knew he was not going away quietly.

"Who are you with?"

"I'm Special Investigator Russell Baker from Madison County," he said while handing the guy one of his really nice business cards. "And I am here with the cooperation of the Gallatin County Sheriff's Office."

In reality, the guy did not have to produce Hector since Russ did not have a warrant and there was no crime in progress and no probable cause. But most people and businesses did not want to attract too much attention by refusing to cooperate with a law officer. The guy leaned over and pushed the button on a warehouse loudspeaker: "Hector Martinez, you're needed in the front office at once."

Hector was putting some pallets on an outgoing delivery and wondered what was so important that he was being stopped at the busiest time of the day. He got off the forklift and walked around the corner to where he could see through the big glass partition separating the office from the warehouse space. He did not like what he saw! The guy looked like a cop or a DEA agent or something like that. Hector's first thought was to run and get in his truck and get out of there. But he calmed himself down. He had been in some shakedowns before and always was able to charm his way out, and he had always managed to have covered his tracks well.

"Yea, Art, what do you need? I'm swamped out there."

177

"This fellow is with the sheriff's office in Madison County and wants to ask you a couple of questions. Mr. Baker, you can have fifteen minutes. Please don't tie my man up more than that. He needs to get through before his shift ends, and we only have a couple of hours."

"Thanks. I'll try to do that," Russ said, trying to sound a bit nicer. "Mr. Martinez, could you step out on the front with me where we can talk in private?"

Hector could see the Glock in the side holster. And judging from what he could see, this guy was carrying a backup gun in a shoulder holster too. Hector usually found a way to carry his gun or have it close but was caught without anything. This guy looked familiar to Hector, but he could not place him right off. Hector was nervous and did not want to make a mistake.

"I don't talk to too many policemen," said Hector. "I guess that is a good thing. What is it you need to ask me about?"

"I believe you have a red Ram truck with Texas license plates, do you not?"

"Yes, sir, that is correct."

"I am investigating the murder of a fishing guide named Warren Cason up on the Madison several days back. Some people have told us that they saw your truck up that way near the Quake Lake area about that time. We are hoping that you may have seen something that will help us. This is a picture of the guide and his truck and boat."

So, the cop doesn't think I did anything. He just wants a witness to help his case, thought hector.

"Well, my truck was up that way. I had some friends over from Utah, Helen Phillips and her husband Jeffery. They had been going around trying to get Helen a singing gig. She sings pretty well, but you know, so do thousands of folks. I went up and we met at a camp of some kind there, had some beers, and that was it. Someone else had rented the cabin, I believe, and I did not see them. I think they went fishing and stayed a while and got tanked somewhere before they came back. Helen and Jeffery were headed to Utah or someplace the last I saw them."

"So you did not see the guide or the truck while you were up that way?" Russ was thinking, *This guy is a very good liar or maybe he is not the guy we are looking for.*

"Sir, I saw a lot of boats and trailers going and coming. But nothing stands out as I remember."

"One last question: have you ever been to the fly shop on S. Black Ave. in your red truck?"

That rattled Hector! He was certain that no one had seen him deliver the envelope to Warren Cason's shop!

This was not good!

"To a fly shop on S. Black? I don't think I've been to any fly shops here in Bozeman. Now, I may have been down S. Black at some time or another. I was looking for a cheap place to stay and have ridden on about every street in town at one time or another, I guess."

Russ thought that question may have jarred him a little, but he was giving good answers, that was for sure.

"Where did you end up getting a place, Mr. Martinez?"

"There is a mobile home park out off of Huffine, and that's where I am."

"How long have you been gone from Oklahoma, Mr. Martinez?" That was another question designed to let the person know his entire background was being looked into and to see his reaction.

"I think we moved to Laredo when I was about eleven." Art, the branch manager, stuck his head out and said, "I need him back now, please."

"Okay. Thanks for the information and the cooperation."

With that, Russ was headed to the car. He knew this guy was one of the two men he saw at the gun range. If he could tie him to the guy in the black Ford truck and to Teresa Walker, man, that would be something.

One thing's for sure: the guy could handle an unexpected interview. Russ did not know Hector had to stop in the men's room. He was about to pee in his pants. He would have a lot to talk to Donny about tonight, if Donny was there.

Hector was sure that he had seen this cop somewhere before. Hector was always keeping an eye on his surroundings, and he thought that he had seen Russ at the gun range. Could it be that cop has been watching him and Donny that long?

Chad called Nancy about doing a shuttle the next morning. After they worked out the logistics of the shuttle, Chad mentioned that he had run into Russ at Betty's. "He sure looks and acts a lot different, Nancy. He has his head on straight now, that's for sure."

"That's great. I guess he was asking a lot of questions about me and Stephen. He saw us together the other day."

"Actually, no. He did not ask any questions. He said he wished you well and that you were a great lady."

That hurt a little, but Chad was not one to sugarcoat things. "How is that new guy, by the way?" Chad asked.

"He is a very nice guy, and it's been fun going out again. He comes from a long line of college professors and teachers. Pretty intellectual."

"I did not hear the word *love* in that," said Chad.

"I did not use that word, Chad. Mind your own business!" She hit the End Call button.

It was getting to be show time at the Hampton Inn. Russ arrived a few minutes before five o'clock and went in and sat down in the lobby. He was very conspicuous sitting there, and the clerk remembered him from his previous visit. In fact, the clerk thought the manager had done a great job of putting Russ in his place on the first visit. He stuck his head in the manager's office and said, "That sheriff guy is back."

The manager got very angry and jumped up and walked out to where Russ was sitting. He instantly noticed something he had noticed on the previous visit: Russ was carrying a service weapon. "I am not going to allow you to sit here and intimidate our guests. Do you have a warrant from a judge? If not, I may call the sheriff and have you removed from here."

"I don't think it will be necessary for you to call the sheriff. He's meeting me here."

"I don't believe you," said the manager.

Looking at his watch, Russ said, "ETA, two minutes."

The manager spun around and went back to his office. In two minutes, six or seven sheriff's department cars came up in front with all their blue lights flashing. The clerk went back and got the manager who came out to the display of deputies all over the front of the motel and stood there dumbfounded. The sheriff came in and asked the manager, whom he knew, to speak with him in his office.

"Please, Sheriff," he said, "turn off the damn lights and I'll see if I can find what you want."

The sheriff said a few words into his shoulder mic, and just as fast as the cars had come, they were gone.

Barry had a good friend in Charlie, the Gallatin County sheriff. He knew how to get things done.

Russ walked over and joined the conversation, and the three went back to the office and the manager's computer. "What is it that you are looking for?"

"We are looking for a murderer," said Russ. "And we think there is a connection to someone named Tess or Teresa or some combination of those who may have stayed here around this date in room 212. All we want to do is see if there is a connection or if that person may have seen something related to the murder. We'll keep your name out of it."

Russ gave the manager the approximate dates around the time that Warren was murdered. The manager had mellowed out and was now trying to be cooperative. He punched in some code and passwords and entered the dates. A name came up for room 212. The name was Teresa A. Walker.

"Well, I think you guys are barking up the wrong tree, Sheriff. I recognize this person. She stays here all the time. She works for the State of Montana and uses a state credit card. Of course, we did not know she went by Tess. We all call her Ms. Walker when she comes in."

Russ and the Sheriff gave each other a questioning look.

"Sir, could you look at one more name? Hector Martinez. Is he in your files?" Russ was asking.

After a minute the answer was no. In fact, Hector had stayed there a number of times, but Donny had always rented the room.

"How long do you keep security videos" asked the sheriff?

"It varies. Five to ten days. The four cameras are on motion sensors, and they get more use some days than others. We would not have videos back that far as the tapes recycle. We only keep a disk if we are investigating an incident of a car break-in, fender benders, etc."

Russell thanked the manager for his trouble and for his help and apologized if he had been offensive.

"Please understand that there should be no mention of this to anyone, especially Ms. Walker."

"Don't worry. She won't hear anything from me!"

The sheriff and Russ walked out the front door, and the sheriff said, "I think we have to have a conference call with Barry first thing in the morning. Can you set that up? We need to tread lightly here until we get more of the facts. What is your take on all this?"

"Sheriff, I believe it is somehow related to the drug drop that the task force was working on. How, I do not know yet."

He did not tell Charlie that they had the scraps of the cushioning material where the drop took place.

"I interviewed Hector Martinez this afternoon. He's the owner of the red Ram and he has a good story. I have to find a way to crack it. We can't be sure that he was at the Cason fly shop at all. He was a cool customer."

It would be a fast-food drive thru and back to Ennis for Russ. All in all, he had had a pretty fair day. The police car ate the miles up, and he found himself flying if he wasn't careful. He made it back a little before 8:00 PM and called Barry.

"Charlie wants us to call him in the morning first thing. It was Teresa Walker in room 212."

"Well, I'll be damned," said Barry. "See you first thing in the morning. Good night."

Russ kicked off his shoes and stripped down to get comfortable with a beer and turned on the TV. He was pleased with the way things had started to turn around. Now he needed to find that black Ford F-150. He would get Barry to help on that tomorrow too.

Hector was a nervous wreck by the time Donny got to the mobile home they were sharing just outside Bozeman. Russ had rattled him when he mentioned Oklahoma because that meant they were looking at his background.

"That hick cop is digging into my shit all the way back to Oklahoma! I know he was watching us at that gun range! That wasn't a coincidence!"

Actually, it was, but there was no one to explain it, and Donny couldn't in his mind either. He needed to talk to Tess and see what she might know about this investigation without bringing up the murder. If it came up, he would play dumb.

In the meantime, he told Hector to go about his daily routine and not get all rattled. If Hector started losing it, he would have to disappear. Disappear one way or the other. But with the cops already talking to Hector, anyone they ever could connect to Hector was a suspect for whatever happened to Hector.

Teresa Walker had two cell phones. One that was issued to her from the DCI and one that was her own that she never kept on during the day much. A call to that number usually went to voice mail during her work hours and when she was working with someone except when she and Donny were having to communicate regularly on some deal going down. He left her a message that basically said, "I sure hope we can get together the next time you are in town."

What that really meant was, "We have to talk so call me when you are going to be here."

Donny wasn't sure how Teresa would react if the fishing guide's murder was connected to him, even if only by suspicion. Tess had this idea that they were going to grab all the money from one of the big deals, run off to the Caribbean somewhere together, and live happily ever after. It made for great talk before and after sex, but he had not lost a thing in the Caribbean and would probably not be going there. Alaska or Canada, maybe. Italy, maybe.

Tess could become a liability, and if so, he could put her and Hector in the same grave when the time came.

16

Russ's phone rang. He wondered who would be calling this late. "This is Russ," he said. It was Miriam, she was obviously crying. "Russ, I am up here in the house all alone and I feel terrible. My husband had packed up while I was at work and moved out. He says he is going to marry this young architect he has been working with and screwing on the side. I was wondering if you could possibly come over here. I'd really not like to spend the night here and my kids are at school and don't know about all this yet. Please."

"Miriam, let's just talk on the phone. I think you are pretty shook up, and I'm not sure I should make things worse by being there. You aren't going to do anything stupid over this, are you?"

"I'm not going to kill myself, if that's what you mean. But it really hurts when someone that you have loved just up and disappears. It's hard to explain. He has been cheating on me and ignoring me for a long time. You'd think I'd be jumping up and down with joy that he's gone. But I'm not."

Russ said, "Believe me I know what it is like to lose someone. I lost my wife, and she never was anything but wonderful. When she died, I almost died too."

"I'm sorry, Russ," she said softly. "I did not know. I guess I'll be okay, and I'll see you in the morning."

"Good night, Miriam."

Russ dozed off and was awakened about thirty minutes later with a soft knocking on his cabin door. He took his .45 off the night table and walked to the door.

"Who is it?" he asked.

"It's Miriam. Please let me in."

Miriam was close to ten years older than Russ. She had married young and now she was an attractive lady about forty and very attractive for her age. They stayed together until the early morning when she woke him, kissing him on the cheek and heading home to get herself ready for work.

"Thank you for being here for me last night," she said. She was better this morning and she was gone.

When Russ got to the office, he was afraid the situation would be awkward with Miriam; but for some reason, it seemed okay. They weren't two high school kids in love. They were two people that for a moment helped each other through a tough time.

Barry came in and asked for a briefing on the past day's events, and Russ filled him in on everything but the part about Miriam spending the night with him. He kept that to himself. They then called the Gallatin County sheriff.

"Barry, how are we going to handle this deal with Teresa Walker? We really don't have much to go to DCI with. This note is the only connection so far, and there is no record of Hector Martinez being at the Hampton. If we go to them now with nothing else, we put her on alert, and we'll never get the thing worked out. The note could have been a purely accidental thing."

"Let's ask Russ where he thinks we go."

Russ responded, "There is still the issue of the black truck that is sticking in my mind. I know I saw Hector with a guy at the gun range in Bozeman. I recognized Hector as soon as we got the driver's license photo, and I confirmed it yesterday. That truck is still in Bozeman, I'd bet. So, if your folks could help me spot it and get a license number, we might ID the driver and I can see if it is the same guy I saw Hector with at the range.

"Also, if we could get a look at the entire background check on Teresa Walker and who she might have associated with over in Butte while in school, we might find a link there."

"How do you know she was in school in Butte? Did she tell you that or have you already done some checking?" Charlie didn't miss much either.

"Our assistant here ran an FBI check on her, but it was not thorough. If she is somehow involved with one or both of these guys, she could be the person tipping off the drug guys, and we have a huge situation on our hands and we don't want to blow it. Also, there is the question as to whether she is involved in the murder of Warren Cason. She was quick to wash her hands of that case."

The Gallatin County sheriff said, "I don't know that I have the clout to get a confidential file, and I don't know anyone there brave enough to get me one."

Barry said, "Charlie, with you, me, and my brother together, we might have enough clout, as you say, and he might know someone who he can ask. I'll talk to him. In the meantime, if you could help us find the black truck, Russ may get us a connection before we spook everyone off. Right now, we just need the license number and where it is, right, Russ?"

"Right."

"I'll get my guys on it," said Charlie. "Good-bye."

Barry called his brother in Missoula.

Teresa Walker met with Donny in the Hampton Inn. He came after dark to avoid the cameras getting a good look and parked in the lot next door, on the other side of the building. He looked like a salesman out for a jog after a hard day on the road, except for the gun hidden in the pants. He was now on alert. Had he known about the cops being there checking on Teresa, he would not have come.

He talked to Teresa about the fact that Hector had been questioned and made it appear that it was because he was seen in the area where the actual drop took place. Some cop from Madison County and Donny had the card that Russ had given Hector. He showed her the card. Teresa was shocked.

"This is a fishing guide that discovered a dead guy over on the Madison River. I interviewed him twice on this case. He used to be a cop in Marietta, Georgia, but no one told me he was a cop here and now!"

She had a very uneasy feeling about this and wondered if she had been hoodwinked by Russ and the Madison County sheriff.

"I will see what I can come up with, but I have to be careful as to how I know about it and his interviewing Hector. That would give me away. I can tell them that I was reviewing the case for follow up, but I don't know why there is any connection. Hector didn't kill the guy, did he?"

"Hell no! He did not kill anybody," said Donny. And that was true of course, at least he had not killed anyone lately, and definitely not Warren Cason. Donny had done that all by himself.

They had some Jack Daniels and went to bed. Donny would be out bright and early in the morning. He might have to find out about this cop. The list of people who could potentially screw up his business plans continued to grow.

Barry's brother was very hesitant to go to the DCI with what they had. There was mostly very circumstantial evidence. There was no direct and confirmable connection of Teresa to anyone, and she was a darling of the DCI community. She was the proverbial pretty and smart woman with brass balls. For them to go after her and fail would injure their relationship with DCI, and they could be put outside the loop. And his county, Missoula, was not directly involved in this situation.

The next morning, Donny put some clothes in a suitcase and told Hector he would be out of town a few days to set up another deal. Hector was never involved at that level and did not see anything unusual about Donny being gone. Donny wanted some space between himself and Hector with the cops snooping around, and he had a place he could lie low in Butte. He had made friends there when he was in school for a couple of years at Montana Tech. He got into his shiny black truck with the chrome step bumper and headed into downtown Bozeman. As he was pulling in to the Conoco station on Jackrabbit Lane at I-90, a Gallatin County patrol car saw the truck and observed it pulling in to the gas pumps. Donny did not use credit cards, so he had to go to the register and prepay for the gas. While he was inside, the deputy took a picture of the truck and the license plate. He pulled around on the side and waited to see who came out and snapped another picture with his dash cam of the guy walking to the truck, pumping his gas, and driving off. He observed the truck as it went to the I-90 ramp and headed west.

Miriam was still working on the scraps of bubble wrap and duct tape and had found a couple of prints, but none got a hit at the FBI. The person who put the tape on, Russ thought, would be some really low-level grunt and would not help them with the case. Russ, Wayne, and Barry kept going over the stuff they had and were in the conference room when Miriam stuck her head in the door.

"Teresa Walker from DCI is on the phone for you, Barry." They all looked at each other.

"When you get through, I will give you the eleven sightings we have of black Ford F-150s from the Gallatin Sheriff's Office. It seems there are a lot of them around Bozeman. They are coming in a steady stream."

Barry said, "Thanks, Miriam. Please close the door." He commented before punching the phone button, "Boy, she is in a better mood the last few days considering what she is going through."

Russ did not comment. In fact, he had been in a better mood too.

"Hello, Agent Walker, how are you?"

"I'm fine, Sheriff. I have been busy the last few days and wanted to see if you wanted me to come by for any reason. Is there anything happening on the murder of the fishing guide?"

"You are welcome here anytime, but there has been little concrete progress made. We have been chasing our tail and riding around burning gas."

It appeared he was not going to address the Russell Baker situation, and she did not want to bring it up as it might give her away.

Then Barry said, "We cleared the guy who found the body and the clients, but I think you know that. What you may not know is that Russell Baker was a cop in the Marietta, Georgia, area before coming out here. He agreed to help me with the investigation on a temporary basis as we don't do murder investigations very much here. So he is asking some questions around about that."

"Well, that is interesting. Have you guys come up with a motive yet?"

"That is the big mystery. No. When we do, we might just catch us a bad guy."

"Well, in that case, I will probably not come by, but call me if you need me or any assistance from DCI," she said.

"You will be hearing from us, I'm sure," said Barry. He hoped she did not get the double meaning!

So, Teresa thought, *they did hire Baker and they are not keeping that a secret. But they hired him to work on the murder and they are questioning Hector in Bozeman. That's interesting. What possible connection could Hector have to a murdered fishing guide?*

Russ called in Miriam to review the truck spotting from Bozeman. There were now twelve! Their work was cut out for them to look at them and research them all and see if they could connect the dots. "I took the liberty of checking to see how many black Ford F-150 trucks there are around our area and the number is startling. There are nearly two hundred in Gallatin and Madison Counties!" said Miriam.

"I knew it would be a big number. The key is the big chrome step bumper. There aren't many of those like the one we are looking for, so we have to be sure anyone looking for the truck knows that," said Russ.

"I will go pull the records on these and any that come in so you will have a picture of the owner if we can find them in the driver's license records," she said.

"There is always the possibility that the person driving the truck is not the owner. But for now, let's just make the assumption they are the same," Russ added. "I may go up and see if I can find that guy Hector's mobile home park and see if there is someone hanging around in a black truck."

The day dragged on, and they continued to get reports of black Fords, and none looked too promising. They had about eight or ten that one of them would go check out in the area and try to interview the owner at his or her residence to see firsthand if the truck and the bumper looked like the suspect's.

Late in the morning, the chief deputy of the Gallatin Sheriff's Department called and said that due to a communication snafu, they had failed to send report on a truck fitting the description of the one on the BOLO to them in Virginia City. He was dropping a video and still pictures of the vehicle into their Dropbox account file, and Madison County could access the files. Miriam took the call and went about sorting out the information. She then went in to where Russ and Barry were looking at some of the material they had already gotten.

"Sheriff," she said. "I think we have something! Can you both come out to my computer screen and look at what Gallatin County just sent?" She spun and walked away in a hurry.

"We'll be right there," called the sheriff as she was leaving. "Man. What a transformation!" said Barry. "Miriam has become a take-charge person. It is unbelievable."

Miriam's husband had wasted no time in filing for a divorce. He wanted to get married to the very successful architect in Salt Lake City. He had offered, through his attorney, a pretty good settlement to Miriam, thanks to his future bride who had provided him money to pay off the mortgage on the Ennis house and pay off the car. Miriam would get the house, the car, and over half of their remaining cash, and he would pay for the kids' college, as well. This was in lieu of alimony. Miriam's local lawyer in Bozeman had advised her to take the offer, and she did. She had told Russ and Barry that she was just a few days away from being a single woman. And for all practical purposes, she was a free woman now. Her ex-husband-to-be was living with his new wife-to-be already. Instead of being devastated, as they had thought might happen, she had emerged from the shadows of a dull and loveless marriage and was now a liberated and self-confident person. In her heart, she credited Russ for some of that. He had become a friend and would acknowledge her and listen to her with respect.

She had worked in Salt Lake City as a part of a larger staff with no real individual identity. She had come to a tiny town, to a small and boring day-to-day job and was living with a husband who was neglecting her. She was now shuck of him, and work had become exciting and interesting, and she was needed there. And there was someone that cared about her. Right now, things were looking good in her life. Her morale and the morale of the entire office had improved. But the person whose light was shining the brightest was Miriam's. She had fought through the pain of getting a divorce and was emerging as a leader. She had no illusions about Russ. He was a younger man and would probably be leaving soon. They were not "in love" but were in some strange and unencumbered relationship, and when time came for him to move on, she hoped they would remain true and loyal friends who would always be there for each other while they found permanent love and companionship with someone else. She thought Russ felt the same.

Russ and Barry went and stood behind Miriam as she tried to get the best angle on her screen so they could see the images they had been sent by Gallatin County. They could see, in grainy and somewhat distant shot from the officer's dash cam, the gas pumps of the Conoco station on Jackrabbit Lane in Bozeman. There was a black Ford F-150 with the big chrome step bumper and a man walked over and grabbed the gas pump nozzle and began putting gas in the truck. He was wearing a cowboy hat, and looked to be a young guy in his early thirties, but the picture was not good enough for a clear look at him. She then showed a couple of still pictures that had been taken by the deputy's cell phone camera. Too tiny to tell much about the man but the step bumper was readily seen.

Then there was a picture of a piece of paper where the officer had written down the license plate number. Russ was fairly certain that this was the guy he saw at the gun range with Hector, although he could not swear in court that who he saw at the range was either of them. The caller had told Miriam that the truck had gotten on I-90 and headed west. But Russ was sure they had the lead he had been looking for.

Then Miriam, who was one step ahead of them now, anticipating what they would ask next, broke the bad news. The man driving the truck was not the person to whom the truck was registered!

"How in the world do you know that, Miriam?" asked Barry.

"Because, Sheriff, the man who owns that truck according to the license number, is a man named Kile Davidson, who lives down in outskirts of Missoula. Here is his picture."

The photo showed a fairly large man sitting in a wheelchair!

The man in Bozeman pumping gas, although they did not have a real clear picture, was not Kile Davidson!

Barry went to the phone and called his brother in Missoula.

"Do you happen to know a fellow there named Kile Davidson?" he asked his brother.

"A lot of people know Kile here. He came here as an army veteran from the Iraq war, I believe. He rode a Harley, mostly, and started making birdhouses, doll house, and most anything someone wanted of that sort of thing. You know, windmills, things they call mobiles for the yard, etc. He took them to arts and crafts shows everywhere. He does a very good job on that stuff. Then one day he got hit by an old guy who turned left in front of Kile's motorcycle. The old guy said he did not see him on the motorcycle and that was that. Kile had severe injuries and has never walked again.

"They had a big lawsuit and Kile got some money from the insurance company, and he just dings around now out there at his house. I think he makes a birdhouse or two and sells them in the yard out there. I hardly ever see him now and haven't in a while. Why the interest?"

Barry explained the whole deal and their suspicions, which were now on shaky ground. Russ asked Barry to ask his brother a question:

"Do you know if he actually has a black Ford truck?"

"I understand your question. Is your guy driving Kile's truck? Right?"

"Right," said Russ.

"I can send a car out and see what we can learn, Barry, if you want us to."

"That would be great if you could. What do you think, Russ?"

"I would like to ride with your deputy when they go, if that would not upset anyone," said Russ.

"It's two hundred miles up here from there. Is it worth your time?"

"Sheriff Steinbrenner, I was fishing and minding my own business a few days ago and now I'm in the middle of who knows what. What looked like simply, if you can use that word in a murder case, the murder of a fly-fishing guide has now seemed to be a lot more than that. There is some connection to something bigger, and I believe it may go pretty deep into some other areas. So yes, it is worth my time."

"Okay. Come on up. When can you be here?"

"How about 8:00 AM tomorrow?"

"Well, if it's that important to you, I'll go with you myself."

Barry said, "Well then, let's make it a threesome. I'll come too. We'll leave after dinner."

The two hundred miles to Missoula were mostly interstate highway, and the Dodge made short work of the ride.

"You have a nice car, Mr. Baker," said Barry jokingly. "You must work for a fine outfit."

"The finest in Madison County, Montana," said Russ. "They could use some better people, though. Maybe they can get a good sheriff and a better investigator when the next election rolls around."

They both had a laugh. But they both knew one thing: Madison County was lucky to have the ones they had right that minute!

The next morning, Russ, Barry, and Barry's brother drove out to see Kile Davidson and try to get a look at his truck, if he had one. They pulled in the yard in the sheriff's older but very nice Ford Crowne Victoria, one of the last of the 9.6 million that were made. They were greeted by two big German Shepherds, which did not seem to be glad to see them. The sheriff tooted his horn, and finally, the door opened and a fellow came out in a motorized chair. He hollered at the dogs, which immediately sat down with their eye on the occupants, and he came down a wheelchair ramp that was made out of aluminum and looked like it could hold up the Crowne Victoria. It also looked very expensive.

"Is it safe for us to get out, Kile?" said the sheriff.

"Sure. If you have a sausage and biscuit for them, you could sic them on me! They respond well to treats. And by the way, I'm innocent of all charges, no matter what they are. What do you need, Sheriff?"

"Kile, these guys are from up in Madison County. That's my brother Barry and his special investigator Russell Baker. We need to ask you about your truck."

"So this is Colonel Steinbrenner, United States Air Force, retired? I read up on you when you were running for

THE DRIFT BOAT DETECTIVE

sheriff up there. Glad to meet you," he said as he reached out his hand to Barry.

Russ could not detect any sense of concern in Kile. He was as cool as a cucumber. He turned his head toward Russ and held out his hand. "Glad to meet you too. Mr. Baker, is it?"

"That's right Mr. Davidson. Russell Baker. Most people call me Russ."

"Now where in the hell are you from, Mr. Baker? Georgia or Texas?"

"Georgia. But how in the world did you know," he said with a laugh. He knew his accent had given him away.

"When I was in the army I was in Fort Benning for a while and later did some special training in Texas. They sound a lot alike."

Barry's brother had enough with the small talk. "Kile, we have an investigation ongoing, and we have a truck that is registered to you that may have been at the crime scene. It was seen again yesterday in Bozeman. We show you have a black Ford F-150. Do you still have that truck?"

"I sure do. I seldom drive it, and the battery is probably dead but it's in that carport around on the side. I can tell you it was not in Bozeman yesterday, and I can't remember if I ever drove it to Bozeman. But if you want to walk around there, I'll go through the house and get the key, if I can find it, and meet you. I have a ramp back there too."

Russ was uneasy about him going in the house and unsnapped the retainer on his holster. Neither the sheriff nor Barry appeared to be wearing a gun. Around on the side in the carport was a dusty but very nice Ford F-150 Harley Davidson series truck. It looked like it had been sitting there a while. And it had no license plate.

199

Kile came out and handed Russ the keys. "See if she'll start. It hasn't been run in a month or two. My buddy comes up occasionally when I have a doctor's appointment, and we used my truck for a while, but the last time or two he drove his Jeep." Russ opened the door and the starter would only do a clicking sound. It appeared the battery was dead.

The sheriff said, "Kile do you know your license plate is missing?"

"Yeah, I think I may have lost it the last time we drove it. But hey, I don't use the thing anyway, so nobody is going to pull me over," he said. "It won't be long before time to get a new one, and I'll get it straightened out then."

They did not learn a lot, but they learned that this truck and Kile were not who they were looking for. Russ asked, "Did it occur to you that someone stole the plate off your truck?"

"Well, I guess I just wasn't that concerned as I have a lot more shit to deal with, as you can see," he said as he tapped the wheelchair.

They thanked Kile and headed around to the front to their car. He went up the ramp and into the house, and as they were getting to the car, he came out of the door onto the porch.

"See you later, guys. I guess I wasn't too much help. Say, Colonel, did you go to the Air Force Academy?"

"Yes, I did."

"Boy that must have been something. I went to Montana Tech in Butte for almost two years, but my folks were strapped, and I quit and went in the army. I didn't learn enough to stay off of a motorcycle, I guess."

They waved good-bye as they pulled out of the yard going back to town. They all felt a little let down as they made the drive and there was not much to say. Then Russ spoke up.

"He said he went to Montana Tech in Butte." A lot of people did, they all knew. "Teresa Walker went to Montana Tech in Butte."

The brothers looked at each other.

The Crowne Vic had barely gotten out of sight before Kile was rolling his chair to a stop in front of an old roll-up desk. He reached in the back of one of the pigeonholes using one of those things people use for a back scratcher. He drug out a throwaway phone and looked at a number he had written inside the desktop, spread out in five places, two numbers each. The ten numbers were entered into the phone, and a voice mail answered.

"This is Donald Bragg with Butte Land and Home Sales. Please leave me a message and I will return the call as soon as possible."

The voice mail beeped, and Kile spoke and left a message: "Hi, Mr. Bragg. This is Kile Davidson. When we were looking at that property a while back, I think I left a part off of my truck in your truck. As soon as you can, I need that back. Contact me when you can. I know you know the number."

This was a prearranged message letting Donny know to ditch the license plate and either use his own or steal another one somewhere. The plate he had from Kile had been compromised. The message would not make Donny happy. *Now, what?* he thought.

Russ and Barry and Barry's brother made it back to the Missoula County Sheriff's Office, and they went inside.

Barry's brother said, "Russ, will you excuse us for a couple of minutes? I need to discuss something with Barry."

"Take your time," said Russ. I have a seriously overloaded bladder I have to see about." The two Steinbrenner brothers were in the office for a long time. Russ was pacing the floor, looking out the window, and was getting very antsy.

Finally, Barry came out and said, "Let's go."

"Barry, do you know what I would like to do?" Before Barry could answer, he answered his own question. "I would like to go code 3 and get back to Virginia City and get a cold one and see if that helps find any clues to solve this case."

Code 3 means that they would use their blue lights and sirens as if going to an emergency.

"Go right ahead and go code 3. I will authorize it. But we are not going to Virginia City. We are going to Helena! We've been on the phone with Bruce Obermeyer in Helena. He is the head guy over all the DCI and all that crap. He is a tough guy, but my brother and he go way back. Hunted and fished together and cleaned out a few bars along the way. My father was always paying for something to be repaired that they broke. He listened to our concern about Teresa Walker. He was really pissed off that we called him wanting to talk about one of his most prized employees. You should have heard the names they called each other on the phone! But he will allow us an eyes-only look at her background file. No copies. No cameras. No sleight of hand. We can look and write down notes, but that is it. I figured we would take what we could get. We have to be there at eight o'clock sharp because he has to leave by nine fifteen."

"I am impressed!" said Russ. And the speedometer climbed on the Dodge. They would make the 114 miles in very short order. After all, 110 is not very fast to an ex-fighter pilot like Barry.

Donny Bragg removed Kile's license plate and put his own plate on the truck. He would have to get rid of the old plate in a dumpster somewhere, but he would keep his fake ID on Kile until he could get some more with a new name. Aggravating, but not really that hard. What he wanted to know was who was asking about the truck and why. He had not heard any warnings from Tess, and if it was that small-town cop from Madison County, he might have to remove that threat, although offing a cop was a little more threatening.

Nancy had not heard from Russ now in several days and was not sure she would. Both of them had been a little too cautious, although she thought with good reason at the start. She had assumed Russ was living hand to mouth out at the Super 8. She did not need a man to look after on top of the store and the shuttle business. It was not too late in the afternoon, and she would like to get an update on the murder case, if he would give her any info. She got his voice mail and stopped short of leaving a message and hung up.

What was she doing? She now had a stable, handsome, and financially secure gentleman friend in Stephen Carter. There was no use messing up the works. If that were true, though, why was she sad that Russ did not answer?

17

To get in to see Bruce Obermeyer was tough. They had left their weapons locked in the trunk of the car. They had to go through metal detectors, leave their drivers licenses, and sign in at the front guard desk.

Barry thought that maybe Bruce had called and told his security people to make it as tough on them as possible. But they finally got to his office at about 7:55 AM, and his assistant announced them.

Bruce greeted Barry cordially and shook both their hands, and they went to a small conference room adjacent to Bruce's office. "Let me remind you of our agreement. You will be allowed to see the file on the agent but no item can be removed from the room and no photos with cell phones or anything else. I will not insult you by taking your phones, but I will be very upset if that agreement is violated. Barry, you have always been a pain in my ass."

Russ could not tell if that was supposed to be funny or not.

"So, let me get this straight, Mr. Baker. You came all the way to Montana from Marietta, Georgia to make my life hell. Is that right?"

"No, sir. I came out here to go fishing. But the lawless nature of this supposedly zero crime paradise blew right up in my face, and I have had to crawl over dead bodies to cast my fly rod."

Barry held his breath! Was Bruce going to take offense to the stern, nonsmiling, and serious tone that Russ had used? He got a quick answer.

"By God, Barry, this guy has been around you too long, already," with a laugh. "Is that Varsity place still open in Atlanta?" asked Bruce.

"Oh, sure. If that place were to close, they would be turning out all the lights in Atlanta. Have you been there?" Russ responded.

"We were there at the Georgia Dome for a football game, and someone said we had to eat at the Varsity. I was sick for two days."

"The hot dogs made you sick?"

"I think it was because I ate about six hotdogs and a pound of fries and two or three fried pies!" Bruce said. "If I ever go back, I will practice some restraint."

Bruce opened his briefcase and put a folder on the table. "Here is the file."

Russ said, "I'm surprised all this isn't stored digitally."

"The official file is stored on the computer system. These are the investigator's work pages. Some are just some notes and some are probably technically illegal from the federal work laws. That's why I can't let this out. It will have more personal info than what we have in the official file. Now we use iPads and fill out a list of questions set up to comply with all the hiring laws. When she was hired, we still did it the old-fashioned way. I will be back in one hour, and I will take the file from you whether you are finished or not. I am leaving, and that will be locked up when I leave."

"Do not leave this room unless you are leaving for good. There is a rest room and water in the little fridge. If you go out, the door will be locked, and no one will let you back in."

Barry said, "Bruce, we are not on a witch hunt. If anything we should find out looks bad, I'll call you before we do anything."

They started going through all the background about school, grades, activities, clubs, drinking habits, drug usage, and her family history. Her folks were your typical all-American, hardworking families that never quite got way ahead financially. The information was mostly dull, and some was embarrassing but most was not going to affect their case one way or the other.

They dug through the file page by page, and then Russ noticed a comment about her friends and associates. Two people were noted, but one jumped, screaming, off the page: Kile Davidson! He was the paraplegic guy with a black Ford truck they had seen yesterday! It seems they hung out a lot, and Kile's friend, a fellow named Donald J. Bragg, dated Teresa for a period of time. He was noted as her "only serious boyfriend" in college according to the notes. And there was a short note saying, "No other serious boyfriends while in school."

Bragg left school his second year it appeared, with no reason given in the notes. Russ and Barry had no idea at that moment that Donald J. Bragg drove a black Ford F-150 with a big chrome step bumper! They still had some work to do.

Barry and Russ made it back to the courthouse where Barry's car was parked, and when they arrived, he said, "Don't bother coming in. I'm going to walk in and give

Miriam these two guys' names and see if we can come up with anything. We'll get on it tomorrow. Go home!"

Russ rode over to the Reel 'Em Inn and got a hot shower and took a well-earned nap after all the riding. He was awakened by his phone. It was Miriam.

"Russ, I am almost a single woman. I got the final agreement done, and all I'm waiting for is the final decree in a few weeks. I want to celebrate! So, I'm asking you out on a date! Just two new friends going to dinner. Are you up to it after all the riding?"

"Will you keep me out late?"

"No, I promise," she said.

"Where are we going?" asked Russ.

"Well, I made a reservation at Daryl's on Main. I hear they have a halibut to die for."

The Daryl's on Main is a restaurant in Bozeman that just happens to be on Main Street.

"I saw it in passing but never got in there. I just took a nap and I am rested up, so let's go," he said.

"I'll pick you up, and I'll drive," she said.

She picked Russ up and looked great and much younger than her years. Dressed to go to a fine restaurant and enjoy her new status: divorcee, almost. Daryl's on Main was a very nice place, and they were just ordering when a couple came in and they were taken to a table across from where Russ and Miriam were seated. Miriam had her back to them and did not notice the couple. Russ noticed. It was Nancy and Dr. Stephen Carter. Nancy was the most beautiful woman there, but truthfully, Miriam was not far behind.

The food started coming course by course, and some wine was poured. It was a great meal and Miriam was very good company and happy to be there. She had not been to a nice restaurant in months.

Nancy could see Russ, and Russ could see Nancy, but they both made an effort to not make eye contact. But they did a couple of times, and Russ noticed a little smile and an attempt to acknowledge him without her date seeing her. At least, that's how it seemed to Russ.

When the meal was finished, they walked to the car, and as they were about to drive off, Miriam reached over and touched Russ's arm.

"Russ, you saved my life, emotionally. No matter where you and I end up in the future, I hope we will always be friends, lovers, or something."

"Me too," said Russ.

She got to the Reel 'Em Inn, and she kept going on until she reached her house. "Come in and let me show you my house," she said.

He did. And he had breakfast there the next morning. They did not talk about murders and murderers. As Russ sat there drinking the coffee that Miriam had poured, he suddenly realized that he was no longer in bondage to the memory of Sarah's death. When he thought of her now, it was about the laughter and the love they had enjoyed and not about the sadness. Miriam had helped him too.

Dr. Carter took Nancy home and walked her to the door after the great dinner at Daryl's on Main. He kept thinking that he would get invited in to spend the night, but then her mother lived there too. A tad awkward. But she gave him little kiss and said good night.

She went in and slammed the door and threw her purse and cell phone crashing to the floor. She kicked off her shoes and went to the refrigerator. Nancy wasn't a big drinker and had about a glass and a half of wine at dinner at Daryl's on Main. Daryl's on Main was a great place, and under ordinary circumstances, this would have been a fabulous evening. But this wasn't an ordinary evening. Russ Baker was there with a very attractive woman. Nancy did not know her but was somehow very angry about it. Russ and the attractive lady had walked out smiling and happy without so much as a wave of the hand to her. The worst part was Nancy did not understand why she was so angry.

She got an almost-full bottle of wine and went to her room and closed the door. After consuming the contents of the bottle, she curled up like a five-year-old and went to sleep.

Miriam had run Russ back to his place to get showered and to get his car. She went to the office and got the coffee going, checked e-mails, and listened to the office voice mail. The radio operator answered the number listed for the sheriff's office overnight, but the internal office phones went to voice mail, telling whomever was calling to call the main number for an emergency. They did have a 911 emergency system as well.

There was a message for the sheriff on the system. As was normal, she listened to the message and made a note for the sheriff regarding the contents. He could listen to the message after looking at the note if he desired. The message was from a person at the Intertek Lab in Seattle regarding the oil rag and shell casing found at the crime scene. The caller said that he knew the sheriff was anxious to get a report on the test results, if there were any results to report.

Did the oily rag and the shell casing have comparable traces of oil? Yes, they matched, and a written report was being sent by registered mail. This was another positive result. This wasn't enough to arrest anyone as it could not be proven that the oily rag and the shell casing were likely from the same person. But this was another plus in their conclusion that the people at that camp had probably had something to do with Warren's death. They still needed the smoking gun.

Russ and Barry arrived, and Deputy Dunkin and Miriam came in, and everyone was briefed. They needed to find out who this Donald Bragg was, and Miriam would go to work on the computer to see what she could find. They knew where Kile was, and he was probably not going anywhere. What was the connection to Teresa Walker and these two guys? That was what they needed to find out. Do they go to Teresa Walker and ask her?

They needed both Donald Bragg's fingerprints and those of Hector Martinez. And who were the couple known as Mr. and Mrs. Phillips?

Russ felt it was going to take some old-fashioned grunt work. Get the pictures of Donald Bragg, if possible, from his driver's license and also Hector's. Get a picture of the two trucks and Teresa Walker. Then he and Deputy Dunkin would canvas the hotels, motels, bars, and restaurants in Bozeman. And finally, he needed both of those guys' fingerprints to compare to those lifted on a couple items from the boat.

Barry said he would assist in that and advise the Gallatin Sheriff's Office that they would be working the case in Bozeman. Neither Donny Bragg nor Hector Martinez had a police record. They had covered their tracks well in everything they had been involved in so far.

Miriam could not find anything there. In searching the names, Miriam got a strange hit. Donald J. Bragg came up on a search as being a representative for a real estate company in Butte. He was listed as a broker/agent. But where was he? As they continued to look, an address came up in Butte for a Donny Bragg. Was this their guy? They had five people they were interested in and one was a highly placed law enforcement officer. They needed something to tie at least one of these to the scene.

Russ had an idea. He would go back and interview Hector Martinez again. He would show him some pictures and try to get Hector to handle them. He had shown Hector the pictures of Warren's boat and truck but did not get Hector to handle them. Should he ask Hector if he knew Teresa? Maybe just show a picture of her and see his reaction. The same with Kile and Donald Bragg. Maybe they could get a break somewhere.

They knew that Teresa knew Donald Bragg. Suppose they tell her that in the course of the investigation, they had run across him and knew he went to the same college and they had dated according to some interviews they had made. They just wondered if she had any recent contact with him. It was a gamble. The whole bunch might take flight and never be seen again.

Tomorrow, the three Madison county officers would start canvassing the Bozeman area showing pictures. It might take two or three days to get around. Miriam had done her usual great job of putting together a list of hotel/motels, restaurants, pool rooms, and bars for each officer and a notebook with the pictures in a plastic sleeve to use in their canvas. Russ had Hector Martinez on his schedule and decided to follow Hector when he got off from work in hopes that he would go to the mobile home park from work. The trio started early with the hotels and then worked their way along as businesses opened. It was a long shot, and it would be a very long day as some bars didn't open until the afternoon.

Some people were not very cooperative and were afraid to say anything if they knew it. Barry found a couple of places that had seen the two men, but they couldn't say if they were in the establishment at the same time or if they were together. The same was true with Deputy Dunkin, and one waitress remembered seeing one or both of them with a couple that was coming in for a while. She thought the woman was a singer. One bartender said that he was sure the woman was named Helen and had asked about a job as a singer, but that they already had a singer for live music a few nights a week.

Hector had told Russ that he went up to the camp/inn to see some friends visiting the area and that the woman was a wannabe singer. Could this be the same person? He had no pictures of the couple, but everyone was sure they had not been in for a while.

Barry then hit a stroke of luck. A bar at the far outskirts of town was frequented by college students. They danced, shot pool, and it was a cowboy environment. One of the waitresses recognized a picture of Donny. "I've seen him in here several times. His name is Kile. He was in here with this guy, pointing to Hector, on several occasions and asked me out, but I am married, but he was always hitting on me."

At last! thought Barry. *We have someone identifying Donald "Donny" Bragg as "Kile." This would make Russ's day when he heard it. Not enough for an arrest, but a big step.*

"He was in here more than once or twice with that woman, but she was wearing glasses and she had her hair pulled up. I'm sure that was her and he called her Tess. I remember because that's my mother's name, and we talked about that. They were very chummy, and once when he was in here hitting on me, I told him I thought he had a girl, and he said something like, 'Aw, she's been my girlfriend, off and on, since college days. And I have been on with her a lot, if you know what I mean.'"

Finally, Barry had been able to put Hector, Donny—or Kile, as he was calling himself—and Teresa together. So Donny not only was using Kile Davidson's license plate, he was using his name and probably his ID.

Russ hung out down the street from the truck terminal. He wasn't sure what time Hector got off, but he thought it might be about six o'clock from what he heard on his earlier visit to the terminal.

At a few minutes after six o'clock, the red Ram truck pulled out and headed out toward the Huffine area. Russ followed at a respectable distance and tried to keep some cars between them to avoid being spotted. Hector pulled in a mini mart and went inside. He came out with a six-pack and got some gas. He then continued on out to the area where the mobile home parks were and watched Hector pull in the driveway beside of one of the double-wides and went in. Russ wasn't sure if there was anyone there other than Hector, but this could be a dangerous situation.

He called Barry on the radio and did not get him. He then called Deputy Dunkin.

213

"Madison County Unit 8 calling Madison County Unit 2."

"Go ahead, Unit 8," came the reply. The radio operator in Virginia City could hear the exchange, and Miriam could hear it in the background and went closer to hear.

"Unit 2, switch to TAC 2. Unit 2, switch to TAC 2. Ten four?"

"Ten four, Unit 8. Switching to TAC 2."

TAC 2 was a scrambled signal not readily available to scanners and other two-way radios. In other words, they could talk in private. The radio operator in Virginia City did not have to switch as the base radio would automatically pick up any of their tactical channels.

"I'm ten seventy-eight off Huffine Road, at the suspect's address on your list. What is your ten seventy-seven this location?"

"Approximately fifteen minutes. Ten four?"

"Ten four, Unit 2. Fifteen minutes. Standing by."

Miriam felt nervous and was worried about the officers and especially Russ. Miriam had been on pins and needles all day about their safety. Somehow, she knew that Russ could take care of himself, but shit happens, and she did not want it happening to a Madison County officer. Especially him.

It was about twelve minutes when Deputy Dunkin showed up. After a quick update, they pulled down to the driveway, and Russ pulled in with his blue lights flashing. Deputy Wayne Duncan stopped his car at the end of the driveway and opened his door and stood so he was partially shielded by it. He removed his service weapon from the holster and stood ready in case there was trouble.

Russ gave him a quick glance and walked to the door. He rang the buzzer and stepped back to wait. Russ had the retainer on his service weapon off so he could get to it in a hurry.

Men and women in law enforcement are trained to do their jobs and sent out into the field with very high expectations. They are expected to possess all the positive and most desirable attributes—compassion, understanding, and patience—but to leave fear and anger at home. They are trained to shoot and shoot well then face the loss of their jobs and possible prosecution when they do. They are supposed to accept danger and verbal abuse and never lose their cool.

When a law officer shoots a perpetrator or suspect, the president of the United States, Jesse Jackson, and Al Sharpton jump on an airplane and arrive to give speeches about police abuse and discrimination if the policeman makes the mistake in shooting someone of a different race. The law officer gets fired, or worse. When a law officer gets killed, the president goes and plays golf, Jesse Jackson gives a fund-raising speech, and Al Sharpton goes to be on TV and talk about how we need some more social programs. The policeman was just doing his or her dangerous job and their luck ran out, and the murderer was actually the victim of social failure. High expectations, indeed.

Yet men and women still put on a badge, strap on a gun, a bulletproof vest, and now a body cam, and try to make it through the day without killing someone or being killed. Here was a Marietta, Georgia, boy who always wanted to be a policeman and tried to walk away from it, standing at the doorsteps of a man who may have put a bullet through the back of a decent young man's head—or at least was party to it in Bozeman, Montana. How in the world did this happen?

Hector had gotten off from work in the warehouse, stopped and bought some beer, and filled up the red Ram truck with gas on the way home. He couldn't wait until he stepped in the shower and had just gotten out when the buzzer sounded telling him someone was at the door.

Who could that be? Donny has a key, he thought as he pulled back a flimsy blind to take a peek out.

Oh, hell! he thought. There was a police car at the end of his driveway and a cop standing there. Hector ran to the bedroom and picked up his gun, which was on the nightstand. The buzzer sounded again, and this time there was sharp knocking on the door.

Fuck! There is at least two of them! he thought. *What are they doing here?* He peeked out the small end window, and he could see the unmarked car with its blue lights flashing and that same damn cop that hassled him a few days back at work.

"Yea. Who is it?" Hector called out.

"Mr. Martinez. This is Russell Baker from over at Madison County Sheriff's Office. Can you open the door and talk to me a minute? I have a couple of pictures I want you to see. We are trying to get a handle on the Phillips couple that you said was there and see if these are them. I won't take but a minute of your time."

"I just got out of the shower. I don't have my clothes on. Come back another time."

Police officers are supposed to use tact and negotiation to diffuse tense situations. No use of force. Hopefully, while the policeman is negotiating, the suspect doesn't open fire.

"I can wait until you get some clothes on or, I can just hand you the pictures through the door and see if you recognize them. I would sure appreciate it."

Well, if that is all he wants, I'll look at them and get him the hell away from here, Hector thought.

"Okay. If you want to hand them through the screen, I'll open the door. Hold on a second."

Hector put the gun under some magazines on the counter and opened the screen. He, indeed, only had a towel wrapped around him and had obviously just gotten out of the shower.

"Mr. Martinez, I have three pictures I want you to see. Here is a man that has been seen in this area, and I wanted to see if this was the Philips person you told me was up at the cabin/camp on Highway 287."

Hector was very nervous but took the picture and was trying to see what the cop was doing. Was this a trick? Was he going to grab Hector when he reached for the picture?

"I have seen that guy around town a couple of times, but that is not Jeffery Phillips. I'm not sure who that is." Russ was certain Hector was lying. Russ took back that picture and handed him a picture of Teresa Walker.

"Well, how about this lady? Could that be Mrs. Phillips?" Hector had seen Teresa Walker several times, but she had always had her hair up and wore glasses. She usually had on a cap. He really did not recognize the picture as the Tess that Donny hung with a few times, although she did look familiar.

217

"No, that's not Helen Phillips. I feel sure I may have seen her, and she does look familiar. You know, in these clubs, everybody looks the same, especially after a couple of beers."

"Okay. One more." He took the picture of Teresa and handed a picture of Kile Davidson to Hector. Hector had never met the real Kile Davidson. Donny Bragg kept his associates apart as much as possible, and this was why. No one could identify anyone else.

"No. I have never seen this guy. Is that a wheelchair he is in?" Hector commented.

"Yes. He is in a wheelchair."

"Well, I sure have never seen him." Russ actually believed him on that one.

"Well, Mr. Martinez, I appreciate your looking, anyway. Sorry to have caught you with your britches down, so to speak." Russ gave a little wave of the hand and headed toward his car with a little wave to Deputy Dunkin that they were ready to leave. The deputy drove up the street to a big post office building and pulled in. Russ pulled in behind and got out carrying the notebook with the photos that he had just showed Hector.

"Well, Wayne, we should have three sets of Mr. Hector Martinez's fingerprints. If you will, take these to Miriam first thing in the morning and let her see if they happen to match those we have so far. Maybe we can put Hector in the boat with Warren!"

"Okay, Russ. What are you going to do now?"

"I'm going to borrow your set of pictures and go by the Homewood Suites and then I may call Teresa Walker and see where she is and what she's doing. I'll see you sometime tomorrow, and you or Miriam can call me if we have any luck with the photos," said Russ.

Barry had already headed for home with the news that they had an ID on Donny using Kile's name. They just needed to tie all these people together and put them in the boat with Warren.

Russ's phone rang. "Hello, Miriam. How are you this evening?" Russ said as he looked at the caller ID.

"I was about to go home and I was worried about you and Wayne going to that guy's house. How did it go?"

"I just gave Wayne three pictures that were handled by Hector Martinez. Hopefully, you will get some prints, and we can see if they match the ones you lifted from the matchbook and the Ziploc bag. There should just be my prints and his on the photos. Wayne will have them there in the morning, and we can all meet in the morning and see what we have. I plan to go by the Homewood Suites and show the photos and see if anyone has seen them around there."

"Glad you are okay, Russ. See you in the morning," said Miriam.

"Good night," said Russ.

Hector had really been shaken when he saw the cop cars, and he did not like the attention he was getting. It might be time to get out of town, but Donny had told him to stay there. Right now, Hector was a lot more afraid of Donny Bragg than Russell Baker, small-town sheriff investigator. Besides, the cop was pretty nice and did not hassle him too much. Maybe that was it for a while. He called Donny's number on a throwaway phone and got the voice mail at the real estate place. Right now, he was feeling pretty much hung out to dry, thanks to the boneheaded and hotheaded actions of his fearless boss.

A quick swing by the Homewood Suites did not turn up anything, and a ride through the parking lot at the Hampton did not turn up a car that looked like Teresa Walker. Russ decided to go to the Brew Works and get a bite to eat before heading back to Virginia City and put off calling Teresa until they all could compare notes in the morning.

18

THE BREW WORKS WAS PACKED, as usual, and Russ went up to the bar as he usually did when he was alone.

"Is this seat taken, Mr. Baker?" a female voice asked.

Russ was startled and even more so when he turned around and there stood Agent Teresa Walker.

"No, Ms. Walker, feel free to have a seat. Can I buy you a beer, wine, or anything?"

"I guess one beer would be fine," she said. "Are you having any luck on that case of the murdered fisherman?"

"We have been up here doing some interviews today. I guess we will all meet up in the morning at the office and see where we are, if anywhere. We haven't arrested anyone yet."

"I know it's a tough one. You may have to face the facts that the killer or killers are long gone."

"I guess you are right."

"How would it be if I stopped by around noon tomorrow and see what you have come up with?" she asked.

"That would be fine with me, but you really should touch base with Barry, if you don't mind. Protocol, you know." As he said it, he saw Nancy coming in alone and taking a table. There was no professor with her tonight. At least, not yet, anyway. She glanced over and saw Russ and immediately looked away. She could not believe he was in here with another attractive woman. Was he just trying to rub it in her face? But maybe she looked a lot like the DCI agent they had met with in Virginia City. Maybe it was just business.

Teresa Walker got down from the stool and said good-bye, and Russ followed her as far as Nancy's table. "Hello, Nancy. How are you this evening?"

"Oh, great, Russ. I'm just waiting for someone. How are you?" She came up with a quick lie to avoid having him sit down.

"I have put in a long day and now I have to drive home. And there is another long day tomorrow, coming up," Russ replied. "I'll be seeing you."

"Are you staying here in town these days?" she asked as he was about to walk away.

"No. I'm a full-time resident at the Reel 'Em Inn! Not that bad for a single guy." He gave a little wave and was gone. Nancy had lost her appetite. Russ got started toward Virginia City and picked up the mic on his radio. "Madison SO, Unit 8 is ten eight." Almost at once he heard, "Madison SO to Madison SO Unit 8."

"Go ahead, Madison SO."

"Unit 1 requests you go to TAC 2. Acknowledge." Unit 1 was the sheriff, Barry.

"Ten four. Going to TAC 2," and he switched the radio to scrambled communications.

"Russ, I have some good news. We have a witness who has been seeing Donald Bragg calling himself Kile Davidson and has put Kile, a.k.a. Donald, in company with the DCI agent on more than one occasion," Barry said.

"That is good news! I have a number of fingerprints coming by unit 2 in the morning for Miriam to compare with the ones we lifted from items in the boat. Maybe that will help. Where do you want to take this?"

"I say we wait until Miriam gets the results, and if they are favorable, we call our contact at DCI and let him know what we have and see if he wants to be here when we talk to the DCI agent. Ten four?"

"Ten four, Sheriff." Russ added, "I'll see you in the morning, Unit 8. Unit 1 is ten-seven."

"Unit 8 is ten-seven seven and going to channel 1."

"What's going on, Hector?" said Donny. "You sound like you are in a panic, again."

"That son of a bitch cop from Madison County was by here again today. He showed me a picture of you and claimed he was looking for the Philips. He had a picture of some dude in a wheelchair and a picture of some girl I think was Tess, but she was all duded up and was not wearing glasses," answered Hector.

"Exactly what did you tell them? Exactly, what?" Donny said in a very hostile and threatening way.

"I told them I thought I had seen you around town at some of the bars and places but that I did not know you. That I had never seen the guy in the wheelchair and I thought the girl was familiar looking, but I did not know her," said Hector.

"What did he do then?"

"He said thanks and left."

223

"Sounds to me like you did good, Hector. Do you want to come over to Butte and stay here for a day or two and let things cool down?"

"That might be good. What about the job?"

"I'll handle the job. It's up to you if you want to come," said Donny.

"I'll be over tonight, then," said Hector.

Donny wanted Hector out of sight and where he could keep an eye on him. He also wanted him handy in case something had to be done about Hector before he caused a major problem. The cops were on to Hector, but he did not know what they had on him or on himself. He had to get hold of Teresa and see if she had any info.

Donny called Teresa. He did not send up an alert and did not want to make any reference to the Warren Cason murder. He told her he was working on something and would be back to her soon. She had no idea that he was involved or in any way concerned about the murder.

By 9:00 AM, the Madison County Sheriff's Office had what they needed to start turning up the heat on Hector Martinez. The prints that Russ had obtained on the photos that Martinez had handled matched those in the Ziploc bag from the boat that the cell phone and keys were in. The two prints they had from the cabin and the matchbook from the boat were not yet matched to anyone. The question was, did they want to bring him in or try to get more evidence? If he was the shooter, could they get a conviction with what they had, which did not put a gun in Hector's hand. The witness had put Teresa and the guy Donny together, and Russ could put Donny's truck at the scene of the crime, but not with a 100 percent match. They did not have enough yet for an arrest, much less a conviction. They knew that

Donny, Kile, and Teresa were at school together and that Teresa had dated Donny. Could Teresa claim to be working undercover? That did not seem likely as she was known by law enforcement and the motel people as being with the state. They needed to call Bruce at DCI and see where he would like this to go. Did he want them to proceed in questioning her or did DCI want to do it?

They went in to call Bruce before Teresa called Barry about coming by. Then Barry would get a warrant for the arrest of Hector Martinez for murder, maybe!

They got through to Bruce Obermeyer at DCI and laid out what they knew so far. Bruce felt they had little to go on as far as charging Teresa with a crime. Her going to school with some guys who were now living shady lives was not a crime on her part if she did not know about their criminal activity. Her having a beer with old friends at a bar might not be smart, but it wasn't illegal. Bruce confirmed that she was not working undercover. Now, if she was giving these guys inside information as to what DCI was doing and they were using that information to avoid detection and arrest, that would get her arrested, and she would be faced with serious jail time. It was apparent that somebody had been doing that. But they had not yet established that beyond a reasonable doubt. Too many loose ends!

Bruce said, "At least we managed to stop a big shipment from coming in the night before the murder. We had enough presence that the drop was stopped."

Barry said, "We don't think that is the case. We believe the drop took place on a grass strip just off Highway 87. We have fragments from the packing they used. We got a positive response on the boat our guide was using from our drug sniffing dog that there had recently been drugs in the boat. We can put the three of them together and there was apparently a couple going by the name of Phillips that was somehow involved. And we know that Donny Bragg was using the ID of a man from Missoula.

"We are pretty certain that Hector Martinez delivered the money to Warren's house in his red Ram truck. We have a witness that saw a truck like that over there. Again, we do not have a witness that can identify him as the delivery man.

"And we have a witness that can put Bragg's truck at the scene of the crime, and going down the street that Warren lived on a day or so prior to the killing. We know from analysis that the murder weapon was cleaned with Outer's Gun Oil at the cabin/camp and that the shell casing found at the murder scene has that same oil on it.

"They weren't deterred, but they moved the drop and probably did not tell Teresa, or if they did, she did not tell you. I believe that our murder victim was killed by the drug crowd and that your lady is knee-deep in this."

Bruce was very surprised that this group had put enough together to know that the drop took place and likely where. He and his department did not know where it was dropped.

"We have prints on the oil bottle, the plastic bag containing the oil and rags from the cabin/camp, and the matchbook cover, and they do not match Hector's. We, as yet, have not found Donald Bragg's prints to compare, and we do not know at this moment where he is.

"We do have Hector Martinez's print on the bag that contained the cell phone and the wallet. We have enough to pick him up now."

Bruce said, "When Agent Walker comes by, why not tell her that you ran across her name during the course of the investigation. And that you are investigating a murder that seems to be related to the recent drug deal bust gone badly and see what she says. I'll be waiting to hear. But I cannot believe that Teresa would be involved in a cold-blooded murder or any criminal activity."

Their case was flimsy, but they could get Hector and maybe they could get him to talk. If he would roll over on Bragg, that would be the leverage they needed. They also felt they might have some leverage with Kile Davidson. A paraplegic would probably like to avoid prison. The case against him on any murder charge could not be made from the evidence they had but they might could get him on criminal conspiracy and identity fraud.

Teresa called and said she could be there around eleven, but Barry told her he would not be available until after two o'clock. She agreed to come after two o'clock. They were going to call Gallatin and tell them they were coming to arrest Hector Martinez today. They set the wheels in motion to get a warrant to pick him up.

Barry and Russ went to Bozeman to the truck terminal looking for Hector and were told he had called in sick. They went to the house where he had been living and went in based upon their warrant. The closets were empty and there was no sign of Hector Martinez, and they guessed that he had fled, spooked by Russ's two visits.

They put out an all-points bulletin on the red Ram and Hector Martinez. They were back to square one!

Agent Teresa Walker of Montana DCI showed up at the Madison County Sheriff's Office as planned and was asked to go to the old conference room that served as grand jury room and jury deliberation room and just about everything else. Barry and Russ met with her, and both

227

made comments regarding the investigation of Warren Cason, and she listened in her normal unemotional way.

Then Russ made a statement that shook her:

"The night before Warren Cason was killed, there was a scheduled drug deal going down. Of course you know that because you are on that drug task force. The drug drop was supposed to take place over around Big Timber, and you and your team were in place to interdict the shipment and arrest the perps.

"But somehow, the drug dealers knew about the drug task force and moved the drop to another location where they successfully brought in several hundred pounds of cocaine." The cocaine part was a guess at this point by Russ. "The drugs were dropped out of a moving and low-flying airplane at a small dirt airstrip off Highway 87, just south of the cabin/camp on Highway 287."

Teresa interrupted.

"How do you know that? We have no record of that happening. It is our understanding that that operation was aborted." But she knew that it did happen.

"Because we found evidence of bubble wrap and duct tape that was used to protect the dropped packages of drugs. Several people were involved in that planned drop: two people calling themselves Helen and Jeffery Phillips who have since disappeared and Phillips is probably not their real name.

"Hector Martinez, who was working at a truck terminal as late as yesterday in Bozeman but who has left town today for parts *unknown,* was in Warren Cason's boat. We have his prints from handling material in that boat. Hector has been driving a red Ram pickup similar to which was seen at Warren's shop."

Teresa Walker was startled that they had pieced so much together! She still could not grasp the idea that there was any connection between the drugs and the murder of Warren Cason. Donny had told her that Hector was not involved.

"And there was someone else involved that you know very well: Donald Bragg, a.k.a. Kile Davidson. You have known Donald Bragg since college where you dated him off and on for two years."

Teresa Walker leaped to her feet!

"Are you accusing me of somehow being involved with drug dealers? You are treading on thin damn ice here for a washed-up policeman from Georgia!"

In spite of her outward incredulous display of anger, Teresa Walker suddenly felt the pressure of the situation, and this guy from Georgia was tightening it more and more. Had Hector and Donny left her dangling in the wind? She moved toward the door.

Sheriff Barry Steinbrenner, a rather formidable-looking guy stepped to block the door and said, "Please sit down, Ms. Walker!" She considered trying to force her way out but decided that was not wise.

"When I call my boss, you will be very sorry about this!" she said.

Barry said, "Go ahead and call if you like. I talked to Bruce about two hours ago. He, my brother, and I have been drinking beer and catching fish together for over forty years."

That was news to Teresa Walker, and it sent a chill up her spine! For the first time in a long time, Teresa Walker was afraid. How much did they know?

Russ continued. "There is also the real Kile Davidson, whom you also know from Butte, who we believe has conspired with Donald Bragg to provide Bragg with a false identity. Davidson was allowing him the use of his license plate and personal identity to throw off anyone looking for him."

"We can put Hector Martinez in Warren Cason's boat with a fingerprint match. We can put Hector's truck at the fly shop on S Black Avenue where it was seen by a witness." That was a little bit of a stretch, but she did not know that.

"He left the $525 in cash to pay for the float in an envelope with your name on it."

"That can't be true. I had nothing to do with any money left at Warren Cason's house. I had nothing to do with any money and no knowledge of it. That's another lie you are making up." But Russ held up the envelope with her nickname Tess written on it.

Oh shit, she thought.

"We can put Donald Bragg's truck on S. Black Avenue two days prior to the murder, probably making sure it did not have cameras and would be safe. We think that is why Cason was chosen. Why they chose to do a fly-fishing float is a mystery. We also have a witness that can put Donald Bragg's truck at the boat ramp where they put in and it was driven by a woman." That witness was, of course, Russ himself.

"We believe that the drugs that were dropped at the Lake View strip were at some point in Cason's boat. We have a set of prints, as of yet not identified, that we believe belong to Donald Bragg from the cabin/camp. We will confirm as soon as we can find Bragg.

"We believe that either Bragg or Martinez took a 9 mm pistol and shot Warren Cason in the head. Maybe because he discovered they had loaded his boat with drugs."

"We have witnesses that saw you on multiple occasions with these men and a note referring to you as being in room 212 at the Hampton Inn and being referred to as Tess that we just showed you. We believe that the records from the Hampton Inn will confirm that. And we believe that you have conspired with these drug dealers to further your own personal and financial interests."

"That's a goddamned lie! I have never done that! It's true; I know Donny Bragg and dated him in college. I ran into him in the lobby of the Hampton in Bozeman one night, and he and I started seeing each other when I was in town. But that was it! Donny Bragg is a successful real estate salesman and would never kill anyone! I am a good DCI agent and would not betray my oath," she was almost screaming at them.

Inside, her heart was pounding, and she could barely contain her fear and anger. Each breath was like torture! All she wanted to do was run to her car and get away from these accusers!

Agent Teresa Walker stood up and composed herself and said, "Are you planning to arrest me? I do not believe you have anything to hold me on, and you know it. The fact that I know some people and ate some burgers, drank some beer, and shot some pool with them is not a crime."

"We have someone who will testify that you did more than eat, drink, and play pool. You were regularly intimate with Donald Bragg." That was also a stretch of the truth based on comments attributed to Donald Bragg. "It would have been easy to give information on your business to them in that environment."

With that, she said, "Arrest me or I'm out of here and I'm going straight to Bruce! I see why you quit your pathetic job in Georgia because you are nothing but a fisherman and you are definitely fishing now!"

"You can go for now, but you need to really think this through. These guys are dangerous! Very dangerous! If you get in their way, you will get what Warren Cason got. If you think you have some future with Donald Bragg, he will eventually end up dead or in jail for many years. And, likely, you will be too, if you live long enough.

"I don't believe they planned to murder Cason at the start. There was no reason. But they did it and as soon as we can get our hands on Donald Bragg's fingerprints and match them up with a set from the boat, we will have enough to arrest him. We went to arrest Martinez today, and he has fled. Bragg probably has too, and you are holding the bag," said Russ.

"You need to tell us everything you know and maybe Bruce and Barry will work to cut you a deal."

She ran out the door and was gone. Russ and Barry looked at each other.

"Now, what?"

"Let's go have another talk with Kile Davidson," said Russ.

"I'll brief Bruce before we go," said Barry.

The screws had been tightened and mostly on Teresa and Hector. There was a chance they would both flee, but the case was too weak without the Bragg's fingerprints putting him at the scene. They needed one of these people to start to crack and Teresa was hanging tough. It seemed clear they had already put the fear of God in Hector. Bruce

Obermeyer could put a shield around Teresa, and then they would not get another free shot at her.

They left for Missoula. Again.

Donny Bragg was trying to decide his next move. If he let this get out of hand, the people he worked for would not hesitate to remove him. Permanently. If they knew he was connected to the murder of the fishing guide with the drugs in the boat, they would not trust him anymore. He had been a very good manager and kept a very low profile, but this was bonehead move, and now he was having to do damage control. If he made Hector disappear, he would probably be the number one suspect, and he wondered why they had not come looking for him yet. It was probably because they could not directly connect him to anything. He needed to talk to Teresa and see if they had made the connection with the murder and the drug drop and do it without alerting her about that connection.

Teresa had pulled off the road to try and stop shaking and crying. She was scared, angry, and in a grave personal legal position. Her career as a law enforcement officer was about to go up in smoke, and she had not made that big deal yet that would allow her to disappear in style. And several years in jail might be all she had to look forward to. But then there was the thought that Donny or his right-hand man, Hector, had possibly added murder to the operation and that was sending chills down her spine! But she could see that Donny would not admit that to her for fear that she might turn on him and he would lose his connection to the task force information. He had the best of everything now: free information and all the sex he wanted, also free.

She needed to think this all through and to do damage control with Bruce. And do it fast. She'd had no idea that Bruce and these local hick sheriffs were buddy-buddy.

She looked down her nose at all the local cops because none were operating at her level. Although by some standards, she had reached a pretty low level.

She called Bruce and maintained a degree of poise. "Chief, I have just been accused of all kinds of criminal activity by the investigator in Madison County. I want to set up a time to come see you. Is that possible?"

"Of course. Come in first thing in the morning. I am out of town today. Eight AM will be fine."

There was no hint that Bruce was overly excited and seemed cool about it. That was good!

19

HECTOR WAS NOW IN THE apartment that Donny had in Butte. The apartment was rented under the name of the real estate shell company to make him harder to find. It was a luxury place like Hector was not accustomed to and had security cameras, flat screen TVs, gym, and video games. A kitchen right out of *Better Homes and Gardens* and was the best that big drug money could buy.

For the first time, Hector was seeing that Donny was high up and well connected. To whom, Hector did not know. And it was probably a dangerous bit of information. Maybe the less he knew, the safer he was. But if he had to hide out for a while, this was as good as it got.

Russ and Barry had the bit in their teeth and were pressing forward. They had asked Barry's brother if he could meet them again at Kile Davidson's house, but he was in court. He told them to carry on without him. Barry's brother asked, "Do you want me to send a deputy or two for backup?"

Barry felt the situation was such that he and Russ would be okay.

"No, we should be fine," he replied. They were going there to try and shake the man to the core and maybe get something on Donny Bragg. But there should not be a confrontation.

They almost accomplished the goal by just pulling in the yard in the unmarked Dodge with the antennas sticking out. Kile did not recognize this vehicle and did not know if it was Feds or state people. It did not look like the locals. Kile let the dogs keep the officers at bay for a minute until he could look at his video screen from the security camera and see who this was.

"Damn it! It's those same guys from the other day."

Kile called off the dogs and invited the men up on the porch and invited them to sit in the glider. They told him that his identity may have been compromised and that a person had been using not only his license plate but his name all around Bozeman and that they believed that person was involved somehow in a murder and they wanted to alert him to check his credit files and be on the alert. But Kile knew they could have done all that on the phone! They were here to rattle his cage, and they had succeeded. But what else did they already know?

"Do you have any idea where Donald Bragg is, Kile? We think he may be involved," Barry asked.

"No. I have no idea," said Kile. And he really did not know where Donny Bragg was at that moment.

Then they set out to tell him that they believed he was part of a criminal conspiracy and that now was the time for him to come clean if he wanted to avoid having to adjust to using his electric wheelchair in prison. They would get to the truth, sooner or later.

On their first visit, Kile was not overly impressed with these guys. They were coming across a lot differently today. He could sense they had picked up a trail and would stay with it, and he had not bargained for getting involved in a *murder* when he made his deal with Donny Bragg.

"And," said Russ, "these people have killed one guy that happened to get in their way. They won't let anyone get in their way."

Kile knew that. He knew what kind of man Donny was. To their surprise, he said, "I did let Donny use my ID. He told me there were some people after him because of a couple of bad real estate deals. I loaned him my tag, and for that, he bought me the black Ford truck sitting out there. Hell, I can barely get in the thing! And I get some cash every month for keeping my mouth shut. He mails it to me in an envelope, and it comes in handy for a guy that can't do much to earn an income anymore. I don't know anything about what Donny Bragg does, and I sure as hell am not part of any murder!

"I am not sure who they are, but I know he works for some highly placed and seriously dangerous people, and they are people who would burn this house down with me in it and roast marshmallows while I am burning! If he finds out I talked to you, I will need to be in some cave somewhere in Siberia. These are not people to fool with!"

They were flabbergasted. He was scared and made no bones about it.

"Are you sure you don't know where he is?"

"I contact him always on a burn phone and always on a voice mail number. He then calls me back when he wants to. I believe he has a couple of people that he works with at any one time, and they are disposable, if you know what I mean." They did.

"Do you need to get out of here, Kile, for your personal safety?" asked Barry.

"I think I am okay for now. As long as you guys don't put me under the bus. But I really don't know where he is. His so-called real estate company is supposed to be in Butte, but with phones and voice mail and stuff, he could be in Mexico for all I know. I do one thing for him and that's let him use my ID. That's it!"

They went back to Virginia City the next day convinced they were on to something big and needed to decide their next step.

Barry decided to call Bruce Obermeyer and update him on their investigation. Bruce had talked to Teresa and was giving her the benefit of the doubt based on the information he had so far. She was just out having some fun with an old friend and not aware of any misbehavior on his part, according to Bruce, and they would keep an eye on her. Barry wasn't buying that but until he got something concrete; he had no choice but to keep pressing with Russ for the facts. They seemed at a standstill. They needed those prints on Bragg but could not find any in any database, and he wasn't coming around to give them any.

They were looking for his truck and they were looking for Hector too. Looking. Looking. Looking.

Russ and Miriam were getting together once in a while, and Russ had not heard from Nancy in several days. He guessed she was doing fine with her new boyfriend. There were no float trips and no fishing. He was fully occupied with the case and seriously needed a little help from somewhere.

Russ was at the coffee machine when Barry called from his office. "Russ, come in here a minute, please."

Russ walked in sipping his coffee, and Barry said, "My brother just called. Kile Davidson died in a house fire last night! Just like he predicted!"

Russ almost poured out the entire cup of coffee; he was so startled!

"They have to do an autopsy to see if he died in the fire or by other means!"

"How did anyone know we talked to him? I did not tell anyone, you didn't, and I know your brother wouldn't," said Russ. He couldn't help but wonder if there were any marshmallow packages around Kile's house.

Barry leaned back and put his hands behind his head and looked at Russ. "I did talk to someone. I talked to Bruce Obermeyer. There is a leak there somewhere, or he told Teresa, maybe. Maybe it's a coincidence."

"Surely he would not tell her!" said Russ.

Russ picked up his cell phone and punched an autodial number.

"This is Teresa Walker. What do you want Mr. Baker?"

"I wondered if you had heard the latest on our investigation."

"I am not following your investigation, as you call it," she said sarcastically. "My boss has told me to stay away from you."

"Well, in any case, Barry and I went to see Kile Davidson, your old friend, to follow up on the murder of Warren Cason. You remember Kile Davidson, I believe."

"Hell yes, I remember him. Did he get a parking ticket or something? Maybe you can pin that on me!"

239

"He died in a house fire early this morning. It's a funny thing because he had told us that would happen if Bragg and his people found out he had talked to us. My guess is the autopsy will show a 9 mm hole in his head."

"Oh my God!" she said. Then she disconnected the call!

Barry said, "Was that wise, Russ?"

Russ gave a shrug. "I don't know."

Donny needed to get things back under control and needed to know what was going on in Madison County and in Helena. He relied on Teresa's inside information and what information he got from the higher-ups to stay one step ahead of the cops. It was time to get with Teresa, and he wouldn't mind a little R & R at some motel with her. With all the scrutiny, he had parked the black Ford truck and was now driving a new Chevrolet Malibu that he used as a backup vehicle and when he wanted to be less recognized.

He called Teresa's personal cell number, and she answered right away.

"Well, it's about time I heard from you," she said trying to sound her usual self. "Where have you been?"

"Well, you know, babe, I have real estate business all over and I have to go where the work is. I have a big deal coming up, and there is a lot of money to be made when I get it all put together."

Donny was talking in such a way that she knew he was referring to another big drug deal coming up.

"Are you going to be around Bozeman the next day or so? If so, maybe we can get together," he asked

"I will be there tomorrow night and maybe the next. I have moved over to the Hilton Garden Inn though if you are coming around. It is just down the street, as you know, from the Hampton."

She added in her sweetest voice, "I would sure like to see you."

She really liked Donny. Maybe, she even loved him. He had made her otherwise dull life exciting and offered the prospects of retiring at some beautiful island paradise with more money than she could count! But as exciting as he was, she could not run away with a murderer if he was one.

She asked him in a low voice, "Did you hear about what happened to Kile?"

"I heard on the news that he was killed in a house fire. Too bad. I guess he could not get out in time," he said.

He did not seem overly sad or concerned. She had to figure out a way to clear up this situation and put the matter to bed once and for all. She would be heading to the Hilton Garden and checking in about 5:00 PM today.

Teresa checked in at the Hilton Garden and in a few minutes, her room phone rang. It was Donny, and she said, "Come on over. I'm in room 206."

When Donny showed up, he had some beer and a bottle of wine plus some snacks, and before long, they were in bed and acting like two high school kids. They talked a little business, and she did not learn much. But she did say she had talked to the Madison County people and they were still working on the murder case but that she had been pulled off that case and was not involved with that right now. That was good news to Donny.

At about nine o'clock, his phone rang, and he had a low conversation. He kept saying, "I understand, I will take care of it." It was clear someone was giving him some instructions. Donny slipped on his trousers, and Teresa got up and poured them a small plastic cup about half full of some whiskey she had.

"One for the road," she said. He turned up his glass and drank down the whiskey and said, "One for the road."

When Donny left, she put her things in her overnight bag and checked outside. She felt all was okay, so she went to her car and headed out of town on the road that went to Virginia City and Ennis.

It was a little after ten o'clock when Russ heard a knock on the door. As was his custom, he picked up his service weapon and asked who was at the door.

"Open up, Mr. Baker," said the female voice.

He opened the door, and there was Teresa Walker! Now this was interesting!

"Can I come in?" she asked.

"What do you want?" Russ asked.

"Let me in and I'll tell you!"

He had only pulled on his slacks, had on no shoes, and was not set up to entertain anyone this late hour.

"So, Ms. Walker, what do you want?"

"I know you think I am a bad person, and maybe I am. I'm not here to make any confessions. But I am not a murderer and have not willingly been part of one. Ever.

"I started drinking, doing some marijuana, and having sex way too early. And I still enjoy those things as often as I can, now. But I still have some small amount of understanding about right and wrong. I got what I thought was a dream job and have done pretty good at it. Maybe I messed all that up now. But I have to know if Donny

Bragg was involved in the death of the fisherman. Then I will know what I have to do. So, I brought you something."

Teresa reached in a grocery store recycling bag and took out three plastic evidence bags.

"Here are two plastic glasses and a beer bottle that have been handled by Donny Bragg tonight. You said you needed his fingerprints. Here they are. How quickly can we get a comparison?"

Russ was almost speechless! One of his key suspects had just rolled over on her lover, so to speak!

"Hold on a minute," he said as he picked up his phone. He called Miriam's number.

"Well, this is a pleasant surprise, Russ. Are you coming over?"

"No. I need to know if you would be willing to come in to the office and meet me there in twenty minutes. I have some prints I need lifted and compared to those from the items we found at the cabin and the boat. We have the oil can from the cabin, the plastic bag with the gun-cleaning items, and the matchbook from the boat. And I need to take a statement from the person who took them."

"I'll be there in twenty minutes. I'll look a mess, but I'll be there," she said.

"Ms. Walker, Do you want to follow me or ride with me."

"I'll follow you," she said.

They all got to the courthouse, and Miriam set about lifting the prints from the glasses. They drank some of the night 911 operator's coffee and waited. About an hour went by and then Miriam announced, "We have a definite match. The person whose prints are on the glasses is the same person who handled the gun-cleaning oil bottle, the plastic bag the gun-cleaning stuff was in, and the matchbook from the cabins that we found in the boat. We also have a match of the oil on the spent shell casing from the murder scene and the oil from the cabin. I believe we can put that individual in Warren Cason's boat and show that he cleaned the murder weapon."

They now had a connection between Donny Bragg, Hector Martinez, the boat, and the gun, but they still needed to be able to put the gun in Donny's hand. Convincing a jury might be tough unless they could actually do that.

Teresa slumped down in a chair. Her lover and crime partner was also possibly a murderer, and she was in deep shit.

"Mr. Baker, he is not driving the truck. He knows that is a hot item, so he has it stashed in a barn somewhere. He is now driving a new Chevy Malibu. It's a dark-gray metallic color, and here is the license number. I can't protect him now."

Here was the breakthrough they needed! Now where was Donny Bragg? Russell Baker could barely believe what was happening.

Russ called Barry at home and woke him up. "Barry, I am at the office. Sorry to wake you up, but I thought you would want to know that we got the prints we needed on Donny Bragg. We have a definite match, and he was the person who handled the Ziploc bag and the gun oil at the cabin and the matchbook we found in the boat. And I have a statement implicating him and Hector in the drug trafficking business in the area."

"I'll be right there. Who gave you the statement?"

"Teresa Walker."

"No frigging way! Well I'll be damned!"

"But she says she knows nothing about Warren Cason's murder, and I am inclined to believe her on that."

Barry came to the office, and they reviewed the statement. Barry had a cell number for Bruce Obermeyer, head of Montana DCI, and he called the number. "I don't care if the fucker is asleep or having sex with Marilyn Monroe!"

"I think Marilyn is dead," cracked Russ.

"It wouldn't matter to Bruce: old or young, skinny or fat. That man has had sex with more women than a Las Vegas gigolo!" Barry didn't say, but he and his wife watched the show on TV called *Gigolos*.

When Bruce answered, Russ went back outside to talk to Teresa. He had not seen her soft underbelly, but it was exposed now, and she was crying with her head in her hand.

"Are you arresting me, Russell?"

"You haven't given me a confession to any crime yet. You told me about Hector and Donny. You have given us a major piece of evidence from a slippery, dangerous, and hard-to-find man. We'll talk to Barry and see what he wants to do. He's talking to Bruce now," replied Russ.

Barry came in following his call to Bruce Obermeyer. "Ms. Walker, I want to get a few things on tape. Bruce says he's okay with us not arresting you and you will be free to go in a little while. But we need to know where you are and you will need to check in with Bruce in the morning."

"If we can prove that you are not involved in the murder, and you agree to testify, Madison County would have nothing to charge you with as all the other activities have occurred outside our jurisdiction. We can get some of the state charges dropped and get you witness protection if Bruce agrees," said Barry.

Teresa slumped back against the wall in relief.

245

"I was with Bruce and the task force the morning of the murder. I was nowhere around here. I was in Billings with a whole DCI and DEA group. I had no knowledge of anything about Warren Cason. In fact, when I heard that you were looking for Hector about this, I asked Donny if Hector was involved and he said no."

"That may be true. It was probably Donny who pulled the trigger," said Russ. "Where is Donny Bragg now?" he asked.

"He was in Bozeman at the Hilton Garden earlier tonight as I mentioned in my statement. He was called away by someone, and that's when I saw him drive out in the Chevy Malibu. He should be on the security cams there," she said.

"Do you have any idea who called?" inquired Barry.

"I have no idea."

"What will you do if he shows back up over there?"

"I will arrest him," said Teresa.

Barry said, "I would not recommend you try that on your own. You could end up dead. Let's find where he is and we will arrest him with plenty of backup."

Teresa continued, "The apartment in Butte is in some remodeled warehouse, but I have never seen it. It is in the name of that real estate company, I know that much. He told me once that they let him use it as part of his compensation. Hector may be there if he is still alive, and I believe that is where Donny has been staying since they cleared out of the mobile home in Bozeman."

"I don't know if it's safe for you to go back to Bozeman alone," said Russ.

"I'll be okay. Donny does not know I am here. If he shows up, I'll just fake it. I'm good at that. I'll just go back to the Hilton Garden tonight, and I may be able to get a lead on where he is headed next."

It was pushing 1:00 AM when they decided to call it a day. Teresa was asked if she wanted someone to take her somewhere or she could stay at the jail if she wanted to avoid driving.

"No, I am okay. I will go to the Hilton Garden, put on my chain, and get some sleep. I will call Bruce in the morning and arrange to see him and surrender to him if that's what he wants." Teresa got in the Ford and headed out to Bozeman.

Barry could have held her for the state or on suspicion, but Bruce had said it was okay that she left for the time being. He was being more than lenient in Barry's mind.

20

THEY ALL LEFT THE COURTHOUSE except for one deputy and the 911 operator. Russ was dead tired and headed to the motel to crash.

At Norris, Teresa headed East on Montana 84, as she always did. It crossed the Madison River as it heads toward Bozeman and runs alongside the river where it is sparsely populated there. Just outside Norris is a camping facility, and it was basically empty of campers. But sitting out of sight of anyone passing by headed east, with its engine running, was a new Chevy Malibu, dark gray. When the tired Teresa Walker went by, the Malibu eased in behind her and waited until he had a good place to pass. He had the window down on the passenger side and an MP5 automatic on the seat beside him. He had done this before, and he had a cardboard moving box held in place with the seat belt to provide a place to rest the MP 5. He could fire it with one hand, and that's what he did as he came alongside Teresa's car. Teresa was hit immediately and swerved to the right and hit the guard rail. The Malibu was forced to brake hard to avoid a collision as the Ford careened to the left off the guard rail across a ditch and into a pasture and rolled up on its side. The driver of the Malibu stopped and opened his door and had the MP 5 in his hand as he was going to go check on his work. But just as he started to across the road, a set of headlights appeared coming out of a side road and were heading his way. He quickly got back in the car and sped away before the truck arrived to avoid being seen.

The manager of one of the large ranches had thrown a going-away party for his son who was leaving for Afghanistan, and it had run late into the night. A truck loaded with workers from the ranch had come out of Cold Springs Road headed his way. The people on the truck saw the car on its side with the lights on, and they stopped to investigate and called 911.

"There has been a wreck out here on Highway 84 just before Norris. We are close to Cold Springs Road. There is a woman here, and she is hurt pretty bad. We think she is alive. The car looks like it has bullet holes in it!"

"Did you say it has bullet holes?"

"It looks like bullet holes. It is a late-model Ford and says Police Interceptor on the back. It has Montana government license plates."

The 911 operator dispatched the EMS people, and a deputy headed to the scene. The 911 operator called the sheriff at home.

"Who in the hell is calling now?" he said out loud as he picked up. "Sheriff Steinbrenner," he answered.

"Sorry to bother you, Sheriff, but we have something going on just past Norris on Highway 84. There is a wreck and a person injured. The people say the car has been shot up, and it's a woman driver in a Ford Police Interceptor with Montana government plates."

"I'm on my way to the scene. Call Units 2 and 8 and have them meet me there. Code ten thirty-two!"

That has to be Teresa Walker, he thought.

The dispatcher called Russ, and he knew at once it was Teresa Walker. "How could we have let this happen? I'll just be a son of a bitch."

He grabbed his .45 and sped to the location. The EMS ambulance was arriving as he pulled up, and they had to work to get Teresa out of the car. Blood was everywhere. The EMS team was very efficient and had her in the big emergency truck and headed toward Bozeman in what looked like record time.

The emergency center in Ennis was not capable of handling this type of trauma. Barry said, "I'm sending Unit 2 as escort to provide security, and I will call Bozeman and ask Gallatin County to have some extra security from them there. If you feel you are not too tired, I want you to go, and if she comes to, see if you can get any information."

They quickly asked the people who had been riding in the truck what they saw, and they told them they saw a car but none could be sure what kind it was. It was dark and they had not been expecting anything like this.

Russ said, "It was a new gray Chevy Malibu! I'll bet my pension on it!"

Barry said, "I'll call Bruce as soon as I get back to the office."

Why he said it, he wasn't sure, but Russ said, "Barry, why don't we wait and talk about that? Other than you and me and Miriam, no one knew she was here but Bruce. It's possible she was followed down here tonight, I guess. Otherwise, how did the shooter know she was here?"

They both stood stunned for a moment, and then Russ was gone in the Dodge with blue light and sirens. He knew one thing: Donny Bragg had to be stopped. He and whoever he was working for. If this had not been personal, it was now!

"Madison Unit 8 to Madison Unit 1," Russ called into his radio.

"Madison Unit 1, go ahead."

"Can we get a *BOLO and advise* on the Malibu? The license number is with the paperwork statement at the office."

"Done! Madison 1 out."

There wasn't much that Russ wanted in life, but one thing he did want: he wanted to come face-to-face with Donny Bragg and have his faithful Beretta when he did! He still had a promise to keep, and now the stakes were even higher. There was one thing for sure: Donny Bragg was a killer, and he would not hesitate to kill again.

Donny Bragg had left Teresa earlier that evening at the motel and gone to make some calls and had still been in the Bozeman area. He was thinking about going back to the Hilton Garden Inn and maybe spending the night with Teresa when he received a call. Not the usual call but an urgent order.

"Teresa Walker is in Virginia City at the Madison County Sheriff's Office and may be spilling her guts. You need to get down there and shut her up." Now, how the caller knew that, Donny did not know.

But Donny Bragg was going places, and he wasn't going to ask any questions. He headed to Virginia City in his newly acquired wheels and license plate to carry out orders. He would not be spending the night with Tess tonight or any other night again. It was his job to make sure of that. Too bad. He had enjoyed their fling. She might have been fun to hang out with in some island paradise for a while, but he would never know now. Neither would she!

After carrying out his orders, Donny swung the Malibu north on 288 and hit I-90 and went west to Butte as fast as the Malibu would go. He would have like to had a chance to check on Teresa at the wreck scene, but he felt pretty good he had done what he came to do. By the time the BOLO was being put out, he was pulling inside the old warehouse turned luxury apartments, and the roll-up garage door was closing behind him.

He had made a call on the way and left a message: "Situation handled." Donny did not think there could be any mistake that Teresa Walker was dead. The MP5 pumps out twelve to fifteen rounds per second, and Teresa had gotten a hail of bullets directed at her. He had put his Ford F-150 in a barn in a remote area near Radersburg, Montana, for now and the Malibu might have to go there once the heat went away. The remote ranch was owned by the people he worked for, and they had it in a shell corporation, so it was not easily connected to them. Radersburg is a community of sixty-six people and plenty of remote places to hide.

Donny needed a stiff drink and a shower. Hector was in his room with the TV blaring, and he was sound asleep. By the time the 7:00 AM news came on, there were several brief news items about the wreck on Highway 84 near Norris and that a State DCI agent had been the target of an assassination attempt. The agent was clinging to life, according to the report, in the Bozeman Deaconess

Hospital. Deaconess hospital is a level 3 trauma center and handles all the emergency cases in the Bozeman area. Hector sat up in the bed and listened to the news, and he knew who had done this. It was the charming guy asleep in the other bedroom, Donny Bragg.

Hector also knew that it was probably Donny that killed Kile Davison in Missoula. He had never met Kile Davidson, but Donny had used that name for a long time as an alias, and he knew that Donny had some sort of deal with the guy to cover for Donny if anyone showed up looking for a Kile Davidson. It would be a case of an identity theft, and the real Kile would act really upset and distraught about it.

The announcer was saying, "A State of Montana Division of Criminal Investigation agent, a Ms. Teresa Walker, was seriously wounded when someone opened fire on her car near Norris last night. Details are sketchy at this time, but it is reported that the car had numerous bullet holes and the agent was struck several times and is clinging to life at Deaconess Hospital in Bozeman.

"This has all the earmarks of a professional hit, and a full-scale investigation has been launched. More details at 6:00 PM."

Hector started to wake up Donny and ask him about it, but decided he needed to think hard about his next move. Hector could see that Donny was cleaning up the trail that led to himself, and Hector just might be next. In fact, there was a high likelihood he would. After all, he was the only witness to the murder of Warren Cason! Laredo and the border were looking very good right now!

Hector had some serious decisions to make, and quick!

Nancy saw the news and immediately knew this involved Russ. It was none of her business, but she was interested in the case, and the shooting was the talk of the town. A big city hit was attempted in Madison County Montana, population, 7,700. They were in the middle of a crime wave with murders and gangland shootings.

Russ had spent most of the night in the corridor outside the surgical unit as the doctors and nurses of Deaconess worked to save the badly injured Teresa Walker. It took a phone call to Barry who woke up the Gallatin County sheriff to get an okay for Russ to be there and carrying his Beretta. After nearly five hours of surgery, it was wait-and-see. Russ couldn't help but feel sorry for Teresa even though she had gotten mixed up with a bad crowd on her own. She had drawn the line on murder, and her conscience had pushed her to bring them the fingerprint evidence.

They moved her to recovery, and there were no visitors. Her mother and father had come in, but Russ only spoke to them briefly. Deputy Dunkin had gone to a local motel to get some sleep and later came to relieve Russ.

Russ was dead on his feet but wanted some quick breakfast, and McDonald's seemed a good place to run in and grab a sausage and biscuit and a coffee. Like everything else in Bozeman, you look on Main Street, and there it is. He picked up a newspaper and Teresa Walker's picture was all over the front page. How did Donny Bragg know she was at Madison County Courthouse? Did he follow her there? Or did he get tipped off? Who could have tipped off Donny Bragg? It had to be someone in Bruce Obermeyer's office. But wasn't he most likely home when

Barry called him? Russ was having a hard time processing the questions he was asking himself. The biggest one: was Bruce Obermeyer behind all of the illegal drug trafficking and the hit on Teresa Walker?

The body count was up to two in this case, and it could be three if Teresa did not make it. And they weren't done yet.

By the end of the day, it looked like Teresa had passed the most critical stage and was stabilized. Barry had gotten a commitment from Gallatin County to help provide around-the-clock protection for her and told Russ to take a day to catch up on his sleep and promised to call if anything turned up on the BOLO.

By most any measurement, Teresa Walker should have been dead. She'd had a rough meeting at the Madison County Sheriff's Office and was only a few hours away from an end to her career and maybe jail. It would have been very easy to have been distracted. What had surprised her was that Russell Baker and the sheriff had seemed willing to help her get a reduced sentence rather than throwing the book at her. She knew they could have booked her that night.

But with the new revelations about Donny and realizing that he had probably killed Warren Cason and Kile Davidson in the past few days, she knew she was in grave danger too if he found out she was now cooperating with the locals against him.

So when the car suddenly appeared behind her from the camping area, she went into a full-alert mode. As it came alongside, she had recognized the Malibu and the dark color as being like the one Donny was driving earlier that evening.

The window was down, and she could see the gun and Donny, and she leaned over in the seat and jerked the wheel to the right on the Taurus just a Donny opened fire. Some of the rounds hit her in the shoulder and upper chest, and one cut a gash in the back of her skull. The pain was beyond description, and then another round hit her in the leg and one in the buttock. Then the car hit the guard rail, and that may have well saved her life because the car careened off the rail and shot back across to the left, almost hitting Donny Bragg's Malibu. He had to slam the brakes as the car came across in front of him.

The Taurus continued across the road, the shallow ditch, and rolled over on its side in the open field. Donny was coming over to finish the job and make sure she was dead when the truckload of farmworkers came up on the scene, and he fled.

The Silver Bow County sheriff, where Butte is located, was trying to find where Donny was holding up. They would meet tomorrow and see what they came up with and Bruce Obermeyer would be there to lend assistance.

Donny had gotten all his personal belongings and loaded them in an old Jeep Cherokee. He had told Hector to do the same, and they scrubbed the apartment in Butte down from one end to the other. Checking and double checking to be sure there was no trace of them there.

Donny needed Hector's help for now. He had feigned surprise and shocked when the news hit about Teresa Walker. His main surprise was that she was still alive and had not died at the scene. Another of Donny's recent screw-ups. He would have to decide how to handle that. But he said to Hector that she must have been on the trail of some real bad criminals to have this happen. That was certainly true, apparently.

Using the two old vehicles, they went separate routes to an old ranch out near Radersburg that was used as a hunting camp by some bigwigs somewhere and was vacant right now. People also came up to that area to fish in the big lake nearby. The ranch house was far off the road and plenty nice enough and the power was on all the time. There was a small grass landing strip, and Donny was going to make arrangements for someone to pick them up and get them far, far away from there.

They could hide their vehicles in the barn with Donny's black Ford. There were several outbuildings that did not contain a lot of farm equipment any longer with room enough to hide most anything in, and at some point, the vehicles would be completely disposed of. Casualties of war. Hector wasn't sure if it was to be Canada or Mexico or just where they might be going. His concern now was if he would be alive to see it happen.

He knew that he posed a real danger to Donny, especially as the Madison County murder investigation kept creeping closer and closer to their door. The next morning, Donny was dressed early and told Hector to hang close to the ranch and keep an eye out. He said he would be gone for probably two nights, and he would be setting up the arrangements for someone to come to the ranch and picking them up in a plane to get them out of the area and the country. He had to meet up with some people and pick up some cash for their departure. There was food, beer, TV, and video games, thanks to the owners of the hunting camp who were so nice to donate its use. A person could stay here a long while with the current stock of provisions.

Hector watched as the Jeep disappeared down the long driveway. He was a long way from anywhere, and limited phone service was available. He picked up the house phone, and it seemed to be working.

Hector had been a utility man for Donny. Running errands, buying food, watching Donny's back, and whatever else Donny had wanted. Donny usually had some temporary help like Helen Potts and Jeffery Bristol. But they had never been so close to having the law come down on them, and Donny seemed pretty calm about it all. Hector could not prove that Donny murdered Kile Davidson, but he would bet money on it. He felt the same with the shooting of Teresa Walker. Who in their right mind would try to assassinate a state cop, especially one you have been sleeping with? But that said volumes about the kind of person Donny Bragg was.

Hector knew a lot more about their relationship than he had let on and had followed Donny on occasion to the Hampton Inn. Hector had no illusions about the likelihood that he could be next. The Feds and the DEA and the locals really had nothing on him, as far as he knew. If they stopped him, they would just have to let him go. He had a clean record. But he was the only witness to the murder of Warren Cason, and that was what would likely get him killed.

21

A S THE DAY STARTED GROWING to a close, Hector had
nosed around in Donny's room and found a few things
that interested him. There was a pad by the house phone in
the room Donny was using. When Hector ventured a look,
he saw some names and some phone numbers. Some of the
names had dollar amounts by them. He had never seen this
note pad before. Some of it looked to be in a code system
that would only be understood by Donny. There were some
receipts like you get when you buy gas, and he noticed
one from down near Missoula with a recent date. It was
probably from when Donny went down to burn down Kile
Davidson's house. It appeared to Hector that Donny was a
little careless in leaving the stuff lying around.

The more he thought about the situation, the more
Hector was getting afraid for his own safety. Not from the
cops, but from Donny. At about 7:30 PM after eating a
sandwich, he made a decision: he had to get out of there!
Would he go back to Laredo or some other place? He wasn't
sure, but he was sure that his only chance of surviving this
was to get away. Now!

As he thought about where to go, he knew that if he
bailed on Donny, Donny would not stop until he found him
because of what he knew about the murder of the fishing

guide. Or the state and Federal authorities and, he guessed, that local sheriff in Madison would track him until they got him. He was being squeezed. He was at that "between and rock and a hard place" stage.

Maybe the state or Federal people would cut him a deal. If he gave them Donny, they should let him off with a slap on the wrist. The cop from Madison County was dogging his trail and did not seem like the kind that would give up on a case. Maybe if he could help them, they could find the big guy in the whole thing and that would make some people very happy. That cop from Madison might be the place to start. Hector did not trust the other agencies.

He felt there was a well-placed person in one of them that could prove to be a serious enemy, and his plan could blow up in his face if he was blabbing to the very guy in charge of the drug business. Spilling the beans to the wrong person would be disastrous.

Hector copied down some of the phone numbers and a name or two that he did not recognize and put them in his bag. He took some pictures of some materials he saw, and he looked at the hunting magazines on the coffee table in the big den. Most were obviously from someone's home or office that they received on subscription, but most had the address labels torn off. But there was one with the label still intact, so he tore it off like the others and put the address label in the bag he was gathering up. It might come in handy. The name did not mean anything to Hector.

Hector Martinez was leaving, and his plan was to never come back. Not to anywhere close to Donny Bragg. He got in his old Chevrolet truck that he was now driving to avoid being seen and headed over to Highway 287 and turned south toward I-90. He got something at a drive-through and continued on south on 287. He pulled over at a pull-out and looked until he found Russ's card with his cell phone. He entered the number. It was about 11:00 PM, and Russ had gotten some rest and Miriam had stopped by for a while. She had just left for home when his phone rang.

"This is Russell Baker."

"This is Hector Martinez. I need to talk to you."

"I'm listening, Hector," said the startled Russ.

"If I come in and turn myself in, can I get a deal?"

"That's not something I can do, Hector. The various jurisdictions—local, state, and federal—would all have to agree depending on the crime. And it would depend on how much they are going to get for that deal in return. I can try and see what we can do."

"Can we meet some place? Not at a courthouse or anything. Just you and me? And then I decide if I want to turn myself in or not."

"Hector, there is a warrant out for your arrest, and I have to arrest you if I see you. I guess you've seen what happened to Kile Davidson and Teresa Walker and you figure you may be next, Is that it?"

"Something like that."

"Where is Donald Bragg now?"

"I don't know where he is. He left and said he would be gone a couple of days and then we would leave the area by plane when he gets back in a couple of days."

"Where are you now, Hector?"

"I won't tell you that until I can get some type of deal. I did not kill that fishing guy. I don't know how we got mixed up with him, but that was Donny's crazy scheme to lay low after the drugs came in."

261

"Hector, I'll call the sheriff and see what he says. He is a straight shooter, I can say that. What number do I reach you on?"

"I'll call you back in an hour." Hector disconnected.

Barry answered, "Is this the way it's going to be from now on…you calling and waking me up every damn night?"

"I thought you would want to know that Hector Martinez wants to turn himself in, and in return he wants a deal."

"You've got to be shittin' me! He called you?"

"Yes. I just got off the phone with him. He says he did not kill Warren Cason."

"What did you tell him?"

"I told him that I wasn't the person who could give him a deal. Any deal would be up to you and various state and Federal folks. But I can tell you he is more afraid of Donny than any of us!"

"I don't blame him for that. I can probably get the murder 1 charge reduced if he testifies against Bragg since that happened in our county, and we can determine that Hector was not the trigger man. As far as any state and federal charges I don't know. I could call Bruce in the morning and see what he says."

"Barry, let's not call him until we get this guy and see what he has to give us. There is a rat in that office somewhere."

"And you think it's Bruce, don't you?"

"Who else could have tipped off Bragg and ordered a hit on Teresa?"

"I hate to say it, but I think you may be right. Proving it, that's another story. It will be one of my life's biggest disappointments if it is true."

262

"I'm supposed to get a call back from Hector in a few minutes, and I'll let you know what happens."

Hector had to try several times to get Russ due to cell phone coverage, but when they finally talked, Hector was unhappy that he was not promised more.

Russ asked him, "Do you know who Donny reports to?"

"No, but I think it's someone in the state government."

"Would that someone be Teresa Walker, Hector?"

"Naw. He got information from her and lots of sex, but he did not rely on her. He was always talking to someone privately and never in front of me or anyone. I got the impression the person he talked to could control just about anything that went on. But Teresa was not the person. I think she was more of a decoy."

"Okay, Hector, what are we going to do? We can probably do something about the murder 1 charge. We can't make any promises for the state or the Feds, but Sheriff Steinbrenner will put a word in for your cooperation. Otherwise, I guess you run until someone tracks you down and puts a 9 MM to the back of your head like they did Warren Cason."

Hector could see that in his head now. "Where can I meet you?"

"Come to the courthouse in Virginia City. I'll go over there and can be there in about an hour, and I'll ask Barry to meet us and we will take your statement. By the way, is Donny Bragg driving the Malibu now?"

"When I last saw him, he was driving an older model Jeep Cherokee. A white one, and it runs a little loud."

Russ had one small light on in the cabin and had to get dressed to go to the office. He gathered up his briefcase and hung his service weapon and gun belt over his shoulder. The fifteen-shot Beretta 9 mm. As he was about to open the door, he thought he heard rumble of a car motor idling. It was now almost 1:00 AM. That was strange to hear at this time of night, and he became very curious. There was no window on the side of the cabin, and his only view out was the front window. He stepped cautiously to the window and took a peek out around the blind but could see nothing but his Tahoe parked outside the door on the right as he would exit and the Dodge cruiser on the left. He did not know why he was so tense about the car engine running. Maybe having a killer on the loose was enough to make you jittery. He opened the door a small crack to see what was going on with the car motor. Just by instinct, he took the Beretta from the holster, and he was now on high alert.

Something was not right! Russ did not see anything until he was stepping out, and that's when he saw the older white Jeep Cherokee, one just like Hector had just described to him on the phone, backed in on the end of his cabin so that the driver had a clear view of Russ's front door! Russ saw a slight movement, and he immediately recognized that the person in the vehicle had the door open and was raising a weapon up toward him! Acting on reflex, he tossed the briefcase out between his Tahoe and the Dodge police car and dived in between the cars just as the H&K MP5 started spitting out 9 mm rounds at eight hundred rounds per minute.

Russ hit the asphalt parking lot hard and with so much force that when his left elbow hit the hard surface, the pain was numbing. The bullets were striking the Tahoe and also ricocheting off the asphalt under the Tahoe and then going up through the floor of the car and out the passenger side. Tires were exploding, glass breaking, and bullets flying! Russ was half rolling and half crawling to the rear of the truck. It seemed like an eternity, but it was really only a few seconds until he had rolled to the rear of the Tahoe and was where he could see the Jeep and the shooter. Without stopping, he fired several rounds from underneath the Tahoe toward the shooter. Russ had practiced these types of scenarios in simulated situations many times, but this was not a simulation! The bullets hitting his car and the asphalt were real this time, and so were the rounds coming from the Beretta! The bullets hit the door and window where the shooter was, and he recoiled into the car. Whether he fell back into the car or jumped, Russ did not know. Russ only had a clear shot for a couple of seconds. The shooter immediately had the car moving, and it lurched out and started turning toward the street. Russ came up to a shooting position and emptied the magazine at the driver of the fleeing car. He had fired fifteen rounds and the shooter had fired dozens at him. Fortunately, the Tahoe had taken the bulk of the hits. Now, instinctively, Russ released the magazine from the Beretta and was scrambling to get another inserted while at the same time getting in to the Dodge, getting it started, and moving to pursue the Jeep and calling in on his radio for assistance! A lot going on at one time. Russ was running on pure adrenaline and training. Not to mention being angry and frightened!

The Jeep Cherokee was speeding away on the little access road that led to Highway 287 and was headed north. Russ was getting the faster Dodge fired up and would chase the Cherokee to kingdom come, if necessary!

Russell Baker had never fired his weapon at a person before. He had shot up a lot of simulated people in the training programs he had attended and was consistently in the top four or five in the county's competitive shooting among fellow officers. But tonight, that training had helped him to react in a deadly contest of survival. A split second later in getting behind the Tahoe and Russ would have been lying dead in the front of his cabin! He could thank Hector for the heads-up on the white Jeep a few minutes before. He would put that in his recommendation for sentencing if he made it that far. Now he was trying to pursue his attacker!

It was a miracle he was alive! Russ turned on lights and sirens and spun the police car around and was heading out and started calling on his radio: "Madison Unit 8 to Madison SO! Shots fired! Shots Fired! I am in pursuit of a white Jeep Cherokee headed northbound in the city of Ennis! Code ten thirty-two! Ten seventy-eight! Ten seventy-eight! Officer needs assistance! Officer needs assistance!

"Suspect is armed with automatic weapon! Repeat! The suspect is armed with an automatic weapon. White male. Approach with caution!"

The radio operator did not ask any questions. She went to work immediately to try and get Russ some back up. She pushed a seldom-used all-units-alert button, which sent a tone to any sheriff's office radio and to their beepers and then she started barking out the information like she did it every day!

"Unit 8, what is your location?"

"Getting on Bauer Lane at the trailer place on access road south of town. Headed north in pursuit! Copy that?" yelled Russ in the mic.

"Copy that, Unit 8!" she replied. "Madison SO to all units! Madison SO to all units! Be advised that Unit 8 is at the trailer shop on south side of Ennis and heading north on Bauer Lane into downtown Ennis in pursuit of white

Jeep Cherokee. White male armed with automatic weapon! Shots fired!

About quarter mile from the motel, Bauer Lane makes a sharp bend to the right, becomes east Main Street, and intersects with US 287. As Russ was making the bend in the road, he saw it. His chase had not lasted long. The Jeep Cherokee had made the bend in the road but then veered off the road to the left. It went across the open field that was beside the road and flipped on its top in front of a large outdoor sign. It was a strange sight under the lights of the sign. The wheels were spinning, the engine was still running, and dust filled the air. Russ slid to a stop.

"Unit 8 to Madison SO! Be advised that the suspect vehicle has overturned at the intersection of Bauer and East Main! I am ten twenty-three that location! Code ten fifty and ten fifty-two!"

Barry had been en route to meet Russ and Hector at the courthouse and had gone into emergency mode when the call came in. Unit 2, Deputy Dunkin, had been getting a cup of coffee nearby when he started toward the location. Miriam's beeper had never gone off before, and she did not respond to crime scenes but was listening and holding her breath!

Barry came sliding to a stop, and Deputy Dunkin, coming from the opposite direction stopped on the other side of the sign and blocked the road with his car. Barry came to Russ's car with a shotgun and his large flashlight. He looked like a formidable force and was all business.

"What's going on Russ? Who the hell is this guy and who has he been shooting at?"

"I believe it may be Donald Bragg. The car matches what Hector told me he was driving, but he did not give me a license number. He was trying to kill me, but he only managed to kill my Tahoe."

"Is he still in the car or has he fled on foot?" Barry asked.

"He hasn't exited since I arrived on scene. I believe he is in the car. I don't believe he had time to get out before I got here. I fired multiple rounds at him but am not sure if I hit him," replied Russ.

Barry spoke into his shoulder mic. Now two other cars and a state trooper were on the scene and all heavily armed. "We are going to approach the vehicle and try to get the guy to come out. Be ready. He has an automatic weapon. If he makes any hostile move, shoot the son of a bitch." Russ had no doubt that Barry would do just that, and he knew he would too. With Deputy Wayne Dunkin on the other side, Donny Bragg had just reached the end of the road. In more ways than one.

As they approached, the sheriff called to the car, "Donald Bragg, show your hands and be advised there are five armed officers here. Do not try anything." There was no response. After calling twice more, the sheriff said, "Russ, I am going up to the car and try to look in. Back me up."

"I'll be right beside you, Barry. I'm not letting you go up to that car alone." By now, the engine had stopped on the Jeep, and there was no sound. There was a strange silence. Barry went toward the front of the vehicle and Russ from the back. They shined their lights into the vehicle and could see who they thought was Donny Bragg lying against to driver's door window, not moving. Donny Bragg was covered in blood and dead, it appeared to them.

The ambulance team arrived and extracted the dead man from the Jeep, and a quick look showed a massive amount of blood in the car and on the victim. There were several bullet holes in the driver's side where Russ's 9 mm had made contact. It was highly certain that the medical examiner would find multiple wounds that led to the driver's losing control and crashing the car. The EMTs said that the man was dead, as far as they could see.

The Madison Valley Medical Center is a ten-bed facility that is staffed 24-7 with one medical provider and is there to help stabilize a trauma patient and to offer nonsurgical assistance for emergency patients and to prepare them for transport to Bozeman if they need major medical care like surgery or intensive care. Since Donny was dead by all appearances, there was no urgency to get him to Bozeman.

22

BARRY AND RUSS MADE A quick decision: delay, for as long as possible, disclosing anything about the incident and the death of, whom they believed to be, Donny Bragg as there was no ID they could find on the dead man. Hector Martinez was already on the way to the courthouse, if he wasn't there already, to possibly give them a statement about the drug operation, Donny Bragg, the shooting of Teresa Walker, the mysterious death of Kile Davidson, and, they hoped, information that would lead them to the head of the organization and the conclusion of the murder investigation of Warren Cason. He was coming to them because he feared that his life was in danger from Bragg. If he found out Bragg was dead, he might feel secure enough to just try to disappear.

They made the decision that the body would be held as a John Doe at the Ennis Emergency Care facility and Russ and Barry would get to Virginia City as soon as possible to meet with Hector. Deputy Wayne Dunkin and the state trooper would start processing the scene at the motel, and Miriam would come join them at the earliest possible time. Another deputy would come and secure the crash scene. The entire Madison County Department was working tonight, and what a helluva night it had been!

"Russ, are you okay? Are you hurt in any way?" asked Barry. "Do you need to go get yourself together?"

Russ had never killed anyone and was shaken by the close call. He knew he was within inches of being killed when Bragg opened up on him. Hector's call and telling Russ about the white Jeep Cherokee had probably saved his life. But he felt he could hold it together until they took Hector's statement. He had bashed his hip and elbow on the asphalt, but he would survive those. If they did not get Hector's statement, they might lose it all.

Donald Bragg had left Hector at the ranch to take care of some details. One of those details was Russell Baker, who had caused him to have to start shutting down his operation sooner than he wanted. His boss had always said he could move out of the country at some point, take his money, and live like a king and be an important cog in the wheel in Mexico or Central America. Costa Rica sounded nice, but maybe Columbia or Panama. Russell Baker had mucked up his plans, and Russell Baker was going to pay for that.

After he finished with Russell Baker, he had to make a trip to a place where he had stashed a lot of cash. This would cause him to be driving to Missoula to a little apartment he had there where he had created a hiding place for cash, IDs, and other necessities like burn phones and guns. A lot of driving, so he had allowed time to be back by the time the plane was coming to Radersberg.

Russell Baker needed attending to, and Donny would exact a little revenge on Baker before he flew away to safety out of the country. His boss had the connections to make

271

getting away happen. He did not like having to do away with Kile Davidson, and his boss would have liked to have kept Teresa Walker in the system, but she had started talking to the local cops and she could not be trusted anymore. His boss still had not connected Donny to Warren Cason's murder and would have considered that very messy.

Part of Donny's plan was to get Hector out of the way but he would wait until they were far away from here. Hector was the only witness to Warren Cason's murder. He had to go. A plane would come for him and Hector at the ranch up at Radersburg, where it had landed many times before. The vehicles would be in a giant car crusher in a couple of days, never to be seen again. He would be living large!

Donny Bragg had not counted on the quick reaction that he got from Officer Russell Baker. A proficient and capable policeman, who had training and luck on his side, and who was also handy with a Beretta.

Russell Baker had gotten his wish too: to meet face-to-face with the murderer of Warren Cason with his Beretta in his hand.

Hector Martinez pulled up beside the Madison County courthouse at about 3:00 AM and halfway expected to be swarmed by a dozen cops. But there were two marked sheriff vehicles and the Dodge that he had seen in his yard in Bozeman. Lights were on in the courthouse. He sat in the car for a minute and nervously tried to decide if he was doing the right thing.

Hector had stopped a couple of times and considered turning around on the way to Virginia City. Donny may have been gone forever, leaving him holding the bag.

Russ had gone in and gotten himself a coffee and washed his face, changed his shirt, checked his gun. He had also gotten a secret hug and kiss from Miriam. He was now looking out a dark window as the old Chevrolet truck pulled up. Barry was watching from another window as Hector got out and came in the side door marked Sheriff's Office.

Barry and Russ were standing there and another officer with a Mossberg shotgun.

"Are you Hector Martinez?" asked Barry.

"Yes," answered Hector.

After checking him for weapons, they went into the conference room, and Miriam sat down with a tape recorder and notepads. They got him a drink from the drink machine, and the questions and answers started. Hector told all about the senseless killing and involvement of Warren Cason. Yes, he had put the money under Warren's door. And he had seen Donny shoot the defenseless Warren Cason in the back of the head with a 9 mm. If that were true, and Russ believed it was, Russ had gotten his wish and kept a promise to a dead fishing guide and a distraught, sick mother. Killing Donny Bragg would not cause him any loss of sleep!

Hector said that he was pretty sure that Donny had been involved in Kile Davidson's death and also the shooting of Teresa Walker but that Donny kept those kinds of things from his associates so that they could not testify against him or spill the beans. He could link Donny to all those people, however. He did not know the name of Donny's boss but believed he was high up in law enforcement.

It was clear that Hector Martinez was at the end of his rope and felt his only chance was that Barry and Russ could help him. He did not know that Donny Bragg was never going to bother anyone again. He told about the drug drop and how the plans got switched at the last minute to drop the drugs somewhere else and the fact that Donny had carried the drugs to Butte, he believed.

Did Donny make that decision alone or did his boss make it? Hector wasn't sure, but he believed Donny had fooled everyone including his boss.

Then they got to the planned extraction of Donny and Hector from the remote ranch up near Radersburg in Broadwater County. With only 5,500 people there, it is even smaller than Madison County but only a third as big in area. Better known for fishing than anything else, this was the home of the large Canyon Ferry Lake, and all Hector knew was the plane was coming to pick them up. There was a small but very well-maintained unlighted grass landing strip at the ranch. Hector said he did not know for sure who owned the ranch, but he had picked up some magazines and notepads with names and some phone numbers by Donny's bed. Also, Russ and Barry had found a couple of phones in the car where Donny had wrecked, and they had not yet had time to check them out.

The pickup, if still on, would be two nights from now. As far as Hector knew, Donny Bragg would be returning to the ranch to meet the plane. He had no idea that Donald Bragg was lying dead in a room in Ennis. Hector's bag was brought in, and he emptied out the contents with the notepads, magazine, and the magazine label that Hector had torn off in a hurry when leaving the ranch. They would go through it all over the next day to try and get some

274

idea of who these other people were and develop a plan, but they would keep whatever they learned to themselves during that time.

It was now 5:30 AM and everyone was dead on their feet. It was decided that Hector would be kept in the local jail, such as it was, and no outside agency would be notified. At the present time, he was being kept in protective custody, and no charges had been filed.

Russ, Barry, Wayne Dunkin, and Miriam would try to get some sleep and come back in a few hours and try to formulate a plan after reviewing anything in what Hector had given them.

Teresa Walker had been in intensive care since her shooting and had not been in any condition for an interview. The doctors were now optimistic that she would recover, in time, from her injuries. Maybe by tomorrow, she would be awake enough to talk. She was still being guarded, and her family had not left her since the incident. Her picture had been in the paper several times, and Nancy Freeman recognized her as being at the sheriff's office in Madison County and one of the women she had seen with Russ in town. She had no word from Russ and wondered if he was involved in any of the dangerous events surrounding Teresa.

She continued to be bothered about things concerned with Russ but could not really decide why.

After a few hours of sleep, the Madison County Sheriff's Department was back at it. A lot of coffee was consumed and a lot of questions were asked and reasked, and Hector was there with a deputy standing guard on the door. Miriam was looking at the phones from Donny's car and trying to compare them to numbers and tracing numbers. The numbers from the ranch had proven to be a dead end so far. They were doing a search to try to determine the exact location of the ranch and who owned it. The ranch owners seemed to be a shell company within shell companies, and the principals were obscure. Of course, Hector knew exactly how to get there.

But looking at the label from the hunting magazine that Hector had torn off was a name that jumped out at them—Mr. Bruce Obermeyer, Director, Division of Criminal Investigation—and the office address in Helena! Sometimes in doctor's offices and other businesses, you will see magazines that have been dropped off for clients and patients to read that the owner or another client had brought from home, and they removed their home address so as to keep people from bothering them. This was one that got missed. Did someone else leave it there? Who knew? It seemed to be more than coincidence. They talked more to Hector, and he confirmed that there were numerous hunting and fishing magazines in the ranch house but all had the address labels torn off. All but that one. This was circumstantial. Maybe Bruce had visited the ranch as a hunting guest and left a magazine behind.

Then Miriam came in and asked to speak to them in the sheriff's office. She had found a private number, unlisted, that was on the personal phone from Donny Bragg. It was listed as "BO" on the ID! Teresa walker's number was also on there and had been called many times, as had the "BO" number. Barry looked at his phone, and to his surprise, and dismay, the number he had for Bruce Obermeyer, his longtime friend, and the number in Donny Bragg's phone were the same! Was Bruce the head man for the drug dealers? Did he order the hit on Teresa Walker, his own agent? Was he coming to the ranch to take these criminals to safety? Barry could see the evidence mounting that suggested his longtime friend and buddy was not at all the fine upstanding citizen that he thought. That was a hard pill to swallow.

Bruce reported to the attorney general and would know just about everything going on with law enforcement in the state. He could withhold or alter information. Most of the major crimes investigations in the state went through his office. He could tip off every criminal group on every type of crime in the State. Unbelievable! He was in a position to pass along information both ways that benefited his operation if he was really involved. He was probably informing the criminals and his own people!

"Now, what?" Barry asked Russ. "Who do we call on this? The state attorney general, who would have a hard time believing this? Maybe."

This was far bigger than the agent Teresa Walker! He would call his brother in Missoula for advice.

Barry's brother could not believe his lifetime friend could be involved, but he knew that Bruce lived large and did have a hunting ranch up that way somewhere, although neither Barry nor his brother has ever been invited there. They decided to contact the local field office agent of the FBI in Bozeman, since he was closest, and they arranged an emergency meeting with him. They laid out the story of drugs, murder, conspiracy, high-level involvement, and the planned escape to Mexico or Central America.

Should they approach Bruce and arrest him? Or did they need to try to build a bigger case before making an arrest? The key witness, the one that could drive a nail in the proverbial coffin, was dead. Donald Bragg was the only one on the list that had direct contact with Bruce, and no one was certain who else might be involved, if any, at the higher levels. Teresa Walker did not have direct contact with Bruce, and neither did Hector. They needed to put Bruce in a position to implicate himself; otherwise, he would deny any involvement, and there may be not be enough evidence that could get them a conviction.

Russ said, "If we could get Bruce to follow up on the plan to pick Donny and Hector up at the ranch in Radersburg, we might be able to get him to say something or admit to something on tape. But he has to think that Donny Bragg is still alive. He won't likely come to get only Hector Martinez alone, and I don't believe he will leave the pick up to someone else. We will have to have Hector's help at the ranch in order to handle any communications with Bruce. Hector has to believe that Donny is still alive too and out there and possibly gunning for him to make that work."

23

IT WAS AGREED THAT THEY would assemble a team to be at Radersburg with the hope that they could get Bruce to show up and maybe get a stronger case. It was another long shot. A plan was developed along with the Broadwater Sheriff's Office to meet at the ranch. Hector would have to lead them back there and would have to play a role in getting the pickup plane to land for the pickup. No doubt the person or persons coming would be very careful. Hopefully, that would be Bruce Obermeyer.

There would be a contingent of law enforcement officers there if and when the plane showed up, and Russ would have Donny's phone if a call came in. Hopefully, it would be a text and no secret passwords would be needed. They would hide their cars in the barns and other equipment sheds. Then they would wait and see.

No doubt the arriving plane would fly over to make sure things looked right before landing. Arriving early in the day, the law officers were in place, and they had now to stay out of sight until the plane arrived, if it did arrive.

Then who would be on it? Did Bruce, if it was Bruce, trust anyone else to do this job? They needed to put a wireless mic on Hector and hope that they could get whoever was on the plane to say something that could be used in evidence before they entered the house where everyone would be waiting. It put Hector on center stage in this act.

Could they get Bruce, if it was Bruce, to admit he was involved? But how? This was a game of bluff. They would really be fishing and trolling deep. Hector would be the key to getting them in the house. He would have to play his part well, and he looked like he was willing to do everything to get off the hook for his participation in the drug ring and get a deal. Hector usually carried a gun tucked in the small of his back in the waistband of his pants and covered by his Western-style shirt that he never tucked in. Now, his gun was in a safe at the Madison County Sheriff's Office, and under the Western-style shirt was a very high-tech microphone/transmitter. It would be hearing everything that Hector and the person getting off the plane said and sending it inside. The hidden microphone could transmit up to one kilometer, and the battery would last for twenty-five hours. The signal would be picked up by a high-tech digital recorder inside and receivers that the officers would be listening to.

An FBI tactical squad of heavily armed men was in the house and barn, if needed. They needed to get some incriminating evidence on the people coming in, and especially if it was Bruce Obermeyer, in order to get a case to stick against him because the person who could directly link him to the enterprise was lying dead in Ennis and listed as "John Doe." Everything else they had was circumstantial. They believed the plane would have to come in before dark to use the grass strip with no lights. Not many people would land on a grass strip in the dark, no matter how good they were.

Then they all realized something: there was no cell phone coverage at the ranch! If there came a call, it would have to be on the house phone. Hector would have to answer and make some plausible excuse as to why Donny was out of the house if that phone rang. Whoever was on the plane probably knew about the phone service, especially if it was Bruce, and was likely prepared. Possibly a satellite phone or maybe his cell would work at altitude coming in.

As expected, about four o'clock, the house phone rang and a well-rehearsed, but very nervous Hector answered and the voice asked, "Who is this?"

"This is Hector Martinez."

"Where is Donny?"

Hector had been given an answer to give the caller should that be asked. "He went to be sure everything was out of his truck and the cars and he will be back from the barn in a few minutes. Do you want me to go find him?"

"Tell him I will be landing there in ten minutes. Be ready!"

The Cessna TT came into view and made its approach to the grass strip, which was in very good shape. The tricycle gear was tested on the bumpy ground, but the pilot seemed to know his stuff. The single-engine plane had a long range for a plane of this size and was perfect for what they had in mind: an illegal border crossing some hours later to drop off two passengers in Mexico about 1,100 miles away. The plane came to a stop, and Hector was standing by the grass at his old truck. He had practiced his lines over and over, but he was very nervous. If he spooked this guy, he could blow the whole deal and maybe get killed in the process. And he did not know who was on that plane and he was not sure where Donny was, but he might show up in the middle of this operation and everything would blow up in their face.

Where in the world was Donny? he wondered. Of course, Donny wasn't going to show up anywhere!

Bruce Obermeyer did not leave much to chance. When he had assembled his team to work in the Bozeman and Billings area, he picked people with no criminal records and with little information available about them. Most did not know each other, so Bruce had used a simple and safe method to make sure they recognized each other when they were meeting for the first time: he sent photos to each of them by mail of the other team members. There was nothing in writing except the name of the person on the back of the photos. He had no trouble recognizing Hector Martinez when he pulled the Cessna to a stop. He did not see Donny Bragg.

Hector was still expecting Donny to show up any minute and wondered why he had not already. He did not know Donny was dead and the lawmen had gone to great lengths to make sure he did not know that until this event was over. They also hoped that they had been successful in keeping the information from getting to Bruce Obermeyer, and so far, that had been accomplished, thanks to the quick thinking in Ennis at the wreck site. No news leaks as yet.

Bruce Obermeyer got out of the plane. "Where is Donny?"

Hector had his lines ready:

"He is in the house. He did not want me to tell you on the phone, but he is injured. He got shot by that cop in Madison County last night. He is wounded but not too bad, but you may have to help me get him in the plane."

Hector thought that this was an entirely made-up story. One made up story by Russ and Barry just to tell Bruce. He did not know that Donny had actually tried to kill Russ. And he did not know that Russ had killed him.

"What the hell are you talking about? He got into a shootout with a cop? What cop? The one from Georgia?"

"Yes, I think that's the one. He was trying to bring Donny in for questioning regarding the murder of that fishing guide."

"Hell. What the fuck is that about? Donny didn't have anything to do with that, did he? I pay Bragg good money to move drugs and not get into shootouts with cops and not to kill fly-fishermen! If he has fucked up my operation, he'll wish he was dead!" Bruce was furious.

"If he's involved in that stupid deal, I may shoot him myself! I'm not letting anybody screw up my business! I've got millions riding on all this! I'll shoot him and leave his sorry ass here!" Bruce was yelling and about to come unglued, he was so angry.

"Donny Bragg has made a fortune working for me by following orders and not attracting attention!" Bruce Obermeyer was storming toward the house.

They got to the house and stepped inside the room that had been darkened by closing the blinds and drapes. As soon as he stepped inside, he asked, "Where is Bragg?"

Instead of a response from Hector, Bruce Obermeyer was greeted by "Hello, Bruce. We've been expecting you."

It was Barry Steinbrenner, sheriff of Madison County, Montana and boyhood friend of Bruce Obermeyer. Along with Barry there were a number of familiar faces, all were heavily armed, including two lifelong friends, the FBI, the local sheriff, and an ex-cop from Marietta, Georgia.

They had him on tape about the drugs and his reason for being there, but they needed more than what they had to have a solid case. Sheriff Barry Steinbrenner, gun in hand, said, "And, by the way, you sound real good on tape. Thanks for speaking so clearly. Donny Bragg will not be joining us. We are holding him down in Madison County. He tried to kill Officer Baker, and he wrecked his car in Ennis trying to escape."

Of course, that was all true.

"We spent a lot of time with him the last couple of days, and we have also enjoyed talking to Hector. We really had a hard time believing that it would be you coming to pick him up."

Bruce still did not know that Donny was dead, and Barry did not say that Donny was dead.

"And we have already gotten a lot of information from Teresa Walker. Based upon the information we have, we are arresting you on drug and conspiracy charges, and the FBI is here to take you into custody."

Barry then read him his rights, and the FBI agent asked him if he understood his rights. "Hell, yes!" he screamed back.

"We think we have a pretty good picture based on everything we learned from Donny and Hector. We have you and your people tied to the murder of one Warren Cason, a major drug drop done in Madison County from an airplane and delivered to Butte, the murder of Kile Davidson in Missoula County, the attempted murder of your own agent, Teresa Walker, and the attempted murder of Officer Baker of the Madison County Sheriff's Department. How about you tell me why you got involved in all this."

Bruce Obermeyer slumped down in a chair, put his head in his hands. His attitude of defiance and anger were gone.

"It was money, Barry, lots and lots of money. It started out small favors and then became a big job. Bigger than you can imagine. But a few more months, and I would be sailing off into the sunset with enough money for the rest of my life. And here I am, at the mercy of three nobodies who will tell you everything to get a lighter sentence."

"No remorse for betraying all your friends and the people of Montana, Bruce?" quizzed Barry.

"A little, I guess. But it would pass pretty quickly." Obermeyer gave them a full preliminary statement of his involvement then and there. It was all on tape, and they could scarcely believe their ears.

The self-confident and powerful state official was now unloading in a manner they never expected. He knew they had him on tape and lots of testimony from his accomplices against him. He told them that he had allowed Donny to approach Teresa Walker because he knew she had a thing for Donny and she would be useful as a "throwaway" in case things got hot. Her involvement was mostly cosmetic and it helped keep Donny occupied in his down time. His plan would let Teresa take the fall for leaking information to the drug dealers when in fact it was him actually doing it. He denied any knowledge of the murder of Warren Cason or the attempt on Russ Baker but did admit to having Donny Bragg try to kill Teresa for cooperating with the locals. Russ, and the Steinbrenner brothers, could not believe how calmly the director of Montana DCI gave out the information they needed.

What did he want in return? He wanted a deal to give them details on his connections in Mexico, Columbia, and Costa Rica. They said that that would have to be done by the US Attorney's Office, and no promises were made. He was arrested by the FBI on conspiracy charges, and more would be coming from the state's attorney and local law agencies. His life as a big-time law officer had just changed to big-time criminal.

"One thing, Barry, I guess Donny will get away with not having to serve a day in jail for turning me in, right?" Bruce asked half sarcastically. After everything he had told them and admitted to, this seemed to be his biggest regret: Donny Bragg might get off scot-free.

"That's correct, Bruce, Donny will not have to serve a day in jail. He did murder Warren Cason and will not be charged for that either. He is getting off without having to go to trial. Donny Bragg made the mistake of trying to kill Detective Russell Baker in Ennis two days ago, and he was killed by Officer Baker while in the act of trying to carry out that assassination."

"You are a son of a bitch, Barry! You tricked me."

"But as you said over in Missoula, I always was a pain in your ass, Bruce," said Barry.

24

THERE WERE MOUNDS OF PAPERWORK and forms to fill out on the arrests and shootings. The press was having a field day with the biggest crime story in the state in years, and cameras and reporters were everywhere. Headlines ran the gamut of the newspapers' imagination.

BIG CRIME STOPPED BY TINY COUNTY SHERIFF

ONE OF MONTANA'S TOP LAW ENFORCEMENT OFFICERS BEHIND BARS

MURDER OF LOCAL FLY FISHING GUIDE SOLVED BY GEORGIA COP

DRUG DEALER KILLED IN A BLAZING GUN BATTLE WITH MADISON COUNTY OFFICER

WILD WEST SHOOTOUT IN ENNIS

HIT ON DCI AGENT SANCTIONED BY STATE LAW ENFORCEMENT AGENCY HEAD

Russ and Barry were ready for the story to quiet down and to get some rest. They had had several days of no sleep, and it was catching up to them. Russ was the happiest about one thing: he had made a promise to the dead Warren Cason and to Warren's mother. He had fulfilled that promise. He had also managed to avoid scratching the new police cruiser, but his Tahoe was full of bullet holes and was a total loss. There might have to be a new vehicle purchased. He wasn't sure who would pay for that! He wasn't sure if that was covered under his policy! Maybe it was time, anyway, to turn that page of his life as he had started doing most of the others.

Russ knew he would not get any rest at the cabin because reporters were everywhere doing follow-ups. People were outside the courthouse, Barry's house, Miriam's house, and followed them around. Russ needed to get out of town for a few days.

Barry told Russ he could take off a few days and then decide if he wanted to stay on with the sheriff's office or go back to fly-fishing. The fly-fishing was sounding pretty good right now. He had not even thought about staying on with Madison County.

Barry gave Miriam some days off too, as she had been burning the late night oil with reports and evidence cataloging. Her work had been invaluable, and she really had not had any time to regroup following her abrupt divorce, which all happened in the middle of the biggest case they had had since she arrived.

"What are you going to be doing, Russ?" she asked as he was cleaning up in the conference room.

"I was thinking about going to Panama City, Florida, and lie around and do nothing for a few days," he said. "I have always loved it there since spring break days. I can't drink that much beer now, but I did have some fun there.

"My father-in-law would fly us down there or to Saint George Island every so often. Occasionally, we went to Islamorada or the Bahamas for bonefishing. Those were the days!"

"I've never been to Florida," she said. "Could I tag along?"

"Of course," Russ was surprised but replied. "That would be very nice, in fact."

Miriam told Russ she would meet him at the Bozeman Airport for the flight to Florida. Russ stopped in at the hospital in Bozeman on the way to the airport and went in to see Teresa Walker. She was in a private room and was essentially under arrest, but everyone felt she was not a flight risk and she was now on her own recognizance and would be released soon with an ankle bracelet until a hearing was set. Barry and Russ felt she should get a minimum sentence since she had come forward and had been nearly killed as a result. Her career as a law enforcement officer was over.

"Officer Baker, thank you for stopping Donny. I had no idea he was capable of killing so many people, including me. I deserve what I get. I really messed up," Teresa said.

Hector was being held pending a hearing also, and would likely get some serious jail time but with a lot suspended for his cooperation in bringing down Bruce Obermeyer.

Bruce was in jail under several million dollars in bond and faced many years in prison on a variety or federal and state charges.

Russ met Miriam at the Bozeman airport, and they were off to Florida. He wondered how Nancy and Chad were doing. He had not heard from either of them in a while. But Russ figured that Nancy was pretty happy with her new boyfriend and that is the way it goes sometimes.

Nancy Freeman had been very busy lately. Between her clothing store, her shuttle business, and her new social life, there was not much time left. But when all the news hit about Russ, she had called his number to say congratulations and how glad she was he did not get hurt in all of the business with Donald Bragg, but every time she called, it seemed to go to voice mail, and she could not bring herself to leave a message. She and Chad had talked about the events on several occasions, and Russ was now Chad's hero. The news of the shootout, car chase, and apprehension of a big-time Montana official was all over the news. Barry Steinbrenner had given due credit to his department and especially Detective Russell Baker from Georgia.

Nancy was enjoying her time with Dr. Carter but for some reason she wished Russ would call. Dr. Carter was a very nice guy. He would be a great husband for someone and knew all the right things to say and was a refined gentleman in a lot of ways. He came from a background of highbrow cocktail parties, political rallies, and academic lifestyle. A lot different than someone like a Russell Baker: a man with a Sage fly rod in one hand and a Beretta 9 mm in the other. But if Stephen asked Nancy to marry him, she would be very tempted to say yes. It would make perfect sense, except for one thing: when he called or came in the room or kissed her good-night, she did not get chills or have a heart flutter. It was just sort of business like. She had not lost any sleep thinking about Stephen.

But she had gotten angry, pissed off, drunk, and frightened thinking about Russell Baker! Now how in the hell could you explain that? She finally got up the nerve to call the Madison County Sheriff's Office and asked to speak to Russ. "I'm sorry, miss, but Russell Baker is not in. In fact, he is out of state at the moment. I believe."

"Okay," Nancy said. "I'm just a friend of his and I haven't seen him in a while. I was in on some of the investigation of Warren Cason's murder and met the sheriff then. Do you have any idea when he is coming back?"

"Well, we are not actually sure he is coming back. He may not," said the person on the phone.

"He may not be coming back! And he did not say good-bye, Chad!" were the words she used to tell her brother about Russ.

"Nancy, you have been full-time with Stephen Carter, and Russ knows that. He had a rough few weeks and was almost killed, and did you contact him or go to see him or write him a letter? Anything at all?"

"No, Chad, I didn't." she said softly.

"Are you in love with the guy, Nancy?"

"I don't know if I know him well enough to love him."

"Well, his boat is still in storage, and he'll probably come back to deal with that, at least. If you want anything from Russ in the way of attention, you'd better let him know because the signals you have been sending were not very positive."

Nancy called the motel where Russ had been staying. "Can you tell me if Russell Baker is still a guest there? I am an old friend of his."

"Mr. Baker is still registered here, but we have not seen him in a few days."

Russell and Miriam were enjoying the beach, fishing around the bay, and sleeping. They enjoyed each other's company, but it was more like "friend with benefits" than romance. Miriam was getting a nice tan, but more than anything,

Miriam had gotten her self-respect back and, even better maybe, a ton of self-confidence. She was proud that she had not let herself be whipped by her sorry husband's behavior, and she owed a lot to the Madison County sheriff and to a cop named Russell Baker.

While they were in Panama City, Russ received a call from Doris McKenzie in Marietta.

"Russ, Dan had a heart attack at work, and they have discovered he has severe blockages. If all goes well, he will have open-heart surgery Monday at Kennestone Hospital. I would sure like it if you were here. Is that possible?"

"I'll catch the next plane to Atlanta, Doris! I'll let you know when I am arriving."

Russ told Miriam that he was sorry, but he needed to go to Atlanta and cut the trip short. She understood and was about ready to leave anyway. They had been having a wonderful time but would have to get back to reality sometime. She had two daughters in Westminster College in Salt Lake City, and she needed to go see them.

"Russ, you need to go to Atlanta and see about your father-in-law. I am going to get a flight to Salt Lake City and see my kids. We both need to take care of some business."

They made it to the Panama City-Bay County International Airport. She had a ticket to Salt Lake and he had a ticket to Atlanta, but they would fly to Atlanta on the same flight, and she would change planes there. She held Russ's hand the entire flight to Atlanta, and they walked to the concourse gate that Miriam was to fly out of, and she gave Russ a hug and a kiss. They might not see each other for a while.

Dan made it through the surgery just fine and was out of the hospital in a few days and walking around. He would start therapy soon, and Russ had been staying at their house where he and Doris had looked at pictures of Sarah and talked about the good times, and Dan gave Russ his financial statements. Russ was astounded as to how Dan had managed them.

Then Dan announced he was taking his retirement option at Lockheed and that he would be traveling and fishing more, and he hoped that he and Russ could catch up.

"That, you can count on," said Russ. "I am seriously behind in my fishing."

"Russ, we need to talk to you about something. Doris and I consider you our son. I hope that is okay with you. I have done pretty well at Lockheed and very well in investing. Quite frankly, Doris and I are loaded! More than we will ever spend. If I die tomorrow, Doris will be well looked after, and at some point, except for a few charitable gifts, it will all be yours."

Russ was speechless.

25

RUSS WAS GETTING READY FOR bed and had decided that it was time for him to get out of the house and let Doris and Dan have their privacy back, and his phone rang. It was Miriam.

"Russ, I have made a decision about some things, and I wanted to let you know. The people here at the Salt Lake Unified Police Department have offered me a very nice position with great pay, and I can be close to my kids again. I have accepted the job."

Russ felt a big knot in his stomach.

"The hardest part of the decision will be not being there to share our friendship together. But I hope you will not forget me and will come to see me as often as you can. Most of all, don't hate me for doing this. I couldn't stand that. That trip to Florida was a highlight of my life."

Russ was not able to speak for a moment and stood in silence with the phone to his ear. He found himself choking back tears. He had lost Sarah, and now he was losing Miriam whom he had always said was "just a friend."

"Russ, are you okay?"

"I'm okay, Miriam. I could never hate you. I care too much for you, and I want the best for you. I am so proud of what you have become and will cherish our time together.

You are my dearest and closest friend, and what you have done for me is not measurable. I love you and you know it, but I guess we both knew this time would come, I suppose. But you will find someone who appreciates you like I do, and I will dance at your wedding. And kiss the bride, of course!"

Miriam had spent many hours thinking about her relationship with the handsome and younger widower. She loved their time together as well, and being with him made her feel twenty-five again. But she wasn't. She had two kids in college and an ex-husband, and she had become disconnected from her kids by being in Ennis where, for the most part, she had been bored out of her mind. Only her time with Russ and working the Warren Cason case was she truly happy. But she was no longer a sad, downtrodden, and betrayed woman. She was capable of standing on her own feet and making good decisions—decisions that would be best for her and for Russ.

"Thank you, Russ. You don't know how that makes me feel. Now, do one thing for me. Will you promise?"

"What is that, Miriam?"

"Do something about that girl, Nancy, in Bozeman before both of you make a big mistake!"

With that, she was gone. Russ wasn't sure about what to do regarding Nancy, but he did need to get back and close out his room, get a better place to stay, if was going to stay in that area, and see about his drift boat. Maybe he and Barry could go fishing one day.

A few days later, Russ headed for Bozeman. When Russ arrived in Bozeman, he had to see about getting a car to replace his Tahoe, which had been in an impound lot for processing. He decided to rent a car and drive to Ennis.

And then he would then figure out where to stay on a more permanent basis, maybe.

When Russ arrived at his cabin, he stood outside for a moment, remembering a night not too long ago when a man tried to kill him on this very spot. He had come very close to doing it! He went in and was surprised that there was a note from Miriam on the bed and two sets of keys. How they got there with Miriam in Salt Lake was a mystery.

> My Dearest Russ,
>
> Here are the keys that I had been using to the cabin. I don't think you will be staying here anymore, and I won't need them. I just happen to have a paid-for house nearby that you have been to several times, and I am leaving the keys here for you. Why not stay there until you figure out what you want? I am in no hurry to sell it, and you can use it, rent it, or buy it if you want. That way, I can keep an eye on you and know right where to find you as I am retaining visitation rights!
>
> Love, Miriam
> (Former lover, now big sister)

Then it came to Russ: Miriam had left the keys and the note before they left for Florida. She had planned on not coming back when they left.

Russ decided to take Miriam up on her offer until he figured out his next move. She was thrilled when he called her and said he would rent her house. He called Barry. "How would you like to go on a float on the Madison and catch some trout?"

"I wouldn't mind that if there was a guide around worth a crap to take me," said Barry with a laugh."

"I think I know one. Let me see if I can set things up for day after tomorrow."

Russ picked up a new Silverado pickup in Bozeman. Somehow, he could not bring himself to buy a Ram or a Ford right now. He hooked up his still almost-new RO drift boat and pulled it to Miriam's house and parked it where he could see it under a boat shelter that Miriam's husband had used. He liked being able to see it out the window.

Russ was in the kitchen making a sandwich and enjoying being in Miriam's nice house when the doorbell rang.

Who could that be? he thought.

Russ was startled and speechless when he opened the door and there was Nancy looking for all the world like a New York fashion model, not the trout bum way she dressed for a fishing trip or a shuttle. Nancy broke the silence.

"I got a call from a friend of yours in Salt Lake City. She claimed to know you well and said you were out here in this big house, and she thought you were really lonely. She said I'd better get out here and see about you, or she would come back to Bozeman and kick my ass. I'm pretty sure she was serious!

"She said I might need to stay here a while to make sure you are okay. I came prepared to stay overnight if you need me to."

"As a matter of fact, I do need a shuttle day after tomorrow. Do you still do shuttles?" Russ said with a smile.

"Right now, sir, I don't know if I will be free day after tomorrow or not. I am working on probably cutting back on my shuttle business to just two guys: my brother Chad and this other fellow that you know. He is a 'sometimes a fisherman and sometimes a cop kind of a guy.' What do you think?"

"Well, I guess you will have to come in and we'll see how things are looking day after tomorrow." And he took Nancy in his arms for the first time. But it would not be the last.

Somewhere, Sarah and Miriam were smiling.

CPSIA information can be obtained
at www.ICGtesting.com
Printed in the USA
FFOW01n0910280916
28029FF